THE

HEARTS
WE
BURN

Also by Briana Cole

The Unconditional Series

The Wives We Play

The Vows We Break

The Hearts We Burn

Published by Kensington Publishing Corp.

THE
HEARTS
WE
BURN

An Unconditional Novel

BRIANA COLE

KENSINGTON PUBLISHING CORP.
www.kensingtonbooks.com

DAFINA BOOKS are published by

Kensington Publishing Corp.
119 West 40th Street
New York, NY 10018

All Kensington titles, imprints, and distributed lines are available at special quantity discounts for bulk purchases for sales promotion, premiums, fund-raising, and educational or institutional use.

Special book excerpts or customized printings can also be created to fit specific needs. For details, write or phone the office of the Kensington Sales Manager: Kensington Publishing Corp., 119 West 40th Street, New York, NY 10018. Attn. Sales Department. Phone: 1-800-221-2647.

Dafina and the Dafina logo Reg. U.S. Pat. & TM Off.

ISBN-13: 978-1-4967-2198-3
ISBN-10: 1-4967-2198-5
First Kensington Trade Paperback Printing: March 2020

ISBN-13: 978-1-4967-2201-0 (ebook)
ISBN-10: 1-4967-2201-9 (ebook)
First Kensington Electronic Edition: March 2020

10 9 8 7 6 5 4 3 2 1

Printed in the United States of America

I dedicate this third book to my three boys, Sean, Elisha, and now Benjamin. Mommy loves you all with everything in me and I sincerely hope you watch me and are inspired to pursue your own dreams. ☺

"Sometimes you have to burn yourself to the ground before you can rise like a phoenix from the ashes."

—Jens Lekman

THE
HEARTS
WE
BURN

Chapter 1
Adria

I never thought I would hate my husband. Well, maybe not hate, because that is such a strong word. Nevertheless, as I listened to his voicemail greeting message for the third time, I couldn't help but feel a strong emotion superseding anger. That's for damn sure.

I pulled the phone away from my ear without bothering to "leave a message for ya boi," as Keon had so eloquently instructed in his greeting. I knew he was doing it on purpose, and that's what was eating at me. He couldn't feign ignorance with this appointment. I made sure of that. We hadn't been speaking, but I had reminded him all week and even this morning before he left for work. So how convenient was it that his phone was off when his truck should've been parked in this deck right along with mine.

Three months. It had been three months since our lives had changed so drastically, three months of this bullshit, and time was doing nothing but driving us further and further apart. I rested my head on the back of the seat and glanced out at the traffic clogging the city streets of Atlanta. Somewhere, a horn blew, a siren wailed, and a slew of pedestrians hurried along the sidewalk through rush-hour congestion, probably to make it home to their families. I swallowed a wave of envy. If only life were still that simple for me. I was too busy dealing with my own losses, my husband included. Fact was, he was showing me he didn't care, and I was slowly adopting those same sentiments.

The phone suddenly rang in my hand, which startled me. Sure enough, Keon's number flashed across my screen. I quickly picked up.

"Where are you?"

"Damn, good afternoon to you too, *wife*."

I rolled my eyes at the smart ass comment. "Keon, today is not the day. Where are you?" I knew what he was going to say before the words even filtered through the phone. Same shit I had heard for our last two sessions.

"I have to work late. Sorry." His tone was anything but apologetic, which only heightened my anger. Maybe hate was the right word after all.

"Keon, I thought you said you would be available. That's why we scheduled this appointment today for this time. Because you said it was convenient for you."

"Why you acting like that, Dria? Therapy was your dumb-ass idea anyway."

"My dumb-ass idea?"

"Yeah, you're the one with whatever mental shit you got going on and I'm trying to work with you—"

"Boy, don't act like you're doing me any favors," I yelled, not bothering to calm my tone. "You act like you're not even in this marriage. Like none of this is important to you."

"You tripping. All because I think therapy is bullshit?"

"No, you know what? This whole damn relationship is bullshit. Keep doing you, Keon. And I'll be sure to do me without you. See how that feels." I hung up and immediately powered down my phone, cursing as my fingers trembled over the buttons. I knew I was arguing from another place because those words had felt completely empty. But as I shut my eyes and struggled to keep my blood from boiling over, regret began to ease its way into my subconscious. Not for the argument. Hell, that had become too common between us these past months. No, regret that I had walked down the aisle to give this man my heart again. Til' death do us part, my ass.

Sighing, I slid weary eyes to the clock on the dash. 5:08, already well into my allotted grace period, so I needed to get inside if I still wanted to be seen today. I grabbed my purse and stepped out of the car.

I bundled my jacket tighter against the September chill as I made my way across the parking deck. The therapist's office was in a high-rise in the hub of downtown Atlanta. But since it was adjoined to other doctors, realtors, and finance companies in the building, I certainly appreciated the discretion.

I stepped into the elevator and jabbed the button for the seventh floor, maybe a little too forcefully, as a sharp pain pierced my thumb. When the doors closed, I could only stare at my piss-poor reflection in the mirror finish.

I still carried baby weight, hadn't bothered to try and get rid of it. Though I still looked the part, to my despair I was very much not pregnant. The realization had sadness extinguishing my anger and I touched my belly. Ghost flutters or something. My OB-GYN had told me it was common to still feel like my babies were kicking or rolling around in there. My head would want to feel there was still someone in there. My heart would *need* to feel it. But I was empty. In more ways than one.

The doors opened to reveal a narrow hallway with watercolor paintings flanking one side and floor-to-ceiling windows along the other. At the end of the hall, a door with the words Waller

Family Counseling etched in the glass automatically slid open to welcome me into the quaint lobby.

The receptionist looked up and smiled. "Good afternoon, Mrs. Davis," she said, sliding the clipboard across the marble desk in my direction. "How are you today?"

I wondered if she really expected a truthful answer to that question. I'm sure it was automatic, but would she be surprised if I actually told her how I really felt one time? *I feel like shit, thank you very much for asking.* But my lips thinned into a polite smile as I scribbled my name on the sign-in sheet.

"Fine," I said instead. No need to blurt out my frustrations to the poor little intern who made coffee and answered phones. Her little college courses probably hadn't prepared her for an Adria Davis. I would do enough of that in just a moment.

Dr. Waller was a brown-skin sister who wore a short curly afro and not a stitch of makeup other than lip-gloss. I always thought she looked entirely too young for this job, like she needed to be taking notes in a black history university classroom instead of being burdened with the world's problems on her shoulders. But she was kind and patient, which kept me booking session after session, even if it didn't initially feel like I was getting better.

"Adria." She hugged me as we stood in the doorway, a genuine embrace like best friends. I held on a moment longer, inhaling the nostalgia of that familiar feeling, before I let go.

"I'm sorry I'm late, Dr. Waller," I said as she closed the door behind me.

"Evelyn," she corrected.

I nodded. "Evelyn."

We sat together, side-by-side on the plush leather couch over-looking the city skyline. In front of us, a recorder and two cups of water sat on the coffee table. Evelyn crossed her legs and folded her hands in her lap.

"Where is your husband?" she asked, though I'm sure she knew my answer.

"He's working late."

"Do we need to reschedule?"

"He'll probably be working late then too."

Evelyn nodded her understanding and remained silent, watching me gather my thoughts.

"That's why I was late," I went on, the argument festering fresh in my mind. "He's just being so damn difficult about this whole thing."

"I want to hear about that," Evelyn said. "But first, tell me about a good time with your husband."

I sighed, already recognizing her tactic. She liked to do some kind of sandwich-method, start with something positive, then let out all my negative energy, then end positive. As irritating as the strategy was, the shit was effective. I let out a breath and closed my eyes.

—◦•◦—

"You look so beautiful, Mrs. Davis," Keon murmured, the words causing my body to heat with anticipation. I did a seductive sway of my hips, slowly peeling out of my wedding dress. The hotel room was nearly dark, illuminated only by candles my husband had placed on the bedside tables. His naked frame looked delicious lying on the white sheets and rose petals, and the light from the flame flickered across the hungry gaze on his face. He licked his lips and I wanted to cream right there.

"I'm in love with you, Mr. Davis," I said, crawling up from the foot of the bed.

"Oh, yeah?"

"Yeah."

He kissed me, caressing my lips with his tongue. "Damn, I'm gon' get you pregnant tonight, girl."

I laughed and let him roll on top of me. This man of mine. My forever. Mr. Playboy, who I had waited through woman after

woman while he got his shit together. Always his little booty call.
Finally his wife. It was about damn time.

———◦•◦———

"He's dealing with it," Evelyn said, her gentle voice breaking
my memory. "In his own way."

"I'm the one having to deal with it," I said on a frown.

"Adria, he lost his daughters, too. And a sister," she added at
my continued silence. The last sentence had me wincing. She was
right. Kimera was his sister, but she was my best friend. As much
as it pained me to admit, it was easier to not think about her. Not
thinking about her made it easier to not blame her, nor feel guilty
about blaming her, since she had lost her life. More memories
flooded through me, threatening to swallow me into some kind of
black hole.

"Tell me about Kimera," Evelyn said. "Before . . . everything."

For the first time, I reached for my water and took a desperate
swallow. Despite the fruit I knew Evelyn infused with the water, it
remained tasteless, the liquid seeming to hit my stomach without
touching my throat.

"I had known Kimmy since middle school," I started. "The girl
was a mess, even then. Always seemed to be in some kind of trouble. But I loved her. More like sisters than friends. I used to tell
her she never took anything serious, but that was just Kimmy. The
epitome of living her best life. But we were always there for each
other. I never even really came out and told her I was feeling her
brother because honestly, I knew I was being stupid for that boy.
Somehow, she always knew though. Just like I knew she was in
love with Jahmad, Keon's best friend. But Keon and Jahmad were
both young and seemed to always be in some kind of competition
on who could sleep with the most girls."

The statement came out snarky but that didn't change the
facts. Restless, I rose and wandered to the window.

"Jahmad hurt her so bad when he moved away. It was clear he

had just been using her for sex, hell, just like Keon was doing to me, but me and Kimmy, we were built different. I dealt with the shit, but my girl, it changed her. There were times I didn't even recognize her . . ." I trailed off at the thought.

"Changed her how?"

"Kimmy met Leo," I said simply. "And well, you know the rest."

Of course she did. I had hashed out the past two years for Evelyn over the past five sessions. How Kimmy had met Leo, a man with two wives. How his long money had prompted her to enter the poly relationship as wife number three, because she would be able to get her hands on enough money so we could open our cosmetic store. The fact that Leo had been harboring a huge secret, and that secret resulted in me and Kimmy being kidnapped and tortured for nearly a week. That was three months ago, but it seemed like yesterday.

⸺⸺◦◦⸺⸺

Pain snatched me from darkness, piercing my body like a thousand blades stabbing from flesh to bone. Everything was throbbing, and a slight ringing in my ears seemed to overwhelm the quiet conversation. Someone was talking. No, several people, in hushed whispers, as if they feared disturbing me. But as the raw memories came barreling back, licking the recesses of my subconscious, I knew it was too late. I was well past disturbed.

I moaned, not bothering to open my eyes to face the dark realities. I was in this mess because of Kimmy—being held hostage, deprived of food, and subjecting my babies to this torture. I hadn't done anything but be a good friend, but now . . . A noise ripped through my thoughts, followed by silence. I could feel eyes on me. Then,

"Adria?" Keon. My husband's voice held the weight of uncertainty. "Babe? You awake?"

I lifted heavy lids, squinting against the sudden glare of the hos-

pital room lights. One by one, the other figures came into view, first Keon, then my mother-in-law, First Lady Davis. And judging by the man in the lab coat at the foot of my bed, my doctor.

He came to the side of my bed, a gentle smile on his lips. "Mrs. Davis," he said. "I'm Dr. Hinton. Can you hear me okay?" He plucked a pen-like object from his breast pocket and shined the light in my eye.

"What happened?" My voice was hoarse, unrecognizable. I cleared it, bracing against a headache that was beginning to intensify.

"You're in a hospital," Dr. Hinton. "We've been treating you for about eighteen hours, but it's good to see you finally came through. Are you in any pain?"

"Yeah."

"On a scale of one to ten?"

"One hundred."

Dr. Hinton chuckled, though I didn't see this shit as humorous. He scribbled something on a notepad, then checked some fluid in the IV bag near my bed. "We'll increase the dosage of morphine," he said. "And I'm going to check on your MRI and ultrasound results."

Ultrasound? My hand went to my stomach in alarm. "Are my babies all right?"

Dr. Hinton's eyes lowered before glancing to Keon on my other side. The panic rose with this silent exchange of information.

"Babe," Keon's voice cracked. "They did everything they could—"

"No!" I shook off his hand and lifted the sheets to eye my stomach. I still had a pudge. My babies were okay. They had to be. "They're fine," I said, sinking back into the pillows in relief. "Thank God."

First Lady Davis turned her back to me, shielding her face from view. I looked back to Keon.

"They're all right," I said with a small smile. "I'm all right. We're all right."

He shook his head and my heart fell as the first few tears rolled down his cheeks. "No," he said. "We're not."

———◆◈◆———

"Do you feel like it's Keon's fault you lost your babies?" Evelyn's voice again cracked through my sordid memory as I struggled to blink back tears.

"No," I shook my head, my voice surprisingly forceful. "No, of course not."

"Then why are you so angry with him?"

"I'm not angry with him. I'm angry with . . ." I trailed off, my heart not allowing me to utter the name. I shouldn't have been angry with Kimmy either. But how could I not? Still, how could I place the blame on a ghost? Yes, my babies had lost their lives in this mess, but so had Kimmy. And my nephew Jamal. So really, whose burden was worse?

"You told me a few sessions ago that you were Christian," Evelyn said. "Have you been praying about this issue?"

I didn't respond, afraid to let Evelyn know I hadn't cracked open a Bible, nor said anything to God since the good pastor, my father-in-law, was killed. I didn't like to admit I had turned my back on Him, but I couldn't really see where He had helped me in any way thus far.

"I want you to go home, and read Psalm 73:26," she continued, scribbling her instructions on a notepad. "And I want you to write down a list of everything you have to be thankful for. I want us to do a little exercise next time you come in."

I shook my head, already dreading the assignment. "Come on, Evelyn. You know that's not what I need."

"What do you need, Adria?"

"Can't you just write a prescription?" I said instead.

"The antidepressants? You're not due for a refill yet." Evelyn stared at me a little longer, making me uncomfortable under her scrutiny. I averted my eyes.

"I know. I just wanted to see if you could write something stronger," I lied. "I'm not sure if it is really working for me."

"Let me be the judge of that," she said with another one of her signature smiles as she handed me the scratch sheet of paper. Defeated, I rose to leave. A sudden swell of anger had me mumbling a quick goodbye before nearly running from the room. Dammit, I had been out of pills for two days, a supply that should have lasted me the rest of the month. I had figured Evelyn could just call in some more to my pharmacy, so I hadn't prepared for her refusal. But fine, let her be on her Dr. Phil rampage. I knew someone who could get me that same medicine for cheaper anyway.

Chapter 2
Kimera

How the hell did I get here?

I sighed as I eyed the chiffon dress still hanging in the dress bag behind my door. I had long since finished my bath but I couldn't bring myself to move from the bed. It wasn't cold in the room at all, but the air tingled my damp skin as I sat naked on the bed. Even though the joyous sounds from the party happening right downstairs wafted up to greet me, still I didn't budge. Exhaustion, stubbornness, or, hell, maybe both, had me narrowing my eyes at the nauseatingly gorgeous garment that probably cost somewhere in the few thousand range. Just another one to go with the hundred others stuffed in my oversized closet.

I couldn't bring myself to look around the spacious bedroom that was the size of a medium apartment. Couldn't bring myself to lay eyes on what I had sold my soul for. Outside my window, a majestic view of the Dallas, Texas, skyline stretched out in the distance. In another time and place, I would have felt compelled to explore the cultural sights and sounds of being in the city for the first time. Instead, I'd been trapped in this place for the past three months. And for what? A lavish mansion and expensive trinkets? My eye had been on the trophy and here I had become the damn trophy. Glass case and all.

A few years ago, I had done something stupid. My very rich and very married boyfriend Leo had asked me to be a part of his polyamorous relationship, being involved with his two other love partners, or wives as he said, in exchange for a happily ever after. It would be temporary as far as I was concerned. Get in, funnel away his money, and get out. Little did I know just how drastically my life would change after I said, "I do."

One of the adjoining bedrooms had been converted to my closet. Open-faced shelves displayed more than a hundred pair of designer shoes and matching purses. A luxe loveseat sat in the middle of the room, nearly buried under a mass of shopping bags and shoeboxes from Leo's last apology.

I crossed to it now, fingering the rows of pastel blouses and tailored slacks, some still hanging in plastic protectors from the dry cleaners. I almost missed being able to just snatch some wrinkled jeans and a faded sweatshirt from the wire hangers. Even though I didn't go any damn where, Leo didn't like me stepping out of my room in anything less than heels and makeup. His father's prosperous status had made him the unofficial king of his country, which had made Leo the recognized prince. So I had to uphold the delicate image of his trophy princess, and at first, I had eaten it up to the fullest. Now it was just downright annoying.

A firm knock on the door brought my attention back to the task at hand. I didn't bother answering because it wasn't like it was a request to open the door. It was Kareem telling me to hurry my ass up.

The man was introduced as my bodyguard, which was complete bullshit. It was more than obvious Leo had hired him to watch me, make sure I kept up the visage as the dutiful and loving wife, not the hostage I really was. It seemed futile to me because it wasn't like I had any clue where I was.

Leo had flown me from Atlanta to Dallas and had taken my phone and every phone in the house. With the exception of the backyard, I hadn't been outside, let alone been able to leave the property. I was miserable, but the tears were long gone. In its place, I just felt hollow, an empty shell of the Kimera I used to be.

"Saida," Kareem called, the command laced in his gruff tone.

"I'm coming, damn," I snapped and rose to my feet.

No, not Kimera anymore. She had died according to the doctored police report. No, now it was Saida, because it meant, what did Leo say? *The fortunate one.* Not *quite* fitting since I was anything but fortunate. And apparently, Saida needed to get her ass down to that party before Leo came up looking for her. And then she would be in an even bigger mess.

I slipped on the dress, not bothering to stop and admire how the tailored fit hugged my curves, not caring how the expensive material felt against my skin. My hair had grown a lot, and now fell in feathered layers at my shoulders. I hated it. But Leo didn't leave me much choice with my looks now. I used my hands to smooth down flyaways and crossed to my vanity for my jewelry.

I ignored another knock as I fastened my earrings. I wasn't surprised when the door opened and Kareem's huge frame stood in the doorway. I rolled my eyes.

"Damn, what did you think I was going to do?" I said, meeting his gaze in the mirror. "Sneak out the window and shimmy down the fire escape?" My tone was sarcastic, though I had considered the idea on several occasions.

Kareem exaggerated a glance at his watch. "Leo's waiting."

I sucked my teeth and stormed to the door. "You would think you had enough balls to follow your own orders instead of just doing what Leo tells you to do," I said. "He tells you to come get me and here you are. Don't you have a mind of your own?" My snide remark didn't seem to faze him as he stepped to the side to allow me to pass. I didn't expect much of a reaction, but his lack thereof pissed me off nonetheless.

Instead of heading to the staircase, I kept straight and continued down the hall, not caring when Kareem followed. The door at the end was cracked and a little sliver of light from the nightlight shown through. I immediately pasted a smile on my face as I quietly eased in and left the door slightly ajar behind me.

Jamal slept peacefully in his crib, his tiny body folded in the Spiderman sheets and comforter. He slept with his mouth open, just like his dad, and it almost made my heart hurt how every day he looked more and more like the man I despised.

I sighed at the thought. No matter how much I had lied and schemed, or how much I didn't want Leo to be Jamal's father, now the resemblance was undeniable. I had been having an affair with the man I loved, Jahmad, during my arrangement with Leo and, for a while, had convinced Jahmad the baby was his. But when he found out the truth, he had left me for his ex-fiancée. Between my deception and CeeCee's pregnancy, I guess she had been the obvious choice.

Another movement shifted my eyes to the toddler bed across the room. Leo Jr., looking like Jamal's twin, also slept snoring lightly. My other son now. I didn't immediately welcome the idea of being Mommy to Leo's other child by his second wife, but now that both his other wives had been killed, who was left? Plus, seeing the boys together warmed my heart. They were the only piece of light in this fucked up situation.

I planted soft kisses on both of their cheeks, and stared a moment longer. When I knew I couldn't stall anymore, I snuck back out to the hall.

Even in the midst of the guests and idle party chatter, I felt Leo's eyes on me as I descended the stairs. Fear, or maybe defiance, had me turning from the crowded great room into the kitchen. I was sure my tardiness coupled with my little escape tactic was going to have him in my ear later. But to hell with him. I couldn't deal with his shit now. And it wasn't like he was going to check me in front of all his precious birthday guests. Not when he had to keep up his perfect image instead of showing everyone what an abusive, low-down, deceptive asshole he really was.

"Mrs. Saida," the chef, Fernando, greeted me as I entered. "Drink?"

"Please."

Technically, I wasn't supposed to be in here. Leo didn't like me in the kitchen with 'the help,' as he described it. Still, this area was one of the few places that felt like home to me. Probably because Fernando was damn near a magician and could make anything from a fried lobster dinner, to down-home soul food fixings with nothing but a skillet and some Lawry's seasoned salt. I hated my situation but his meals were always something I looked forward to. Even now, he and his staff had the delicious aroma of Italian spices hanging thick in the air and my mouth watered.

As was customary, Fernando went to the bar and within minutes, had sat his little signature fruit cocktail on the marble countertop in front of me. I downed it in two gulps and relaxed as the buzz immediately took over. That was another thing I loved about this man. He had a heavy hand when it came to the liquor.

"Dinner will be served at eight thirty," Fernando said, taking his place back behind the stove. "I hope you like. Fernando special recipe." I smiled, the first genuine smile in what seemed like forever.

"Fernando, every recipe is your special recipe," I said. "And you know I always like it."

My grin widened when the hint of a blush colored the man's cheeks.

"Saida."

Leo's voice chilled the air and I turned and stared at the man framing the doorway. Funny how the features that had attracted me to this man all those years ago were the same ones that disgusted me now. Hell, just his presence made me want to bend over and toss up the acid in my stomach.

I didn't move as Leo closed the distance between us, placing his arm around my waist. He kissed my cheek, reeking of cigars and alcohol. "You were gone for a minute," he said, and even though his voice was hushed, I still heard the edge of his temper lacing the words.

"I couldn't decide what to wear," I said. "And I wanted to check on the boys."

I caught a sideways look at him as his eyes turned to narrow at Fernando. "Looks like you're in here flirting with the cook."

I rolled my eyes and tapped my finger on the empty glass in front of me.

"I was just getting a—"

His grip tightened around my waist and I inhaled sharply at the tight pinch on my flesh. He smiled at me, his words seeping through teeth. "It's my birthday," he said. "And I need my wife by my side." He pulled me closer until I was nose-to-nose with him. "Get your ass to the party. Now." This time, he released me, but instead of letting me walk alone, he let his hand brush down my arm to lace his fingers with mine. He led the way, half-yanking me along.

We entered the great room and all eyes immediately turned to us. A few pictures were snapped and, because he expected it, I forced my lips back into a tight grin. "I found her," he announced. "You know I can't go too long without my lovely wife." A few "aaawws" and chuckles lifted and Leo leaned in to kiss me softly on my lips. A huge contrast to the vice grip he had on my hand.

It seemed like Leo had flown all of his family over from Ivory Coast. Why, I didn't know. It wasn't like they were even close. These same people I hadn't seen since our little faux wedding two years ago, not even at our little courthouse ceremony a few months ago. The whole thing felt like some kind of three-ring circus act as opposed to genuine interest in Leo's celebratory event. I guess it really was no different from my own presence here be-

cause Lord knows if I'd had a choice, I would have been anywhere else.

I thought again about the little marriage thing (because that's
really the only label that made sense, a *thing*). It was almost me-
chanical and I was just physically going through the motions as I
again pledged to love, honor, and obey this man I could barely
stand to look at. He, on the other hand, had seemed too damn
happy, like he had finally won his prize. I didn't know whether the
reason for his smile was me, or the fact that Tyree, his boyfriend,
stood right next to him as his "best man." Either way, he was
clearly relishing my misery.

I stood stiff as a few people hugged and gushed over me, told
me how beautiful I was while enfolding me in entirely too much
perfume and African garb. They asked me about my life and my
babies and, if I wasn't mistaken, I detected a hint of jealousy in the
overly-cheerful smiles. I wished I could ease their little envy and
tell them that they could have every bit of this shit. A few people,
Leo's aunts I believe, even went as far as to kiss my forehead and
I cringed under the pleasantries, fighting back tears as Leo pulled
me tighter. No one seemed to notice, or care for that matter, my
obvious disdain. That would be too much like right.

"Son." Obi Owusu, Leo's father, walked up, his arms outstretched for a hug. Leo let me go long enough to embrace his
idol and the two shared a grin, like some secret family language.
Obi then turned in my direction and wrapped his arms around me
next. I shrank under the awkward gesture. "So good to see you
again," Obi said, planting a huge kiss on my cheek. "Saida, is it?"

"You too, Mr. Owusu," I said, because I felt obligated to. The
little exchange was forced because I was certain the man knew my
name. Both this one and my real one.

Obi nodded to three women who lingered by the bar, giggling
among themselves. "You remember my wives, right? Amora,
Yana, and Natasha?"

I nodded, noting the new face among the group. Leo's mother had passed of cancer and it looked like Obi had already secured her replacement.

"Aren't they beautiful, Son?" Obi turned to Leo and gave him a slap on the back. "Wait until you get you some more. I know Saida here isn't enough."

Leo chuckled his discomfort and I could only roll my eyes at the accuracy of the statement. Of course, I wasn't enough. Not when he was sneaking off to Tyree every chance he got. Still he couldn't very well tell his father that. Leo had made it clear he had to keep his relationship with Tyree hidden because his father would disown him, leaving him vulnerable to whatever danger and consequences that were tangled up with the Owusu bloodline, and there seemed to be a lot of both. So, his bright idea was to have me, his public and true wife, as his cover to hide his little male plaything on the side. The idea was revolting but after he had threatened the life of my best friend Adria and my son Jamal, I hadn't had much of a choice.

Immediately, the thought of my friend brought on a wave of sadness. The last time I had seen Adria, she had been beaten, tied up, and left in a storage closet. All in an effort to get me to cooperate. Of course, it had worked and though Leo assured me and reassured me he had sent help for Adria once we boarded the plane to our new life, I had absolutely no way of knowing for sure other than his word which didn't mean a damn thing to me. So every day I was left with the uncertainties and it was killing me. Had she been saved in time? What about her babies?

"I got a call." Strangely, Leo was now whispering to his father and the two were leaned in so close I didn't even know if I had actually heard the words or just read his lips.

Obi turned his eyes on me and sitting his hand on the small of my back, steered me in the direction of the bar. "Saida, why don't you go over there and say hello," he suggested with a smile. "Let me and my son have a little privacy."

Grateful for the reprieve, I made my way through the crowd to the bar. I could use some privacy of my own. "What are you having, Beautiful?" the bartender asked as I leaned on the countertop.

"She'll have one of these." One of Obi's wives, I couldn't remember which one, lifted her glass in the air. Obediently, the bartender pulled out various alcohol bottles to begin the mysterious concoction.

"Saida, right," the woman said with a smile, her thick French accent weighted under each word. She didn't bother waiting for a response. "I'm Yana." She gestured to her companions, all equally beautiful. "This is Amora and Natasha Owusu. You're Leo's wife, right?"

I smiled my response, but didn't bother opening my mouth. I immediately got that this one was the self-proclaimed leader of the trio. She reminded me of Leo's first wife, Tina. She knew good and damn well I was Leo's wife.

The bartender handed me the drink and I took a hesitant sip, decided the liquor was too weak, but kept on sipping so as to keep my mouth occupied. Maybe then, I wouldn't have to play nice with these women.

"Good, huh?" Yana continued with a wink. She tapped her glass to mine. "Cheers. To love and happiness with the Owusu men."

I wanted to throw up. Point me to the love and happiness because it damn sure wasn't here.

"How long you been married to Leo?" Natasha spoke up, her English broken.

Maybe it was the alcohol getting to me but I didn't bother trying to sugarcoat my answer. "Too long," I said boldly. "And it's not like I have a choice."

Natasha glanced at the others in confusion. "I don't understand."

Before I could comment again, Yana grabbed my forearm and pulled me away from the other two. Gone was the confidence she previously exuded. Her face had paled to nearly sheet-white with fear. She lowered her voice as we found a quiet corner away from the chatter. "Look, I know you're new with this," she said. "But trust me. You don't want to go advertising that."

"It's true," I said. "I'm being held hostage. Leo won't let me go. I need to get home to my family."

Yana *ssshhhed* me and quickly glanced around. "Listen, I get it," she said. "But you can't say things like that. Obi would kill you."

The comment stopped my ramble and I just watched Yana, unsure how to digest the news. She went on. "Look, I know it's not easy. But in time you'll forget your family when you realize we are your family now. If Leo is anything like Obi . . ." She trailed off, shaking her head, and after a moment, pulled me into a hug. Her voice was barely a whisper as she murmured in my ear. "Just be careful." She kissed my cheek and pulled away, heading back to her little group.

"Wait, Yana." My words had her turning around to face me again. "You believe me though, don't you?"

Her smile was now sad, bent in sympathy. "It doesn't matter," she said. "Because no one can help you. Or me. So just enjoy it. It is what it is. You need to behave and be careful, Saida." And with that, she turned away.

I had never felt so sick before. This time, I couldn't attribute this to the fact that I had now reached cruising altitude on this private airplane. Any other time, the plush, beige leather reclining seats, champagne, and chilled shrimp cocktail at my elbow would have me immersed in the lap of luxury and basking in every bit of it. But as the clouds glided past my window, all I could do was squeeze my eyes shut against the horror. With every passing second, I was traveling further and further away from my life, and closer and closer to my prison. The realization had me dying inside.

"Something else to eat, Miss?" I heard the voice, but didn't

bother answering the flight attendant's inquiry. She got the hint and I heard her gentle steps as she padded away, probably to ask the same thing to Leo and Tyree.

I hadn't even acknowledged them since we had boarded, and thankfully, they had left me alone as well. They sat together a few rows in front of me, their heads huddled together and speaking in hushed whispers as if I gave a damn what they were talking about.

The swell of nausea in the pit of my belly grew and I suddenly rose on shaking legs. As if on cue, their heads whipped up and they tossed suspicious looks in my direction. I smacked my lips and snapped, "What the hell do you think I'm going to do? Jump out the plane?" Neither of them spoke, but I could feel their eyes on me as I made my way to the back of the plane, bracing against the seats for support. I needed to get to the bathroom before I redecorated all this pretty, expensive shit in here.

I made sure to let out my frustration when I slammed the door behind me. That gave me a little liberation, but not much. The rest came as I stooped over the porcelain toilet and let the bile do its business. As I continued to dry heave over the bowl, I let the tears flow again. Was this my karma? Did I really do something so messed up that this was the punishment considered to fit my crime?

I sank to the floor, weak from throwing up and exhaustion. Physically, I felt as empty as my heart because Lord knows Leo had snatched everything from me. In a matter of minutes, I had to give up everything I loved, to save everyone I loved. The irony.

"My love," Leo's voice came soft through the door. "Are you okay?" What the hell kind of question was that? The man was staging my death just so he could keep me all to himself, a prisoner in my own body. Yeah, I was overfuckingjoyed. His knock was just as soft, but persistent, enough to have me groaning and peeling myself from the floor. If I thought I was about to have any peace, I would have been better making good on my threat and jumping out the plane for real.

I snatched open the door and stared into Leo's face. He had the nerve to actually offer a smile and that pissed me off even more.

"Do you need anything?" he asked.

"Yeah, for you to leave me the hell alone," I snapped and shoved past him, feeling a little triumphant when he bumped against the wall. I stormed back to my seat, slightly surprised when Leo followed and sat next to me. I was even more surprised when he grabbed my hand and lifting it to his lips, kissed my palm. His signature. Part of me was hoping I would just piss him off. Maybe then, he would realize he was much better off without me. I damn sure wasn't trying to make this easy on him.

"You know I love you," he said.

I tried to pull my hand from his but he held on tighter, now gripping my fingers until they nearly hurt with the pressure. I winced and struggled to keep my face neutral. The last thing I wanted to do was give him the satisfaction. But my lack of response must have been enough for him because he smirked, kissed my fingers where he had just tried to squeeze them broken, and let my hand go.

"I like Saida," he went on after a moment. "I think that fits you, my love."

I frowned. "The least you can do is let me keep my real name."

"Kimera Davis is dead. I made sure of that." He rubbed his knuckles against the side of my face and I turned my head from his touch.

"Did you do what you promised?" I asked. "Did you send the police to help Adria?"

"Yes."

"How do I know?"

Leo shrugged. "Guess you're going to have to trust me." He started to stand and I grabbed his arm, almost desperate.

"Leo please. You promised. Let me just . . . talk to her or—"

"I sent the police. I got word. Your friend is safe at the hospital."

"And the babies?"

Leo shrugged. "Don't know and really don't care. She's been admitted. They'll take care of her. I did my part. Now you just have to do yours." He left, leaving the statement, which seemed more threatening than I liked, hanging in the air.

Maybe I had pushed his buttons too far. I couldn't be sure. But either way, later that evening, we had touched down in Texas. And though I wasn't finished with the conversation, I damn sure wished I had been.

"My love." His accent licked each syllable in the two-word greeting as he entered my room. I turned my head when he met me in the closet, the kiss intended for my lips instead planting gently on my cheek. He smelled of overly-splashed cologne. Cuba. It used to be my favorite for him. But now the stifling aroma merely masked the stench of sex, and did nothing but turn my stomach knowing where his body, and lips, had just been. Obviously not fazed by my evasive gesture, he turned and headed for the bathroom.

I met him in there and he was leaning in to the shower stall. For a brief second, I eyed the bends and angles of his well-toned physique. I watched him until he disappeared behind the frosted shower glass. I waited, half expecting him to speak, but heard only the water echoing off the stone walls.

"Leo, do you love me?" I asked finally.

"Of course, my love."

"Then why are you doing this? Why won't you let me go?" His silence had me snatching the door open and gasping as the hot steam slapped my face. Leo turned, and on a smile, wrapped his wet arms around my waist. "Leo . . ." I struggled, suddenly angered as he pulled me into the shower, pinning me against the wall.

"You know I love you," he murmured, his lips brushing mine.

"Leo, stop it." I was furious as I shoved his chest and as if on instinct, my hand snaked out and connected with his cheek. The slap of skin echoing in the stall was enough to snap me out of my instinctive daze, ripping a fearful gasp from my lips. "Leo, I'm sorry,"

I said as his eyes narrowed in restrained anger. "Leo. I didn't mean it. I'm sorry."

"Bitch," he growled.

I hadn't even had time to brace for the punch. His knuckles connected with my jaw with enough painful force to snap my head back and slam it against the wall. Crippled with pain, I slithered to the floor. My face was throbbing and I was sure I felt a trickle of warm blood pooling from my scalp. Or maybe that was the water from the faucet. I couldn't be sure. But I folded myself into a ball anyway and braced for the next round of punches I knew was sure to come.

I screamed when I felt his fingers grasp the back of my throat and drag me from underneath the spray. "You want to act like a bitch," he said, his voice low and menacing. "I'll treat you like a bitch."

Leo held me down by the neck as he yanked me across the linoleum. Our soaking wet bodies left a trail of water on the floor as I struggled to keep up in a half-crawl, half-slide type of maneuver, to keep from breaking every bone in my body along the way. "Leo, please," I could only muster a whisper as his grip tightened. "I'm sorry. Please don't." But I knew I had fucked up.

He pulled me through the bedroom and into another room down the hall. A thirty-six-inch dog crate sat on the side of a futon and Leo threw me against the metal wire. I winced as it bit into my flesh. Confused, I shook my head fiercely. "Leo, please," I cried. I ate my words as the sole of his wet foot jammed so hard into my mouth that it felt like my teeth came loose from my gums.

"Shut up," he said. "And get your ass in the crate."

Weak with pain, I crawled into the tiny cage and folded myself tight against the confined space.

"My father told me I needed to get a better handle on you and he was right. You come out when you're ready to act like my love and not a little bitch," Leo said closing and locking the door. With that, he padded away.

I didn't know exactly how many hours he left me in there. But *when the sky turned to night and moonlight spilled into the room, I knew it had been all day. Leo didn't say a word when he finally came back and opened the cage door. My muscles were tight as I crawled out of the cage and it was enough to have me whimpering in agony. "I love you," Leo murmured. "Are you ready to behave?"*

Too exhausted to speak, I merely nodded. Leo scooped me into his arms and kissed my tear-streaked face. My body felt numb. Even as he carried me back into the bedroom, laid me on the California King Bed, and began to undress me, I couldn't even feel his touch on my skin. When he licked my neck, the gesture had me bursting into a fresh set of tears. What had I done? What had I agreed to? I had to get away . . .

"You are never leaving me again, my love," Leo's throaty whisper came as if he had read my mind. "You agreed and now, we have our happily ever after. Tomorrow, we'll go to the courthouse and make it official. I love you." The silent threat was enough to have me shuddering as his lips took possession of mine.

⇒•⇐

I tried to stay to myself as best I could for most of the evening. But as I stood by the bar and nursed glass after glass of wine, I couldn't help but notice my "precious husband" had all but disappeared from the festivities. Funny. I was gone for 3.5 seconds and he insisted on sending my little bodyguard to come drag me from the bedroom. Yet here he was, absent from his own party for, I had to think for a moment the last time I actually spotted him among the crowd. Yeah definitely over thirty minutes. Which could only mean one thing.

My eyes lifted to the ceiling, as if I could almost see Leo getting a little birthday gift from his secret boyfriend Tyree in the upstairs bedroom. The thought alone had me finally setting my half-empty glass on the bar.

Shit was pathetic, if I could be completely honest. Tyree was content with hiding in the shadows while Leo paraded me around like the trophy. It was socially acceptable but both men acted as if the world would end if someone found out Leo was on the down low. I sure as hell didn't care. But what I did care about was that they expected me to be just as content with this arrangement. Of course I wasn't, but for the safety of me, my kids, and my family, I had to fake like I was. So Tyree lived in the huge house with us as well, only coming out when all of us were in private. Then, he and Leo didn't hesitate to display their affection freely and publicly. All within the confines of these walls. But when guests came, Tyree was nowhere to be found. He knew his role. I frowned at the huge wedding ring glittering from my finger. I guess I knew mine too.

I must have spoken Leo up because not even ten minutes later, I caught him inching down the stairs, his eyes darting around to make sure his entrance wasn't too obvious. He even had the nerve to be stuffing the tail of his dress shirt in the waistband of his slacks. Damn, I wish someone other than me was watching this. Leo easily blended back into the crowd and before I knew it, he had re-emerged, this time heading straight in my direction at the bar. I rolled my eyes.

"My love," he leaned to kiss me and I just as smoothly, shifted my body away from his so his lips couldn't make contact.

"Already opening your birthday gift, I see," I murmured, my voice hushed.

Leo ignored my comment, instead gesturing toward the bartender. His poison of choice was placed in front of him and he downed it in one quick swallow. If I cared to really pay attention, it was more than evident Leo was uneasy about something. He used the small paper napkin to dab at the sweat on his forehead. I didn't say anything but inside, I couldn't help the small gloat that had my lips turning up. Good. Whatever Tyree had told him, I'm glad it worked. Leo turned to look at me and that's when I saw it for the first time, a sliver of fear that had him readjusting the neckline of his shirt. And because I figured he really wanted me to, I chose not to speak any further on my observations.

"We need to talk," Leo said finally. His touch on my arm was light, so light in fact, I had to look down to confirm that it was indeed a slight tremble in his fingers that I felt.

"Are you letting me go?" I asked.

He seemed confused by the question. "No, it's something important."

"Well if it's not about you letting me and my children go, I really couldn't care less."

"My love, listen." He turned me by my shoulders to face him. "I think I—may, no *we* may be in danger. All of us."

The statement chilled my blood. "What are you talking about?"

Leo opened his mouth to speak again and quickly shut it, as his eyes slid to someone behind me. I turned as Leo's father walked up, gently kissed me on the forehead, and draped his arm around Leo.

"It's time, Son," he said, and it was obvious he could barely contain his excitement. I didn't know what was going on, but it was clear Leo did by the way he allowed his father to lead him away. Together, they walked to the massive fireplace and bowed their heads together to exchange a few words. Then, Obi turned to the guests.

"Attention please," he said, his voice carrying through the room and immediately silencing the party chatter. All pairs of expectant eyes turned to Obi, their king. In their expressions you would think the man was Jesus himself. Obi continued, "Today is a very special day. My only son has reached a milestone year. I must admit we haven't always had the best relationship, but I couldn't be more proud of this man." As if on cue, "aawws" wafted up to accentuate Obi's words. "So, happy birthday, Son. May you and your lovely family enjoy all the blessings the world has to offer." Now claps and cheers as Leo stood uncomfortably in the middle of the attention.

"So to celebrate this special occasion," Obi continued, once the applause had died down, "I wanted to do something I knew he would appreciate. I know this has been a tough few years with the death of his other two wives, and I have to applaud Leo's wife Saida for stepping in to support her husband in this time of need." Now more applause, this time in my direction as everyone grinned and cheered. As if I had a choice. "But now," he continued. "It's time for me to give my son a little bit of the sunshine he's lost. Son, meet your new wife Naomi."

People seemed to part to let someone through, and the cheers of approval only intensified as little Miss Guest of Honor made her way to Father and Son. I didn't see her face, but from the back, I could tell she was wearing the hell out of the Vera Wang beaded gown and her hair, in brown and blond highlights, was cascading in voluptuous waves down her bare back.

She hugged first Obi, then Leo, and they shared a passionate kiss as if they'd known each other for a long time rather than a first-time greeting. When she turned, her face finally came into view. I couldn't really tell how old she was, but she looked like she could've passed for my age, twenty-seven. She looked to be mixed, but I couldn't make out her racial background.

For a brief moment, the woman almost reminded me of myself. The way she quickly snuggled up to Leo and seemed to relish the attention from everyone took me back to one of the first times I started dating Leo myself.

I had met him while working at the bank. He had just strolled in to open a new account and made a large deposit while grinning and flirting with me the whole time. And me, in all my naïveté, had flirted right on back. It wasn't really the male attention I was seeking. No, more than his looks, the man had money. And according to the commas in the deposit I was keying into the computer, lots of it. After dropping out of college and moving back in with my parents, it was money I was lacking; so suddenly, this mystery man had my undivided attention. Not even Adria could talk me down from my stupidity.

I watched Leo lean over and whisper something in Naomi's ear and she giggled playfully. Yeah, that was me all right. Two years, two babies, and a lifetime of common sense ago. If only I had known better. And now, apparently the circle of life continued because here was Naomi, parading around, confidence masking her ignorance. And when she finally found my eyes through the crowd and a bright smile touched her lips, I too smiled, already working on a plan to use Leo's new wife to finally get me the hell out of here.

Chapter 3
Adria

Eerie. That was really the only word that could describe the air hanging so thick and still in the afternoon. As if the wind carried the weight of the death surrounding it and was now buried under its suffocating pressure. I should have been used to it by now. But of course that was a lot to expect of myself.

The smell of damp soil and moss clung in my nostrils as I made my way across the grass, my sneakers crunching on the fall leaves littering the ground. Headstone after headstone trailed past my peripheral, each one with names, dates, and words I had seen so much they had been committed to memory. *Gloria Renee Malcolm, a grandmother and best friend. Kimberly Pastor, daughter and wife.* And who could forget Leonard. No last name, just Leonard. His stone was void of the loving sentiments and instead just read *Good riddance.* I remember first seeing that one and having to pause in my own trek, frowning at the simple harshness. "I'm sorry for whatever you did Leonard," I had mumbled to myself.

We had buried my daughters together, wanting them joined in

death as they had been in my womb. Their names were also together on one headstone, inscribed in an elaborate cursive font
that was both beautiful and angelic. Just like I knew they would
have been. *Britain and Brooklyn Davis.* At the base were two sets
of angel wing figurines and beside those, a bouquet of daises that
had begun to wither with either age or weather, or both. Two baby
dolls, still wrapped neatly in their plastic boxes were propped
against the headstone, evidence that Mama Davis had come by re-
cently. A smile touched my lips.

I knelt down beside the grave and pulled out the fresh bouquet
of flowers I had brought, silently picking up the old ones and setting the new ones in their place. I sighed, surprised when those familiar tears didn't come. Maybe, just maybe I was beginning to
heal. Or becoming numb to the despair.

"Hey, Mama's angels," I started after an extended moment of
silence. "I see Granny came by to visit. Y'all weren't acting up,
were you?" It helped, the light jokes. As forced as it was, I had to
take this time not to wallow in my grief of their deaths but uplift
the beauty in their lives, their presence. Even if it wasn't here with
me. At least I was trying to take Evelyn's advice. "Mommy hasn't
been working a lot," I went on. "Just missing you girls, really. I
sleep in your nursery all the time. I dream about you every night.
And Daddy and I talk about you. Which one of you would've had
their first tooth, crawled first, who would've said 'Mama' first. My
vote was on you with that one, Brooklyn." I paused again and
looked to the street when I heard a car engine. I swallowed my
disappointment when the white Nissan Camry gently eased by
and disappeared through the gate.

Had I really expected Keon to come? After our heated argument, the fourth this week I might add, had I really expected my
husband to be the bigger man and put our issues to the side for
just a few hours while we visited our girls? Saturday morning, like
clockwork, he knew this was what we did. What we had agreed to

do. And yet, here I was alone. Surprised? I really shouldn't have been. Hurt? To my core.

I tore my eyes from the now empty street and glanced a few plots down to the other names I would have to bring myself to visit shortly. My time with my girls was special, albeit short, but the other grave never felt the same.

"It's strange," I murmured almost to myself. "I come out here every week, I sit and talk to you girls, and I'm still just as broken as I was months ago when they told me you two didn't make it. My therapist assures me it'll get more bearable as time goes on. Not easier. 'Bearable' was her word. But I don't know. It's like I leave a piece of myself here each time I visit."

Tears clogged my throat and I released a heavy sigh. "Of course, not saying any of this is your fault, Babies. No, never that. For the rest of my life, you know I'm going to come see you. Even if it means one day, I'll never leave."

I said my goodbyes, and slowly rose to my feet, taking in an extra moment of silence. I felt guilty as hell for not wanting to make the short walk across the gravesites. I wondered if there was some kind of curse I was laying over my life. Probably why I was in the predicament I was in. Nonetheless, I blew silent kisses to my daughters' memorial, dabbed at the tears beginning to form at the corners of my eyes, and prepared myself.

Kimmy had been my best friend, probably long before I was hers. Our chance encounter at the lockers at Lakeview Middle School had resulted in years of laughter, tears, and a sisterhood bond that had only strengthened over time. I had moved on past denial into that acceptance phase that left a raw bitterness gnawing at my insides.

". . . Breaking news. A woman and child were killed when a predawn fire tore through the mansion estate in a neighborhood overlooking Lake Spivey . . ."

At the mention of the location, the familiar location so close to my own home, I turned my head to the TV to watch the newscaster continue her story.

"Twenty-five-year-old Kimera Davis and her son, seven-month-old Jamal, died in the blaze, Sgt. Paul Roberson of the Henry County Police Department said. Neighbors recounted a chaotic scene as flames engulfed the house and firefighters tried to rescue those inside. The fire started on the first floor in the back of the home, according to Stockbridge police. A Cleveland firefighter and an EMS worker were also injured . . ."

I didn't realize I had been screaming until I felt hands struggling to restrain my arms against the hospital bed. I was sobbing, my head was throbbing and all I could focus on was the image of the house burned to a pile of charred wood flashing on the screen. And knowing Kimmy and Jamal had been inside. Then I felt the tiny pinprick of the needle on my forearm, and just as quickly, the horror subsided and my eyes fluttered closed, the tears coming in quiet trails down my sunken cheeks.

The church had been thick with mourners for their funerals. A mix of family and members of Pastor Davis's church congregation stood in clusters under umbrellas on the steps outside, speaking in hushed whispers, and dabbing at their cheeks with soiled tissues.

I had felt eyes on me as I entered the building and slid into one of the back pews. Two coffins rested at the front, angled diagonally from the altar, and a picture of each of them rested in a frame on top of the powder-blue stainless steel. Just looking at the headshot of Kimmy, and then Jamal, those eyes that were gushing with warmth and innocence, had more tears falling.

Once everyone was seated, the pastor stood at the front adorned in a cream and purple robe. He signaled the musician to lower the music. "Good afternoon." His greeting was met with a few solemn murmurs. "We are here today to seek and receive comfort. Not one, but two souls have been called home to be with the Lord and though our hearts ache, we must find peace in trusting and relying *heavily on God. Not just in this time of need, but always. Proverbs 3:5 says 'Trust in the LORD with all thine heart and lean not unto thine own understanding.' We are going to move past the tears, the questions, and the doubt. For God does not make mistakes. And the Holy Spirit is here today to comfort and strengthen each of our hearts. And He will continue to be with us as we continue to live for God."*

The pastor quoted a few more scriptures, then someone belted a tear-jerking rendition of Yolanda Adams's "I'm Gonna Be Ready" that had a mass of sobs erupting.

Even as the woman trailed on the last note, the instrumentals continued to play. I slipped from the pew like putty, my body weakened with grief.

A shadow fell across the headstones and I immediately knew by the wide build who it was. I had asked him to meet me here. It had been an act of desperation but I was surprised when he obliged.

"How you holding up?" Barlow's voice came out rough as he stopped at my side. His shoulder bumped against mine, his hands shoved in his pockets. Both of our heads were lowered looking at the graves of my family and from a distance, I'm sure it looked as if we were grieving together. Certainly not conducting drug transactions.

Hearing his code to make sure we were still good to handle business, I nodded my head. "Doing good today," I answered as usual. I removed my own hand from my pocket, clutching the folded two hundred-dollar bills against my palm with my thumb. To keep the distance between us closed, I rested my head on his shoulder and his arm immediately circled my back to rub gently. Barlow took my hand and for a moment, we just stood in that platonic position while he expertly switched out the money I held for a Ziploc bag of pills. The trade was one fluid motion but as a pre-caution, we stood a moment longer before breaking contact.

I immediately released the breath I was holding. Even after months of buying these pills on the black market, it always caused me a little anxiety. What if we were caught? What if Keon found out? But I had to reassure myself it wasn't like I was a crackhead or buying heroin. It was merely the same meds my therapist had already prescribed. It was just never enough. I knew the shit I was going through so there was no way she could tell me how much medicine I needed to make me feel better. So, thank God I had met Barlow. It was my idea to start meeting at the cemetery. I was probably being paranoid, but something just didn't sit well with me doing this in back alleys or anywhere out in the open.

"So, when you gone let me take you out, little mama?" Barlow turned to face me for the first time, a sly grin on his lips. The man was the epitome of thug with the stocky build and face tattoos and arm sleeves coating his dark complexion. It was clear though his hustle was doing well for him because he always looked clean, yet not flashy enough to draw attention. It was as if he smelled like money, if he let you get close enough in his space to take a whiff.

"Come on now," I said, my smile sympathetic. "You know I'm married."

"Yeah, but he obviously ain't taking care of you like I can." Barlow nodded to my side pocket where I was now gripping the bag of pills in my fist. "He know about your little problem?"

I frowned. "I don't have a problem."

Barlow nodded, at the same time pulling out a blunt and a lighter. He fired up, lifting his head again to blow a steady stream of smoke in the air.

"Yeah, aiight," his voice laced with sarcasm. "All I'm saying is, I can make you happy, Ma. Give me a chance."

I didn't really know how to respond. No, this wasn't the first time Barlow had tried to come on to me, but it was becoming more and more persistent. And I was running out of ways to decline his advances without making it awkward between us.

Barlow must have taken my silence as permission because before I knew it, his hand was on my face and he was planting his lips on mine. I froze, shocked.

Surprisingly, his lips were soft, gentle, a stark contrast to his image. And, if I let myself admit it even for a second, I did enjoy the attention.

A moan escaped my lips and the sound had me snatching my eyes open and stepping back to break the kiss. I was breathing heavy, the taste of his weed still fresh on my mouth. Barlow seemed satisfied with my reaction and he grinned again, putting the blunt back to his lips to take another drag.

"Barlow . . ." My voice came out much weaker then I intended. Still, I pushed out the words. "Don't do that shit again. We can't—I can't . . . I'm married."

His nod was quick, his face neutral. "Yeah, I got it, Ma." But did he get it? He was now staring at me, a little too long for comfort. What did that mean?

When he turned to leave, my hand quickly snaked out to stop him. I prayed like hell this didn't mean he was done with me. "Is this . . ." I swallowed, my eyes almost pleading as he turned to look at me. "Are we . . . can I still call you? You know, if I need you?"

"Yeah, I'm not about to fuck up business," he said. "Hit me *when* you need me."

I didn't like his verbiage. As if he knew I was going to call. He knew I needed him. And dammit if he wasn't right. Still, I was satisfied just the same so I let his arm go and watched him make his way back to the waiting Escalade he had parked behind my car.

But what had my heart quickening was another vehicle easing by on the graveled road, the familiar license plate like a glare against the crisp black paint he had just gotten detailed. I know because he'd said that's where he was headed when I talked to him this morning. But here he was, in prime sight to witness everything that had just happened between me and Barlow. Shit, now I just had to figure out what all my husband had seen.

I couldn't bring myself to go home. Not yet. I tried to psych myself up by telling myself that it wasn't Keon I had seen in the cemetery. No, he'd told me he wasn't coming. I know because we had argued about it but I had settled on making the trip alone. I had been so upset that I had called Barlow, though it wasn't "time" for more medicine. I figured might as well take advantage of the opportunity. So why, then, had Keon's car been there? Had he been trying to surprise me? Did he know something and had been trying to catch me?

He hadn't bothered stopping and with good reason. I hadn't thought a lie all the way through just yet so, though I was in full-fledged panic mode, I couldn't help but sigh in relief when the car had turned the corner and disappeared from sight.

So now, in a weak attempt to prolong the inevitable, I knew, I maneuvered my car in the opposite direction from our house and headed to my mother-in-law's instead. I just needed more time to think. To come up with something. Anything that wasn't the truth but sounded reasonably like it could have been.

We had ended up moving Mama Davis to an assisted living facility. Keon and I couldn't bear the thought of her alone in that home she'd shared with the good pastor, consumed with grief and aging memories after his death. She was adamantly against moving in with us, though I could have used the company just as much as she could have. So this was the next best thing.

Golden Gates was known in the community for being the crème de la crème so Keon and I hadn't hesitated to move her there. Of course, it was expensive but the peace of mind was worth it. To our surprise, Mama Davis hadn't put up a fight. Probably due to the exhaustion of everything she had been going through, which only saddened me more.

It was hard enough for me losing my babies, but I couldn't even begin to imagine what my mother-in-law was going through. A few months prior, her husband was murdered and now, to lose her daughter and grandson. It was more than obvious, however, the circumstances were taking a toll on her. She was clearly a different woman than she was last year.

I parked in the visitor parking lot and walked along the stone pathway through the beautiful landscaped lawn. A man tended to the shrubbery and lifted his shears in the air to greet me as I walked by. I smiled in return.

Inside, the lobby looked like something out of the W Hotel, with its marble floors, floor-to-ceiling windows, and chandelier dripping from the dome ceiling. Yes, it was more than obvious what the money we handed over each month was going towards. But again, we were comforted by the round-the-clock care she was receiving, the amenities, and the sincere attention the residents received from the staff.

I checked in at the front desk, flashed the receptionist my ID in exchange for a visitor pass, and walked back outside toward the housing units. Residents had their pick of the style of their home, from Victorian to contemporary luxury. They were grouped together, joined on either side like condominiums, with a common gardens area and gazebo right in the heart of the units. They were all one-bedrooms and despite being a substantial downgrade from her house, still just enough for what Mrs. Davis needed.

I knocked on Unit 1302 and waited for her to buzz me in. I had a key but I wanted to respect her privacy. Especially because she wasn't expecting this little impromptu visit from me.

"Who is it?" Her voice cracked through the speaker beside the door.

"It's me, Mama," I said.

The buzzer signaled she had unlocked the door and I stepped inside her quaint cottage. The furniture was included and as minimal as it was, Mama Davis had brought her mementos and keepsakes to make the home her own. Her Wall of Fame held a collection of pictures from over the years, family, friends, and church members. It almost seemed like another life entirely. A two-way fireplace was against one wall but for safety reasons, was there for decorative purposes only, and above that, some Lifetime movie on mute played on the wall-mounted flat screen TV.

The smell of soup steered me to the kitchen and sure enough, Mama Davis was gingerly removing a bowl from the microwave using oven mitts. She sat the bowl on the counter and I inhaled the delicious aroma.

Again, due to safety, the residents weren't allowed any appliances in their homes other than a microwave and a refrigerator. However, with the food included every month, the chefs made meals the residents could indulge in within the common areas or bring back to their homes to enjoy alone.

"Hey Mama," I greeted and stepped into the kitchenette to give the woman a kiss on the cheek. Her smile was tiny, but a smile nonetheless.

"So glad to see you, Adria," she said, searching her drawers for a spoon. "I wasn't expecting you and Keon until next weekend."

"I know. I just . . . decided to drop by and surprise you. Check on you and make sure you were okay. You were on my mind." It wasn't a total lie. She was always on my mind. Never mind me using her as an excuse to keep from going home and facing my husband.

Mama Davis nodded and braced against the counter. My smile immediately turned into a frown when I caught her face wrinkle in pain.

"Mama, what is it?"

And just like that, the brief flicker was gone and her expression was once again neutral, except for that small smile on her lips. "Nothing, Sweetie," she said. "You don't have to come check on me. They're taking good care of me here."

"I'm glad," I said. I took her elbow and led her to the two-seater dining table. "You were fixing yourself some lunch?"

"Yes, they had this vegetable soup for dinner last night and it was so delicious. Have some. There's more in the refrigerator."

I obliged, taking out the covered Tupperware to make my own lunch. I poured us both some lemonade, grabbed us some slices of bread from the loaf on the counter, and brought everything to the table.

I hadn't made myself comfortable in the chair before Mrs. Davis grabbed my hands and bowed her head. Her grip was surprisingly strong for her feeble frame.

"Father God, thank you for this food we are about to receive for the nourishment and strength of our bodies," she prayed. "Please bless the hands that prepared it, bless our minds, hearts, and bodies." She paused before adding, "And Lord whatever my children are going through, please give them peace, for Your Comfort is with them always, and let them lean not on to their own understanding but look to you for guidance and strength. Thank you for a long fruitful life, Father. Thank you for mercy, love and grace. In Your Son's Heavenly name, we pray . . ."

I joined her with the last word. "Amen."

I felt a little uneasy with Mama Davis's prayer. It was as if she knew. But of course, being the First Lady and a devout follower of Christ for so many years, she was bound to have spiritual gifts of her own. She didn't even bother addressing the words she had felt led to speak just now, and I didn't bother bringing them up either. I guess it was true. What was understood, need not be explained.

"Soup is good, isn't it?" Mama Davis said after a few sips.

Honestly, I hadn't tasted the liquid easing down my throat. My mind was everywhere but here. But I nodded just the same.

"How are you feeling?" I asked.

Mama Davis looked at me, her eyes almost boring into my soul. I shifted uncomfortably under her stare.

"I should be asking you that same question," she said.

"I'm hanging in there," I admitted.

She nodded. "Same here," she said and reached across the table to pat my hand. I felt there was something else in the gesture, something she wasn't telling me, but I knew long ago not to push Mama Davis. She opened up when she felt like it. And if she didn't, well that was just something you dealt with. She had always been so giving of herself, so concerned with others, that she once admitted to me she didn't feel comfortable opening up about herself.

We continued eating in silence, our spoons clinking against the tableware as we polished off the soup. I hadn't, and still couldn't bring myself to mention anything to her about Keon. As far as she was concerned, we were still going strong, our family's ordeal only bringing us closer and deepening our love and support. Mama Davis was dealing with so much, with death after death, trauma after trauma, that I couldn't bear to add to her plate of disaster. Sure, Keon and I were severely estranged, but Mama Davis was only but so strong. One more tragedy and she was liable to break completely.

"Detective Terry came by to see me," Mama Davis broke the silence.

My head whipped up, my eyebrows lifted in hopefulness. "When? What did she say?"

"Couple days ago." She sighed. "She came to tell me they closed the investigation about the fire. A gas fire, they said. No signs of arson or anything other than a simple accident."

I swallowed, trying to digest the information. It had been my idea to call the police after Kimmy and Jamal's death. Something just didn't sit well with me regarding the circumstances. Leo and Tyree had taken her from that storage room where we had been held captive. Now suddenly, their bodies were found? Where were Leo and Tyree?

"Did she say anything else?" I asked.

Mama Davis shook her head. "What else is there to say, Sweetie?" she said. "It happened. Unfortunate yes, but I'm not one to question God. We grieve, we move on." Her eyes were pointed as she stared at me once more. It was clear her words were more directed at me than herself. Oh, how I wish it were that easy.

I didn't say anything but I told myself I would have a little chitchat with Detective Terry myself. There had to be something more there. Too many coincidences. Too many unanswered questions. And shit wasn't lining up. I couldn't help but feel like Leo and Tyree had something to do with these deaths. And if they did, their asses needed to be found. But if the police wouldn't do it, well then, I would have to handle it myself.

By the time I pulled into the driveway, I still hadn't settled on a story for Keon. To my horror, and relief I had to admit, I wouldn't have to worry about it for the time being. CeeCee was leaving out my front door, making her way to the truck parked against our curb. If she was over there, that could only mean one thing: Jahmad was there too. Which would give me a little more reprieve for now, because if Keon was hanging out with his best friend, then he wouldn't have time to be bothered with me.

I had to admit, it was weird seeing these two coming around more. Kimera had been so deeply in love with Jahmad, and obviously, he with her, because despite his fiancée CeeCee, he and Kimmy had carried on a full-blown affair before he eventually called off his engagement. Now how mighty convenient for this chick to pop back up in his life when he and Kimmy started having problems, namely over the question of Jamal's paternity. So when it became known that Jahmad wasn't Jamal's father, as Kimera had assured him before, he was gone and right back in CeeCee's waiting arms.

And the shit had pissed me off . . .

"I just don't understand how you can still be friends with that dog ass nigga," I yelled, pacing so hard in our bedroom that it was a wonder I hadn't walked a hole in the carpet. Keon didn't seem fazed by the outburst as he continued tying his basketball sneakers.

"That's my boy," he said, as if I needed to be reminded. "Me and Jay go back since middle school. I don't even see how it is a question. Or how it's any concern to you who I'm hanging with."

I whirled on him, my anger ignited by his nonchalance. "Don't see how?" I snapped. "Oh, do we forget that Kimera was my best friend? How Jamal was my godson and nephew, how 'your boy' was so quick to betray them both by jumping back in CeeCee's bed before trying to make it work with his family? That's the type of influence you want to be around? You don't see nothing wrong with that?"

I saw Keon's jaw tighten, evidence that I was crossing the line with my words. But I didn't give a damn. If he didn't want to see the truth, I was sure as hell going to show it to him.

"First, we ain't gone talk about my sister like she was some angel," he said, his voice low. "Now I love her, and I hate what happened. Shit is messed up but we all make mistakes. Kimmy included. Now it's not my place to speak into Jay's relationship, just like it ain't his place to speak into mine. How would you feel if he was in my ear trying to convince me to divorce you?"

"Then you would be a damn fool," I shot back with no hesita-

tion. "I've been right there for you even when you were doing me dirty. I'm not in the wrong about anything."

Now, Keon's eyes lifted and he stared at me long and hard to the point I had to replay my own words. "And I guess I'm in the wrong about something, Dria?"

I opened my mouth, shut it again. "I'm not saying that," I backpedaled, a little calmer. "I'm saying that Jahmad would have no reason to be in your ear about anything having to deal with me. He has no right."

"And neither do you."

"Kimmy was my friend!"

"And she was my sister," he yelled back, finally climbing to his feet. "What makes you think you loved her any more than I did, huh? You lost in-laws. I lost family, Adria. Shit doesn't even compare."

That stung. I closed my eyes against the threat of tears. "They were my family, too, Keon," I said, swallowing against the lump in my throat.

His back was to me now and when I saw his shoulders slump, it took everything in me not to run forward and cradle him in my arms. "We are all grieving, Adria," he said, his voice lower. "Jahmad included. He loved Kimmy, and he loved Jamal as if he were his own. You can't tell someone how to grieve or how to find peace in all this turmoil. Just like you can't tell anyone your grief is more than theirs. Because you just don't know what everyone else is going through Adria. That's what I mean by you have no right." He turned then and his next few words stunned me to silence. "And no, he can't be there for the child he lost. But the least he can do is be there for the one he's got coming."

———※·◆·◈———

When CeeCee turned, I narrowed my eyes at the hint of a belly protruding underneath the flowy maxi dress she wore. Apparently, she had been all too eager to take Jahmad back and seal the deal with him now that Kimmy wasn't around to stop them. It hurt like hell too. She was clearly happy and glowing with this pregnancy, just as I had been only a few months ago myself. But now, my twins were gone and here she was with the life I had been robbed off. Life was a bitch for sure.

I would have continued driving down the street and waited until she left but not realizing she was there, I had pressed the garage door opener too fast. Now, she turned and locked eyes with me through the windshield and I had no choice but to turn into my house and face her. She even had the nerve to offer me a pleasant smile, which sickened me even more.

I turned into the driveway and pulled up into the garage. It probably would have been rude to close the door while she patiently stood there so instead, I dipped my head, pretending to search for something in my purse.

She didn't get the hint. A minute or two later, there was a gentle knock on my window and I groaned inwardly before letting down the glass.

CeeCee's smile was still in place, small but genuine. "Hey Adria," she greeted.

"Hey."

"I didn't mean to bother you. Just wanted to speak before I left."

I nodded. "What are you doing here?"

"Just dropping Jahmad off. His car is in the shop and I think he said he and Keon were going to run out for a bit."

I nodded again. Good, good. More time to myself. More time to think. To take some medicine. To cry and grieve and wallow in my own despair.

CeeCee flinched a bit and her hand went to her stomach. As much as I didn't want to, I felt obligated to ask. "Everything okay with the baby?"

Her smile was one of surprise as it brightened her face. "Yeah, I've just been having some cramps that's all. Doctor says it's normal. Thanks," she added after another awkward moment of silence. "For asking I mean. I appreciate it."

I nodded again, silently wishing she would hurry this up.

"I wanted to also tell you," she went on. "that if you needed anything, to please give me a call. I'm not Kimera, I'm not trying to be. And I know you probably don't care for me, I get that." She sighed as if her next thought was taking all of her strength to speak. "I just . . . know what you're going through. I've had four miscarriages myself. That's why I'm a little afraid with this one. But I don't want Jahmad to be concerned so I just keep my fears to myself."

For a moment, I almost felt sorry for her. Damn, four? I couldn't imagine dealing with this tangle of emotions four times over. How was the girl still sane? I was at a loss for words.

"Thank you," I murmured finally.

That was obviously enough, and CeeCee gave a little wave before returning to her car. I watched her in the side view mirror until she backed out of the driveway and disappeared down the street. Keon was right. You never knew what other folks were going through, that's for sure.

I caught snatches of Jahmad and Keon's conversation as I entered the house through the garage. The moment I heard my name, Kimera's name, and some other choice words describing their mutual feelings and trying to get through this whole ordeal, I just let them have their moment. Besides, after the little encounter with CeeCee, I just needed my own relief.

So instead of going through the living room and having to see them, I headed to the kitchen and took the back stairs that led to the master bedroom.

The first room outside of ours was the nursery, still decorated as if the girls occupied the room even now. We had painted the walls gray and pastel pink with little elephants and sheep. Twin cribs sat on either side of the room with matching bedding. Over their beds, their names were spelled out with white letters. I had done those letters myself, taking the time to paint each one with loving strokes. By the time I had added the gemstone embellishments, I had been so proud of myself I had actually cried. Those damn hormones, I swear. But what I would give to have those moments back. It hurt to go in the room, seeing their beds, toys, and baby things completely untouched, tags still attached, signaling everything would remain showroom new. Like some kind of museum or shrine, it felt like. But it hurt just as much to not go in.

Part of me thought that maybe we could just try again. Have another baby and all of our problems would be solved. I had even attempted to on several occasions, desperate for anything to fill this void.

<hr />

I opened the bathroom door and glanced at my husband, lying asleep in the bed. Without hesitation, I slid between the tan sheets. My wet body dampened the silky fabric as I shifted closer to Keon, sliding my arm around his waist. "Baby," I whispered, pressing my breasts on his back just like I knew he liked. I flicked my tongue across his earlobe and felt him stir underneath me, his body humming to life. "Sweetie. Wake up." Keon was fully awake then, and he sat up, his face reflecting clear frustration.

"Adria, what the hell are you doing?" he said getting out of the bed. I only watched him in disbelief as he went on. "And why the hell are you wet? Damn, Girl, you play too much."

I sat up in the bed, almost feeling guilty. "I'm sorry Key, I just wanted to try again, you know. The doctor said—"

"Damn what the doctor said Adria." He was still seething as he rose and made his way across the room. "You can't just up and get pregnant and think it'll replace our daughters. That's not how this shit works."

"I'm not trying to replace them," I said, swallowing tears. "We

could never replace our babies. But we can try to move on. Pick up the pieces of our lives. What's wrong with that? You want a child just as much as I do."

Keon leaned on the dresser and shook his head. He released a frustrated breath. *"That's not how we're going to heal. Trying to hide our pain under sex, hoping and praying we have another kid. Shit sucks, it hurts, I know. But if that's your motivation for wanting to have another, you're going about this the wrong way."*

I stood up then, folding my arms against the cold air. I waited for Keon to grab my robe from the closet. When he made no move, I sighed and walked past him to retrieve it myself. *"I'm too old for this, Adria,"* he went on as I belted the robe.

"You're acting like you have to go through this on your own Keon. It's not like I'm as young as I used to be. I'm hurt and grieving and want to fix this, fix us. It's like we're wasting time." As soon as the words dripped from my lips, I regretted it. Keon's face frowned in controlled anger and he stared at me for a few seconds without speaking.

"Fuck you, Adria." He spoke a little above a whisper now. *"Since me grieving my daughters is wasting your precious time."*

"I didn't mean it like that," I defended, watching him snatch the comforter and a pillow off our bed. *"I meant it like our time could be running out. Pretty soon, we may not want kids anymore. Or we may not have time. Or—"*

"We may not even be together." Keon tossed the cover over his arm and headed for the door. *"You're right. Our time is running the fuck out."* He slammed the bedroom door shut behind him.

———◦◦◦———

I sat in the rocker next to the changing table and finally pulled out the Ziploc bag Barlow had given me. Without thinking, I pulled three from the bag and popped them in my mouth, dry-swallowing them in one gulp. I laid my head back and closed my eyes, letting the tears fall as that familiar feeling of calmness washed over me. It seemed now it took longer and longer to achieve this feeling, and that euphoria didn't last as long as it used to. Maybe I needed something stronger. But for now, no matter how temporary, at least it was something.

Chapter 4
Kimera

"Mommy," the voice squealed in delight. I opened my eyes as Leo Jr. threw his little body in my lap, giggling as if his little adventure was the funniest thing ever. His carefree spirit brought a smile to my face and, much to his amusement, I hoisted him onto the lounge chair with me and enveloped him in a bear hug.

"Kissy face," he demanded cupping my cheeks in his tiny palms.

"Kissy face," I echoed, pretending to consider the offer. "Are you sure?"

"Yes!"

"Are you really, really sure?"

"Please."

Because I knew the type of kiss he was requesting, I planted my lips on his fat cheek and blew a raspberry against his skin. His laughter was infectious and I couldn't help but chuckle myself. This little boy definitely brightened my days.

I had to admit, at first it was strange taking on the role of Leo Jr.'s mother. But my heart ached for the poor child. His biological mom, Lena, had died during childbirth; well, she was murdered if we wanted to get technical. Then there was Leo's main, conniving wife Tina, who hadn't been much of a mother to him at all. And Leo was so busy keeping his eyes on me and his body on Tyree, he didn't have time to step into the father role like he should have. But his apathy could be attributed to the fact that he wasn't biologically Leo Jr.'s father. So where did that leave the baby? Hell, I was pretty much all he had. Me and Jamal.

At first, I felt compelled to correct Leo Jr. when he tried to call me Mommy. But what if one day he got up enough courage to ask me if I wasn't his Mommy, then where was she? But he was nearly two, too young for the truth. It was easier on all of us if he just called me Mommy since that's how he saw me. And that's all I had been to him. No matter how false the reality, the perception was there.

"I'm sorry, Señora." The nanny, Lupé, walked up balancing Jamal on her hip. She looked tired and completely out of breath as she struggled to communicate her exhaustion through her thick accent. I didn't blame her. These two little ones were certainly a handful. "I turned my back for five minutes and he was gone."

I grinned, nodding my understanding. "You can leave them here with me," I offered. "I was just taking a nap but I'm up now."

"No, it's okay." Lupé gingerly took Leo Jr.'s hand and helped him to his feet. "Señor Owusu insisted I bring them inside and get them ready for bed. He says I shouldn't disturb you because he wants to talk to you later."

I frowned, not liking the sound of that.

Lupé turned to leave, then suddenly remembering something turned around to face me again. "Oh, please make a shopping list for me, Señora," she said. "I have to go to the store tomorrow since Señor Fernando is out sick."

I nodded and watched her head to the French patio doors with my boys. When she had gone inside, I leaned back against the pool chair once more. I felt Kareem's eyes on me and knew he was just a few feet away, sitting under the umbrella table with sunglasses shielding his eyes. He had been like that since I'd come out to the pool an hour ago and frankly, his brazen surveillance, or stalking as I liked to put it, was pissing me off more and more.

Across the glistening infinity pool, I lifted my hand as if to wave, then flipped it around until only my middle finger jutted upward. I couldn't even be sure he had seen the little snide gesture until the corners of his lips turned up in an amused smile. I sulked and rolled my eyes, turning my face away from his stare. My thoughts turned again to Leo. What the hell did he want with me tonight anyway?

Suddenly feeling uneasy out here alone with Kareem under the beginnings of nightfall, I rose and wrapped the beach towel I was lying on around my waist. The one-piece bathing suit was enough to cover everything worth looking at, but still, knowing Kareem's eyes were on me drinking in my every move made me a little self-conscious of my post-pregnancy body.

I stepped into my flip-flops and started inside the house. Again, for sheer amusement, I pulled the door closed behind me and locked it, leaving Kareem's ass outside. Was I being childish and petty? Hell yeah. Maybe if I annoyed him enough he would get fed up and quit this little babysitting job of his.

I journeyed into the kitchen and grabbed a Coke from the refrigerator. Leaning on the counter, I popped the top and took a deep swig, just as Kareem appeared in the doorway.

"You think you're funny," he said.

I shrugged. "Not trying to be."

"Well what are you trying to prove?"

"How much I can't stand you all down my back," I answered. "I mean, damn, can I get a little privacy sometimes? You don't have anything better to do?"

"You need to take that up with your husband," Kareem said,

stepping forward to the counter. "I get paid to do a job. And if he wants me to watch you take a shit, shower, and shave, then that's what I'm going to do."

I rolled my eyes, disgusted by his little smug demeanor. "Not many people would brag about being another man's bitch," I said. "But hey, do you Kareem."

Mission accomplished. The smug grin was gone and his eyes lit with the anger I knew my words had ignited. Served him right.

Just as quickly, as if remembering something, the flame was gone and something else was in its place. Something . . . sexual. He leaned closer and I drew in a breath. His cologne smelt delicious, like a masculine fruit. I inhaled and had to angle my head to meet his gaze struggling to ignore the embrace of his scent, his hard eyes, his body nearly touching mine. I watched his gaze drop to my gently parted lips and linger before they held my eyes again.

"Cute," he said, and I wasn't sure now if he was referencing me or my comment. I didn't like feeling like I was slowly being steered into some kind of mouse trap. Suddenly I didn't have the strength to form words so I could only shake my head. He smirked then, and stepped back and as if on cue, my breathing returned to normal.

I snatched my eyes from that hypnotic smile. Intrigue. Maybe that was it. I was now intrigued by this man that was all up in my face and space. I think I had been too annoyed with his presence to notice before, but now something was different.

Rather than risk it all and explore these new feelings that had decided to surface, I left him there alone and headed upstairs to the boys' room where Lupé was getting them settled in bed. I just stood quietly for a moment in the doorway as they each put up their little fights about not wanting to go to sleep, all while stifling yawns.

"Boys, it's time for night-time," I said walking in the room to assist. "You know the drill."

"Mommy, story please," Leo Jr. said, immediately sitting up in bed.

Lupé gave me a look, indicating she had already gone through their little story routine.

"Tomorrow," I promised. "If you go to sleep right now, I'll give you two stories tomorrow. How about that?"

Satisfied, Leo Jr. threw his arms around my neck and squeezed me tight. I hugged him back, wishing like hell this could be somewhere else. A different time, a different place. Anywhere but here.

Jamal was standing up in his crib, bouncing on the mattress and blowing spit bubbles. I *sshhed* him and laid him back too, planting a kiss on his forehead. "Night, night," I whispered.

I then joined Lupé in the hall, pulling the door to a crack at my back with the nightlight shining through.

"They are so sweet Señora Saida," she was saying, muffling a yawn of her own. I nodded my agreement. "I go to the store early in the morning before I come here if that's okay."

I started to nod again, then stopped as an idea sprung forward like it had been waiting for the most opportune time. I had to bite my tongue to keep from blurting it out.

"I'll make you a shopping list," I said, trying to keep the excitement out of my voice. "Where are you going?"

"Wherever you need me to go," she said. "I needed to pick up some groceries too."

I nodded, the plan beginning to formulate in my mind. Of course, why hadn't I thought of this sooner? And because Kareem was lurking nearby (I didn't see him, but I sure as hell could feel him), I kept my voice as casual as possible.

"Okay great. The boys need a few things. Can you swing by in the morning before you go to the store? It's going to take me a moment to make the list and I don't want to forget anything."

"Sure, Señora. I'll see you in the morning."

At that point, if it wouldn't have looked too suspicious, I would have hit a back handspring. Lupé had never gone to the store before and if she had on the chef's behalf, she certainly hadn't asked me if I needed anything. But it looked like an opportunity had finally presented itself. I definitely needed something. And it sure wasn't going to be on a grocery store shelf.

Still trying to contain my excitement, I walked to my bedroom, already working out the words I would need to write for Lupé. Sure, I could pass it off as a shopping list. Kareem wouldn't check it or anything, right? But when she got in the car, she would read the truth. That I was being held captive, that I needed her to de liver my exact location to my family in Atlanta, that she couldn't tell anyone for the safety of me and my children. It should work, shouldn't it? No reason why it shouldn't.

As soon as I clicked the bedroom door closed behind me, I turned, nearly running to my dresser to find some paper, and damn near screamed at the sight of Leo in my bed. I stopped in my tracks, watching him lift his body from the pillows propped on my headboard, the sheets pooling at his waist and exposing his naked, chiseled chest.

Almost in reflex, I took a step backwards as Leo extended his arm in my direction. "My love," he said, the words more of a de- mand.

Understanding his intent and swallowing my own disappoint- ment, I removed my towel and bathing suit before sliding into the warm sheets alongside him. Immediately, his arm came around me and pulled me close and he turned my face towards his. I cringed. No telling where this man's lips, hands, or body had been for that matter. Well, given the circumstances I had a pretty good idea. And the thought had my stomach turning because now here he was trying to get a piece of me.

"Leo," I whined as he tried to pepper my face with kisses. "Please. I'm . . . not feeling well."

Doubtful, he pulled back searching my face for any shred of the lie I was telling.

"I saw a little blood earlier," I barreled on. "I think I'm about to start my cycle and it's got me cramping." It was weak, but what was he going to do, ask me to prove it?

Whether he believed me or not, Leo let it slide and he turned me around so my back was against him and his arms were around my waist in a spooning position. I cringed again as he kept kissing, first the back of my neck, then my shoulder, his hand massaging my thigh. Damn he was getting too comfortable. I hoped like hell he wasn't planning on sleeping in here tonight. Where was Tyree anyway? Why was he insisting on bothering me tonight?

For a moment, we just laid there in silence, snuggling. Well he was snuggling, I was trying to shrink into the mattress so he wouldn't have to touch me. He was quiet so long that I had relaxed thinking he had finally fallen asleep. Then, "We need to talk about some things."

Shit. "I'm a little tired," I said, laying my acting skills on thick. "Can we talk in the morning?"

"No, I have some decisions to make," he was firm, clearly signaling there would be no negotiating about having this conversation.

I sighed. "What's wrong?"

"How do you like Naomi?"

I frowned. Is this what was so important? "I don't really know her," I said honestly. "I guess she's okay."

"You're right, you really don't know her yet," Leo said, almost to himself. "But I would like you to."

I remained quiet. What was he getting at?

"What would you say about me bringing her into our marriage?"

I'm glad it was dark. Otherwise he probably would have seen me roll my eyes so hard it was a wonder they didn't get stuck in their sockets. As if we needed more complication.

"It would make my dad happy," Leo went on quietly. "And if it makes him happy . . ." He trailed off, obviously waiting for my input.

I shrugged. "Leo, do whatever you want to do," I said. "Not

like I have a say-so in any of this. So what difference does it make what I think?"

Leo turned my body to his and now we were facing each other, illuminated only by the moon shining brilliantly through my open window.

"That's just it," he said gently, rubbing his knuckles on my cheek. "I do want your say-so. I want to make you happy, my love."

I blinked back tears, refusing to be vulnerable again with this man. A bunch of bullshit I knew because he already knew what would make me happy. And yet still, he was too selfish to care.

"Maybe we should all go out," he went on at my continued silence. "Get to know each other a little better. What do you think?"

The suggestion had my ears perking up. Out? As in out of the house? Hell yeah, that's what we needed to do. I hadn't been off of this property since we got here. Maybe, just maybe if I was somewhere public . . .

My mind was already calculating, so much so that I didn't notice when he had pressed gentle lips against mine. "What do you say? Would that make you happy, my love?"

I nodded, trying to keep from seeming too eager. "Yes, I would like us to go out and get to know each other better," I said. "I want to give her a chance. She seems like a nice young lady."

Leo smiled, obviously pleased with my words. "I think so, too," he said. "Though I don't know how happy I am about taking on another partner."

"Why?"

This time, it was Leo who pulled back. "I like what we have here," he admitted. "I like . . . us. You, my boys." He stopped there as if that were all parties involved. I wondered if he had said the same thing to Tyree.

"Well, just tell your dad," I suggested for lack of anything else to say.

Leo shook his head. "You know I can't do that."

"I don't get it. You're grown. Why do you have to always do what he says?"

Leo's sigh was heavy and he leaned back even further from me, completely breaking contact. I appreciated the space.

"You didn't grow up with him," he said, finally. "There's no arguing or objecting him. His word is law. And if you don't go with it . . . well you let me know if you find someone alive who has gone against him."

His words sent a chill down my spine.

"He's powerful," Leo continued. "Let's just leave it at that. So when he moves here, you don't go against him. Understand, my love?"

"Wait," I sat up. "What do you mean? Moving here? In this house?"

"No not here, but to this neighborhood."

"Why is he leaving Africa?"

"For our protection."

I didn't like the sound of all this. "What is going on Leo? Protection from whom? For what?"

Leo sat up next to me and folded me in his arms. His weak attempt to provide some sort of pseudo-comfort only angered me.

"Nothing to worry about my love. Only as a precaution. And it's temporary, until we put some things in place to move."

"Move? Where?"

"To Côte d'Ivoire."

I shook my head, my hope diminishing bit by bit. If I moved to Africa, my family would never be able to find me. Then what would I do?

"But why, Leo? What aren't you telling me?"

"I'm telling you what you need to know," he said giving me a reassuring kiss. "The rest, I'll take care of it."

"But when?"

"Soon, my love."

Now tears did come, desperate as I struggled to calm my rising panic. Whether it was dark or Leo was wrapped up in his own thoughts, he appeared not to notice.

Then he turned and again, as if suddenly remembering I was there, smiled and wrapped his arm around my waist.

"So, tomorrow then?"

His words had rattled me and I racked my mind trying to figure out what the hell he was talking about now.

"Tomorrow?" I echoed, frowning in confusion.

"You, me, Naomi," he said. "We'll go someplace nice."

I didn't respond. Instead I was trying to figure out all this new information Leo had thrown at me. And what the hell was I going to do now?

Chapter 5
Adria

I wasn't crazy. No matter how much I mourned my children and my best friend, I damn sure could pick up on the subtle changes with my husband.

Of course it wasn't anything major or glaringly obvious. But I did notice when Keon would come home and jump straight into the shower without so much as a glance in my direction first. I noticed how he spent a little extra time in the mornings getting dressed for work, how he seemed to be in much lighter spirits and I knew I hadn't put him in that place. Why wasn't he grieving with me, wallowing in mutual misery that could only be felt by parents suffering a loss? No, he was past that. And I needed to know how. Or better yet, with whom.

Fortunately, I had gone down this road with Keon before, this little playboy phase of his. So I recognized the signs. Unfortunately, I had gone down this road with Keon before. So I also recognized the heartache.

Keon didn't expect to see me in the living room when he came home from work. Probably didn't expect to see me anywhere outside of the nursery. That room had become my tomb and my altar. So I could see the sheer shock when I turned from my position on the couch to greet him as entered the room and tossed his gym bag on the floor.

"Hey," I said, leaving the single word to hang between us. Keon looked at me, then to the empty kitchen as if trying to assess how much of me was "back to normal," if that was such a thing. Seeing that I hadn't cooked, hell, hadn't so much as dusted off the cobwebs on the stove in months, he sighed, almost like he was disappointed.

"How you feeling?" he asked.

How was I feeling? Hell kind of question was that. Empty. Dead. How was I supposed to feel?

Instead, I murmured, "Fine," since I knew that's probably all he would tolerate right now to alleviate an argument. I was uncomfortable. This was uncomfortable. "How was work?"

"Fine."

"Good."

Silence. Then, "I'm going out for a bit. I'll be back."

The signs, the signs. I would be an idiot to ignore them again. "Where are you going?"

"Out."

I was just as appalled at him. Never had he been so evasive since we had gotten married. Then again, I hadn't been so inquisitive either.

"With Jahmad?"

"Why?"

"I was just asking, damn. Why you getting so defensive?"

Keon smirked, almost amused at the question. "You haven't paid any attention to me in a long time, Adria. Honestly didn't think you cared."

That hurt but I ignored it.

"Yeah," he went on. "Me and Jay will probably take care of some business."

I rolled my eyes. "Don't know why you still fooling with that asshole. After—"

I stopped short when Keon mumbled something and abruptly left the room. I was right on his heels. "What?" I pushed. "Don't want to hear the truth?"

"Adria don't start that shit tonight. Please."

"Then don't go out with him."

"And what?" he countered, turning to face me. "Stay home with you while you sit in the nursery like some mindless zombie? No, thanks. I'd rather go out."

I followed him into the garage, still warm were he had pulled his truck in just moments before. Hadn't even been home five minutes.

"Who you going to see?" I said as Keon jumped behind the wheel of his car. "Huh? You bastard who is she?" I was yelling now, my frantic screams bouncing off the cement as the garage door rumbled open. I'm sure I looked like a lunatic banging on the hood of his truck before he slammed it in reverse and out of my arm's reach.

Before I knew it, I was running back inside to grab my phone and keys and jumping in my own car to follow him.

Keon had a good five-minute head start on me but I was able to catch up to his truck with its custom Falcon plates at Camp Creek Parkway. He was at the light and I could see he was on his cell phone. But since mine wasn't ringing, the fact that it was someone else only infuriated me even more. The bastard.

I kept my distance, easily navigating in and out of traffic so I stayed at least two cars behind him, no more no less. Yet still, my phone didn't ring so I assumed he hadn't realized I was following him. Not yet anyway. At one point, I chanced calling him, pissed when his voicemail message immediately rang in my ear.

I steered with one hand and texted with the other, 'WE NEED TO TALK. PLEASE.' The notification next to my sent message indicated READ, and yet still, no return reply.

It was times like this I wished desperately I could call Kimmy. She always had some words to talk me off the ledge with her brother. Even if in my stupidity, I didn't listen, she was still there. But now here I was alone. Tailing my husband like some predictable scene out of a Lifetime movie. I had become the wife I always despised, had always said I would not be.

Keon's car slowed and my heart cracked and bled out my shirt when I saw him ease into the parking lot of the Hilton Hotel near the airport. I knew for sure he was not meeting Jahmad at a damn hotel.

Just as he parked in the visitor lot and stepped into view, I dialed him once more, silently pleading that he'd answer. I was past angry. I was devastated and most importantly, afraid.

I watched him glance at his phone before swiping the screen to reject my call and shoving the device in his back pocket. He walked right in front of me. Clearly, his mind was on his destination in that hotel because he didn't even look my way or he would've seen me through the windshield, tears dribbling down my face like a faucet. Because I was remembering a time when we were at this very same place, a special time when we both were actually happy.

<hr>

Excitement wasn't even the word I would use. Elated. Ecstatic. Euphoric were more like it. Keon had finally invited me on our first official date. And even though we were still sneaking around sleeping together behind Kimmy's back, it was definitely another level I had been yearning for.

I settled into the black leather seats of his truck and smiled at the two steaming Styrofoam cups of coffee resting in the cup holder. "Look at you." I tossed Keon an appreciative smile when he slid in the car and handed me one of the cups.

"Figured it would help a little."

I nodded and took a sip, not bothering with the cream cartons and sugar packets he offered. The caffeine already seemed to be kicking my energy up a notch. Even just being around him had lifted my spirits and dispelled all doubts of his sincerity about me. This was exactly what I had needed.

"So where are we going," I asked as he maneuvered the vehicle out of the complex. "I wasn't going to ask but you got me curious."

"Can't you just sit back and ride?"

"Not really. For all I know, you could kidnap my ass."

Keon laughed. "I assure you. You would go willingly. You must not like surprises," he concluded.

"Negative. I do like surprises."

"Well, you must not like me."

I smirked at the loaded question. "What's your point," I asked, instead.

"My point is, if you enjoy surprises, and you enjoy me, then you should be able to relax and know you're going to have a good time. Don't we always have a good time?"

That much was absolutely true. A charmer. "Do you always get what you want, Keon?" My amused grin froze when he took my hand and lifted it to his face. The kiss was gentle; a reassuring brush of lips on my knuckles, but enough to have my heart stuttering.

"I'm not going to say I usually get what I want," he answered. "But I will say, anything I want, I go for it." Damn, he was good.

Keon drove with leisure. The windows were down to let the comfortable breeze drift through, the radio soft enough for conversation, but loud enough to have me murmuring along to the music. When he placed his hand on mine on the armrest, I didn't budge at the casual gesture.

After a short drive, Keon eased the car to the back of the Hilton Hotel, up a brick driveway and under the arch of a stone building. A Spa Jadore sign hung suspended between two columns, and large windows allowed a glimpse of the elegantly decorated reception. A valet was already opening my door and extending his hand to help me out.

"Welcome to Spa Jadore," he greeted, before rounding the hood to the driver's side. I was surprised to feel my body almost heating with anticipation.

Inside, candles, plush cream couches and ottomans, lap throws, and glass shelves adorned the lobby. Someone had lit the fireplace and a mellow flame cracked the air as it licked a stack of firewood, filling the room with the smell of hickory.

Keon headed to the reception desk while I wandered to a set of French double doors towards the back of the room. I peered through, admiring the pool, hot tub, and rock formation waterfall, all surrounded by an assortment of palm trees, hammocks, and patio furniture.

"Gorgeous, huh?" Keon touched the small of my back as he joined me at the door.

"It really is," I agreed, turning to share a generous smile. "Thank you for this."

"No problem. First things first, a couple's massage. Then you can do your girly thing."

I laughed. "What's my 'girly' thing?"

"You know, your nails. Face."

"Oh yeah," I flirted. "And what's wrong with my face?"

"Too damn sexy," he responded and had me laughing again.

We were shown down a spiral staircase where the young attendant led us to our respective areas.

I noticed the women's changing room carried the same luxury and high-end finishing as the rest of the resort; from the deep, chocolate lockers lining each wall, to the patterned tile floors with rich shades of rust and saffron. When I removed my socks and shoes, I could only smile as the under-floor heating radiated gentle warmth to each of my feet.

As instructed, I moved to change into the monogrammed spa robe, savoring the distinct smell of honeysuckle that infused the locker room and drifted suggestively into the attached bathroom. Damn. The depth of this serenity had my body nearly throbbing in appreciation. Yes, I would allow this place to spoil me for the day. I deserved it.

Keon didn't bother with subtlety as his eyes wandered over my body when I emerged. Turned on, I fingered the lapel of his identical robe, catching the hint of chest hair peeking through the opening. "Well, don't you look nice," I commented. I was surprised when he mimicked my gesture, his fingers brushing my neck in the process.

"You too," he said.

I smiled. Is this what real couples did? I was beginning to enjoy the volley of flirtation between us.

The attendant led us into a European-style room, dimly-lit with a range of earth tones and two massage tables. "If you two will get comfortable on the tables," she said, adjusting the lighting on the wall, "your masseuses will be in shortly."

As soon as the door closed, I watched Keon turn his back to me and I couldn't help but smirk. Did he call himself now being respectful? After all the sexing we had done with each other over the years?

"What's the matter," I teased. "You afraid to see me naked?"

Keon chuckled and glanced over his shoulder long enough to toss a wink in my direction. "No, I'm afraid I won't be able to lie down flat on my stomach."

I laughed as I loosened the belt on my robe. I let the robe slip *from my shoulders and pool at my feet. My breath quickened and my eyes remained fixed on Keon's back. He had to feel the sudden spike in sexual tension that nearly had the room vibrating. I didn't give a damn what we had previously agreed to. I wanted him. So, I waited.*

When his own robe fell to the floor, I sucked in a breath. Damn, the man was cut. I appreciated his body each and every time I saw him. I could easily visualize my nails raking over each chisel of his chocolate frame; from the defined angles in his back down to those ripped thighs, taut with what I knew for a fact was enough aggressive power to handle even my wildest orgasm.

I climbed onto the table facedown and adjusted the sheet to cover my waist and legs. We rested in silence for a few moments, a soft jazz melody breezing through an in-ceiling speaker.

"Do you like to travel?" he asked.

"That is an off-the-wall question." But, I did appreciate the change in subject. I looked at him, watched his lazy grin spread, and could only smirk in return.

"Not off-the-wall if I'm trying to get to know you, Adria," he commented. "Isn't that what we said we were going to try to do? No more casual sex? Building a real relationship?"

"True," I said, appreciating how he quoted my request word-for-word. He was listening. And complying. "Well I do like to travel. I just don't get to do it as often as I would like."

"I hear you. Kimmy and I used to do more traveling together but that kind of died down."

"She probably got tired of your silly ass."

"Probably so." Keon's raspy laugh was just as erotic as his smile. "I guess that's something we can do now."

My smile flourished. Oh, he was saying and doing all the right things. "I guess so," I agreed.

A man and woman walked through the door, dressed identically in crisp, white t-shirts and white cargo shorts. My masseuse was Jude, a young blond with a stocky build and huge hands. I closed my eyes, enjoying the feel of warm oil dribbling on my back. I couldn't be sure if Jude was actually trying to hold a conversation with me and honestly, I couldn't care less. Instead, I focused on my body beginning to come alive with his delicate presses, his fingers gliding over my skin like satin.

I pictured Keon's hands on me, kneading my back, easing down to squeeze my ass, slap it, then massage the sting with gentle strokes. He would replace his hands with his tongue, using the tip to coat my skin and lap the oil. Then, he would trail down. Down. And he would moan and lick his lips, preparing to devour. When I wiggled in anticipation, he would dive in—

"Ma'am?"

Jude's nudge snatched me from my dream. I eyed him, curious if I had made some outward display of the damn good fantasy my mind was playing for me.

"You're all done," he said.

But I couldn't help but smirk at the double statement. Because no, I was not all done. Keon and I were just getting started.

I don't know how long I sat out there after Keon went inside. I do know the sun began to set and pretty soon, a hotel valet was knocking on my window to move me along because I had probably exceeded the limit on parking in this drop-off only zone. He was right. I had long since dropped off my husband to another woman. Now what was I waiting for? For him to come out and tell me how good she was?

I drove around with no purpose or destination for a while. Didn't recognize the streets and by the looks of the thugs clustered on each corner, I didn't need to stop and ask either. I couldn't bring myself to go home but home was where my pills were. And now, more than ever, I needed something to relieve the pain.

Barlow's number was scattered in my call log more frequently than Keon's. Maybe he had been right. I needed him more than I needed my husband right now. And, shit, he had proved time and time again he had been there for me more than my husband. Tonight was no different.

"What you need, Ma?" he answered after he picked up on the first ring.

"Something to take the edge off."

"You calling out of routine, Ma," he said with a chuckle. "I'm at the crib." I had been around Barlow enough to know that was code for one of his trap houses counting money, so apparently I had caught him at a bad time.

"Can I come by?"

That caught him off guard. "Here?"

"Yeah. I . . . need to see you." I didn't give a damn how it sounded. I was desperate at that point and right now, Barlow had what I needed.

"Where you at?" he asked after a minute.

"Honestly, I don't know."

"The hell you doing out this time of night anyway, Ma? You lost?"

"I think so."

Barlow smacked his lips. "What you see? What street names?"

I squinted as I eased up to a four-way stop. "Glenwood Ave.," I read.

"Ah shit, Ma. Don't move. I'm on my way. Lock your damn doors 'fore somebody snatch yo' ass up." *Click.*

It almost sounded like he was joking but I quickly did as I was told. He appeared to know more about this area than I did anyway.

Thirteen minutes later, I know because I was counting, a black

Honda pulled up alongside my car, blacked out from the windows to the rims. I didn't look over until I saw the driver's side window roll down and I breathed a sigh of relief when Barlow's head came into view. He gestured for me to follow him and he waited while I turned my car around to get behind him.

Barlow led me through several neighborhoods before we pulled up to a decent size one-story home. He pulled his Honda under the single carport and I pulled behind and cut off my engine.

I waited while Barlow unfolded his body from the car and walked to me. He opened my car door and I felt his eyes gaze up and down my body, nodding his head in appreciation of my simple yoga attire. "You coming in?"

I felt a danger alarm going off and I tried my best to tune it out. "You don't want me to just wait out here?"

There was that chuckle again. Barlow must've been entertaining himself because I sure didn't see anything funny.

"Nah, Ma," he said. "Not in this area. Come inside for a sec. Don't worry. I got what you need."

He turned then, confident I was going to follow. He was right. All that talk about this being a bad neighborhood was scaring the hell out of me. I locked my car and half-ran to catch up with Barlow. At least I knew I would be safe with him.

The inside was definitely a different atmosphere than outside. Outside felt like an older home that belonged to someone's great grandmother. Inside looked completely renovated, a clear indication of where they had invested their drug money. Two women were sitting at the dining room table bagging pills, and a man was hunched over the coffee table counting money. It all looked too obvious in my opinion, having everything out in the open like this, but what did I know about the drug game?

No one spoke and we didn't even bother stopping at the tables but instead continued to the back of the house. Barlow opened the door to one of the bedrooms and stepped to the side to allow me to enter first.

The room was enveloped in darkness with the exception of a red light bulb coming from a floor lamp beside the bed. Through the red tint, I could see a bed in black sheets that dominated the center of the room and a single dresser pushed against one wall. That's it. Nothing on the dresser, not an article of clothing laid out, nothing to indicate the room was actually lived in.

I took a few hesitant steps in, whirling around when he closed the door behind us. There was that smirk again.

"You need to relax, Ma," Barlow said, stepping around me and taking a seat on the bed. "You act like I'm about to do something to you."

I watched him kick off his shoes and reach underneath the bed for something. He pulled a magazine into view. On top was a bag of white, powdery substance I instantly detected was cocaine. Dipping his pinky in the bag, he brought the powder to his mouth and rubbed some on his gums. I just stared.

"You looking like you want to hit this," Barlow said.

I shook my head. "No, I really just want some more pills."

"Damn you running through them shits quick."

I didn't know why but the comment put me on the defense. I crossed my arms. "Forget it. Let me get out of here," I said even though I made no move to go. We both knew I wasn't leaving this room without my medicine.

Barlow sat the magazine on the bed beside him and gently patted his lap. "Come talk to me for a minute, Ma." He licked his lips and though I didn't tell them to, I felt my legs moving in his direction. I don't know whether it was me or the drugs in the air but I was beginning to feel a little buzzed. So I didn't object when Barlow pulled me down on his lap and brushed my hair behind my shoulder.

"You know you sexy, right?" Now I could smell the weed on his breath and unconsciously I leaned closer to inhale the scent deeper.

Barlow closed the distance between us, assaulting my lips with his while his hand found its way under my t-shirt. I tasted remnants of the cocaine powder on his tongue and, like an addict, I lapped it up eagerly. This felt so wrong. So forbidden. But so damn good.

He laid me back on the bed and sat up just enough for him to pull his shirt over his head. He was muscular for sure, but I couldn't help but notice the healing cuts crisscrossing his midsection. Then he was lying on top of me and I felt the heat waking up every organ in my body, each humming to life with an intense ache that left me quivering. Had it been that long?

Barlow licked and sucked me dry while my hands fisted in the sheets and I moaned every syllable in his name like a lullaby. My legs tightened around his neck as he used his tongue to coax the orgasm from hibernation and I bucked and arched to let him feast on every part of me. Every part that, up to now, had been exclusively for my husband. But after seeing his little hotel rendezvous, I didn't care. Even when Barlow slid in me raw and I felt every painstaking inch massage my walls, I didn't care. I didn't think. Just rode on the ecstasy until my skin was in flames and slicked wet with our chemistry.

Barlow emptied himself and collapsed beside me, completely spent. I waited until my breathing subsided before turning to climb out the bed.

"Where you going?"

I paused and glanced over my shoulder. "I was just . . . I thought we were done."

"Nah, come here Ma." Barlow held out his arm for me and I obediently snuggled in the crook. "I got your shit," he assured me stroking my hair and back. "I want you to try this other stuff first, then I'll give you your pills and follow you home."

I angled my head to look up at him. "How much I owe you?"

Barlow's grin was huge in the dim light. "You paid up, Ma."

I nodded, more satisfied with that than the actual sex. At least I would be leaving with two things that made me feel better. If only for now. I couldn't speak for the next time.

Chapter 6
Kimera

I was torn tonight.

Part of me was excited. It had been a long time since I had been out of the house so I was going to take advantage of this opportunity for sure. Leo had gone out and bought me a sexy Michael Kors dress with a red beaded corset and a hi/low hemline, shorter in the front to show off my legs and trailing long to brush my ankles in the back. I had done my own makeup, taking extra care to contour my cheekbones and blend the colors on my eyes until they were a smoldering dramatic gray. Having the brushes back in my hand almost had me forgetting my circumstances. Almost took me back to a time when makeup was my life, and Adria and I had wanted to open our own cosmetic store. I take that back. Not just wanted to, had actually done it. But that, along with the rest of our dreams, had vanished up in smoke. Literally.

I stood back, admiring my work. Had to admit, I still had it though. My hair had grown long enough for me to be able to pull it into a loose bun with simple strands cascading down the sides of my face. I was smelling good, looking good, and even feeling good despite the news Leo had dropped on me last night. I would deal with that later. One day at a time. And for now, I needed to be focused and alert. If I played my cards right, maybe, just maybe I could get myself out of this predicament and none of that 'moving to Africa' mess he revealed would even matter to me.

But the other part, and I had to admit this was almost outweighing the excitement, was fear. I had been able to give Lupé the note this morning. Because Leo seemed to be scrutinizing my every move, I had resorted to writing the note while I was in the tub and hiding it in the pocket of my robe. I had tried to appear as casual as possible, swallowing bits of the fresh omelet I had been too nervous to taste for breakfast while sneaking looks at the security monitors to see if Lupé's car was pulling up to the gate.

Finally, Lupé had arrived and I told her to come with me to check on the boys. Then, since Kareem was up my ass as usual, I had to slip the note in her purse the moment we stepped in the room. With luck, she would find it while she was in the store and get the message back to Atlanta. At least that's what I was praying for. It seemed like it would work. No, *should* work. Then why was I so afraid?

Because I didn't know who I could trust, I admitted. After everything I had gone through, it was hard to say which side people were on. If word got back to Leo about my little escape attempt, well, I shuddered to think what he would do. So, basically, I was functioning on hopes, faith and prayers here. And a splash of alcohol as needed.

Speaking of which, I grabbed my drink from the dresser and knocked back another glass of merlot. My third one. I was on edge and the wine was doing nothing to ease my anxiety.

Lupé had never returned from her store run this morning. The items she had picked up were delivered earlier this afternoon by some errand boy that Leo seemed to know. As hesitant as I was, I finally got up enough courage to ask, considering the boys had been looking for her too.

Leo just shrugged it off. "She said something about going to the hospital to visit her sister," he said. "We'll check on her tomorrow. Amora is going to come by and babysit the boys tonight," he added, referencing one of his dad's wives. I didn't remember which one she was but that wasn't my concern right now. I just hoped by hospital, she meant post office to send off my letter. And I hoped like hell Lupé didn't go running to the police. The kind of pull that Leo, and even his father, had around here, I couldn't trust officers either. No, that letter had to get home. That was the only way I could be sure everything would be done to find me.

But no Lupé today, so no news. I would have to wait until she came over in the morning. And pray like hell this was the beginning of the end as Saida Owusu.

I glanced up from the vanity mirror just in time to see Kareem open my bedroom door. I whirled around then, a slew of curses already on my tongue about his abrupt invasion of my privacy. But I could only stare.

I had never seen the man outside of a sweat suit or black jeans and a t-shirt. But damn he could wear the hell out of a Hugo Boss. The suit hung just right on his body, as if it were personally tailored to accentuate every bend and angle in his frame. Of course, it was his signature color, black with a crisp, white collared shirt underneath. He had apparently gotten a fresh haircut too, his beard thick and rich like some kind of pristine muzzle that had me staring entirely longer than I intended.

The glint in Kareem's eyes was one of amusement and embarrassment; I rose to cross to my closet. Anything to get the oxygen circulating in my lungs again.

"What do you think you're doing?" I asked.

"What do you mean?"

I turned then, tossing an absentminded gesture to his outfit. "Why are you all dressed up tonight?"

Kareem frowned. "I thought we were going to dinner."

Now it was my turn to frown. "No, *I'm* going to dinner with Leo. You're not invited."

"You sure about that?"

But I wasn't sure. Kareem had obviously gone through so much trouble to get suited and booted tonight, but for what? And now he had the nerve to stand here grinning at me like I was the butt of some kind of joke. Was I missing something?

Slightly flustered, I stormed to the door, ignoring the cologne that smelled of delicious fresh mint and cinnamon, and descended the stairs. I couldn't be sure but I felt like I almost heard Kareem chuckling as he followed close behind me. Damn him.

Leo was at the bar and immediately turned when he heard me enter the massive living room. His eyes lit and he took me in from head to toe. His lips peeled back into an approving smile.

"You look radiant, my love." As customary, he took my hand and kissed my palm.

"Thank you," I struggled with a smile myself. "Leo, didn't you mention dinner would just be us tonight?"

"And Naomi," he added.

I nodded. "Yes, of course. And Naomi. That's it, right?"

Leo started to nod, then as if remembering, he lifted his eyes to the man who hovered so close behind me. Too close for comfort.

"Ah yes, I thought it would be a good idea if Kareem came along."

I pouted. "But why?" I knew I sounded like I was whining, but dammit I was whining. Kareem wouldn't do anything but watch me the entire time. It was uncomfortable enough. How was I going to get away then? Plus, and this I didn't want to admit even to myself, he was a distraction. I hadn't noticed so much before but my body was certainly noticing now.

Leo handed me a glass and clinked it against mine. "Relax, my love," he said, kissing my forehead for reassurance. "We are all going to go out and have a great time. Can we do that?"

I frowned into my drink and again, felt Kareem's eyes staring into my back. I couldn't bring myself to turn and face him but I would bet my life he was gloating like hell.

I opened my mouth to voice my objection but saw Leo's eyes had again shifted from me to someone behind me. This time I did turn and saw Naomi enter the room, looking unbelievably stunning in a beaded mini cocktail gown. She had piled her hair into a high, messy bun and accentuated her dress with subtle jewelry at her ears and wrists. Sensing all attention was on her, she stopped and did a twirl, exposing the deep cutout back and her sculpted calf muscles.

She looked good. Okay, she looked damn great. I felt my self-consciousness creep up a little because standing beside her, I felt like the older woman, trying to be young and sexy.

For a brief moment, I caught a whiff of déjà vu. Only this time, I was Tina and Naomi here, she was me. Did she really know what she was getting into? Was she prepared to handle the consequences? Lord knows if I could turn back the hands of time . . .

"My world," Leo side-stepped me and opened his arms to greet Naomi. I took note. I was his love. She was his world. Interesting.

Naomi nearly leapt into Leo's embrace, throwing her arms around his neck and kissing him passionately. No, of course she didn't know what was she getting into. She saw Leo and saw dollar signs, just like my stupid ass.

"I missed you sweetie," Naomi crooned in her baby voice.

"I always miss you," Leo said. He kept his arm around Naomi's tiny waist and turned to me, holding out his hand. I obliged taking hold of his and stepping into his embrace as well.

"Naomi, meet Saida. Saida, Naomi."

I nodded as Naomi's smile widened. "So glad to finally meet you," she said. "I've heard so much about you. You're so pretty."

Well, this was certainly awkward. As fake as it was, I smiled for lack of anything better to do.

"Leo said you know how to do makeup," she went on. "And yours looks so good. Can you please do mine?"

I hesitated, not really sure how to respond.

Leo spoke up for me. "Of course she can. You don't mind, do you my love?" He eyed me as if daring me to object. Keep the peace, keep the peace, was all I could tell myself. The quicker we could get this over with, the quicker we could be on our way. And maybe, if I showed my compliance, Leo would be more trusting of me going out in public.

"Of course I would love to," I said. And for good measure, I added, "It shouldn't take too long. You really don't need much."

Naomi let out a little squeal and surprised the hell out of me when she folded me into a hug. "Oh thank you! You are so sweet. Leo, I love her already."

She kissed Leo again and led me to the huge master bedroom behind the staircase. So this was where he had her staying. The room was majestic and took up nearly half of the downstairs square footage. Across the canopy king bed and even on the floor, Naomi had thrown several dresses, evidence she'd had a hard time picking her attire for the evening. The entire room smelled like her, orange blossom.

"I really appreciate this," Naomi said as she stepped out of her shoes and headed to the bathroom. "I can't do a lick of makeup. Never have. Not even in high school."

I glanced behind me, surprised when neither Leo nor Kareem followed. Good. Maybe this little girl time would work out in my favor. For extra measure, I closed the double French doors and followed her.

"No offense, but you look like you're still in high school."

For some reason, Naomi found that hilarious. "Aw, thank you so much. Why would I take offense to that compliment?"

She plopped down on the bench in front of the mirror and gestured to the large spread of makeup and brushes scattered across the marble counter. Most had never even been opened, but the brands let me know this was all top-shelf cosmetics. "Leo let me go shopping," Naomi explained. "So I just went to the store and asked the saleslady what I needed to buy. As you see, I'm new to all this."

I picked up the primer and removed the cap. But as much as I loved it, makeup was the last thing on my mind. Here again, I didn't know if I could trust this woman. She seemed so wild and carefree. And it was obvious from their interaction that she adored Leo. So wouldn't she be in his corner despite what I told her?

"So how did you meet Leo's father?" I started, beginning to apply her makeup. "He presented you at Leo's birthday party so I'm assuming you've known him before?"

"I met Obi a few weeks ago. I was waiting tables and he sat in my section. He made me laugh and I thought he was just the sweetest man."

I frowned. So what? She was just looking for a sugar daddy or something? Why would this sexy thing come on to Obi Owusu, unless she smelled the money?

"So he said he wanted to introduce me to his son. I said sure. I haven't been having much luck in the dating field."

"So, how much do you know?" I pressed, trying to make my questions appear like casual girl chat.

Naomi tossed me a questioning look.

"Like, about me," I clarified, quickly. "Me and Leo. Us. This whole thing."

Naomi shrugged. "A little I guess. He told me Leo had a wife but was looking for someone else too. I asked if he meant you two were looking for somebody to have a threesome with."

I shook my head. This girl, here.

"I mean, you never know nowadays, right?" she went on. "Or if y'all were swingers or were into some *Fifty Shades of Grey* kind of kinky stuff, you know."

"And what did Obi say?"

"He said it was nothing like that. That his son was looking for another partner in a poly relationship." Naomi's shoulder lifted in a careless shrug. "I said sure, why not. How bad could it be?"

I had to pause so Naomi didn't feel my hands shaking on her face. How bad could it be? How about murder, down-low men, kidnapping, faked deaths, crazy lovers, and physical abuse, just to name a few. Hell, I had even done a little stint in jail after I'd been framed for trying to kill Leo. Oh, it could be really, really bad.

"You know, I wasn't sure if I could do it," Naomi said. "Like, be his wife while he goes out to get other women. You're strong, Saida. I hope I'm as strong as you. Does it get any easier?"

It wasn't what she meant, but I had to agree. To endure all of this, I had to be strong. If only for my kids. But, easier? That was certainly a loaded question. Had any of this really been easy at all? "No," I said simply and left it at that.

I finished her face in silence, letting Naomi ramble on and on about whatever. By the time I was done, I had learned naïve little wife number two wasn't the sharpest knife in the drawer. She didn't have much family with the exception of a half-sister she barely spoke to and a dad who was always too drunk to notice she wasn't doing anything with herself since she barely graduated high school. She had moved to Texas from North Carolina to be with some boy she met online, but it turned out she had been catfished. And because she really didn't have the money to go back home, not that there was much of a home to return to, she settled for a little waitressing job and paid some girl she met on Craigslist $75 a month to crash on her couch. She loved to party, that much was certain. For her to be twenty-six, she spoke about clubs and parties like she was still in college. Had I been like that? I couldn't help but wince at the comparison.

So, when Obi had been seated in her section at The Capital Grille restaurant, she had jumped on the opportunity because, in her eyes, she had hit rock bottom and it was only up from here. Classic damsel in distress and here comes the African knight in shining armor.

"I need your help," I blurted out suddenly.

Naomi frowned and it was clear I had interrupted whatever she was talking about. Proof I was no longer listening to a word she was saying.

"With my makeup?" she said with a laugh. "Girl I told you I can't—"

"No. I need you to get me out of here."

The door startled us both and I turned as Leo crossed the bedroom and entered the bathroom. He looked first to me, then Naomi. I held my breath. *Had he heard something?*

When Leo looked to Naomi and grinned, I could do nothing but sigh in relief. "Beautiful," he said. "Both of my women. I'm so in love."

Naomi hesitated a moment longer before turning on the stool

to look at my work in the mirror. Her eyes met mine in the mirror, her expression unreadable. Then, she too smiled. "I love it," she said. "Leo was right. You're like an artist with makeup."

"Thank you."

Leo held his hands out and we each took one. "Shall we go?"

Chapter 7
Adria

I shouldn't have felt guilty. It wasn't like this was special or anything.

I did a small turn in the mirror, observing the way the fabric hugged my curves and was short enough to show an ample amount of leg. The heels only further accentuated the muscles in my calves and the little pieces of jewelry I'd added to my ears and neck further solidified what I didn't even want to admit to myself. Yeah, I had every reason to feel guilty.

Of course I hadn't meant to keep seeing Barlow. The way I saw it, our little arrangement was merely business. He had something I needed and hell if that meant me having to spread my legs to allow him his fill so I could have a steady supply streaming, then so be it.

Tonight was no different. He'd invited me over for some kind of party. I didn't plan on going to mingle or any of that. I was going to pick up my prescription and then I could come back home. Period. The fact that he was making a special request about my attire, well was that really a big deal? So what if he wanted to see some legs? They were one of my best assets I had to admit. And if I could use them to my advantage, well then why not?

I had to keep telling myself why I was involved in the first place. It wasn't for the sex. And it damn sure wasn't for Barlow. I don't know, I guess a part of me felt satisfied. Not necessarily happy, satisfied. I remember once I had asked Kimmy what the difference was, back when she first told me why she was doing what she was doing when she got involved with Leo in the first place. I couldn't understand it. Not then, but now . . . wasn't I justifying my actions with the same excuse? Did it really matter that I wasn't happy, as long as I was satisfied? Because at the end of the day, if it meant I wasn't depressed, that I wasn't wallowing in my grief and self-pity, wasn't that a good thing? Hell, that's what everyone seemed to want. Especially Keon.

The thought of my husband halted my movements. He was out. Again. Was I really surprised? I had seen so little of him that I often wondered if we were even still married. Just my luck one day I would have someone knocking on my door to serve me some divorce papers. Then where would that leave me?

I took another long, hard look at myself in the mirror. I no longer saw the woman I used to be. I looked older, more fragile, hell my hair didn't even have the same volume that it used to. Could I really blame him for his lack of interest? For his stepping out on me, again? The medicine made me feel better on the inside, well better than how I felt without it, but on the outside it was clear it was damaging my appearance.

I crossed to the bathroom and pulled open a drawer. Even the makeup looked foreign. I hadn't bothered to use any of it in a long time. Did it really matter how I looked? Just seeing all the cosmetics immediately had my mind turning to Kimmy. Makeup was her thing. I had been the businesswoman between us. The levelheaded, sensible one. Now look at me.

Still, I popped open a lipstick tube and spread the color across my lips, watching the fire red hue pop against my ashen skin. I then moved to my eyes, spreading a little color over my lids since my dress was a sheer black. I stepped back, admiring my work. I didn't do much. I was damn sure no Kimmy Davis with the makeup. That girl had been like a magician. Still, this would do.

I had driven this route to Barlow's trap house too many times to count in the past few weeks, down to the point where I even knew the hustlers on the corners along the route. Barlow had made my position with him clear to his homeboys. I was his, what did he call me? His Lil' Thick? Whatever the hell that meant, it was enough clout so no one bothered to mess with me.

Chevy Malibus, Expeditions, and other baller-type vehicles lined the driveway and curb outside the house and men spilled out into the street amidst smoke and loud music. I had to park a little ways down and walk back.

"Hey, Shawty." A dude with a dirty looking afro called out to me. I ignored him as another guy nudged Dirty 'Fro and gestured to me with his blunt.

"Nah, boi. That's Barlow's girl."

That statement did make me a little uneasy. *Barlow's girl.* Was I Barlow's girl? With a whole ass husband at home? I had been a mother, a wife, and now this was what I had been reduced to? Right then and there I should've stopped in my tracks and turned around. Should've gone back to the comfort of my car and driven to my house. But what was back there for me? A nursery, devoid of life but filled with the ghosts of my dead children? I kept strutting to the porch. Fuck that. Barlow's "girl" or not, I couldn't bring myself to go back. No, not when just inside, was my answer. My pacifier. My feel-good.

The house was consumed in darkness and smoke. If I hadn't gotten so used to the smell of weed while dealing with Barlow, the thick cloud of it would have made me sick. Instead, I squinted through the dense curtain and was able to make out numerous bodies either grinding on each other in the middle of the living room or laid out together on numerous couches and fold-out chairs. The bass of the music drowned out the actual music itself and was causing the beginnings of a headache to brew. Not long, I assured myself. Let me just find Barlow, give him some, and leave. This was definitely not my scene.

Someone's hand brushed my ass and I turned to see a woman in a skin-tight neon yellow catsuit and big weave grinning and licking her lips. She was close enough I could see her eyes looking me up and down appreciatively.

"You looking for me, Ma," she asked, her words slurred by the alcohol. I noticed she kept flicking her nose and no matter how casual the gesture, the coke use was clear.

"Where is Barlow?" I yelled over the noise. The name obviously held weight and seemed to bust her high. She nodded towards the kitchen and turned around, disappearing in the crowd.

I maneuvered through drunken bodies and made my way towards the tiny galley kitchen, also stuffed with people propped and sitting on the dingy counters. Despite the congestion, the person stirring something on the stove, the money not-so-discreetly changing hands, it was obvious this was still business. Of course.

I could make out Barlow at the round dining room table. He had a woman on his lap, some busty chick who looked to be only in a bathing suit, hunched over the table. When she sat up, I saw the bit of white residue on her nose and the rolled bill in her hand. A mirror rested in front of them with a few more lines of coke dribbled across the glass. I paused.

Barlow had mentioned this several times, me doing coke, but I was adamant on sticking to my pills. Anything more was just too much, too far and I certainly wasn't prepared for it.

Miss Busty leaned back on Barlow's shoulder, her eyes closed and Barlow used his finger to swipe the remaining power substance from the side of her nose into her nostril. She sniffed and flinched before sighing.

I started to back up, though there was nowhere for me to go

without bumping into folks. Barlow looked up and seeing me, he smiled and gestured for me to come over. And that was all it took. Hell he was like a drug in and of himself and like I was gravitating to my own addiction, my feet propelled me forward until I was standing directly in front of him.

Without speaking, Barlow nudged the woman from his lap and obediently, she rose before stumbling forward. He pulled my arm until I was now seated on his lap and he kissed my neck, his breath and body reeking of liquor. I cringed.

I leaned down close to his ear so he could hear me over the chaos. "You got my stuff?" I asked.

Barlow chuckled to himself and took a sip of whatever was in a red, plastic cup at his elbow. He held the drink out to me. I hesitated before taking a sip myself. The brown liquid burned my throat and brought tears to my eyes. Thankfully, Barlow polished off the rest of it.

"You need to loosen up, Lil' Thick," he said and brought a dollar bill in front of my face. I shook my head and gently pushed his hand.

"You know I don't do that," I said. I then leaned in and kissed him, hoping to cause a little distraction. His tongue was rough on mine, almost possessive, and I felt his hand reach up to clasp the back of my neck. His grip tightened and to my surprise, he pulled my face away from his and angled it towards the table.

"Try it," he said, his voice laced with aggravation. "You been coming more and more to get stuff from me so you obviously need something stronger. This the shit you need."

I blinked and could only stare at the powder not even an inch from my face. This seemed wrong on so many levels. But hell the whole thing was wrong. I shouldn't have been here in the first place. Sitting on the lap of a drug dealer, kissing and letting him feel me up while I begged for pills. But in my mind, as long as I stayed away from the illegal narcotics, I was good. I slept better at night knowing I hadn't stooped to that level. I had never had a desire to do hard drugs. Hell I had seen enough movies and TV shows to know what it did to people. But was I that much different? Just got my little fix in a different type of way, but I needed a fix just the same. And would this really make me feel better? Because truth be told, I felt I was slowly becoming immune to the effects of the pills. Barlow was right. I was frequenting his place more and more and knocking them things back like candy that was for sure. Was my pain just that abundant? Or was I slowly becoming numb to any kind of relief?

I didn't realize Barlow had, again, placed the rolled dollar bill to my face until the paper grazed my cheek. He kept his hands on my neck, my face positioned down to the drugs on the mirror and I could only stare at my reflection between the jagged lines of powder going across my distraught face. But I moved almost mechanically placing the tip of the bill to my nostril and angling the other end to the coke powder. I didn't know what I was doing, but I had seen Barlow do the same thing on numerous occasions.

I inhaled, the immediate sting hitting my head with the consumption of the drugs. I couldn't even make it through the whole line before I dropped the dollar bill and rose, gasping for air. My nose was burning and I suddenly felt dizzy so I stood, hunched over the table and squeezing my eyes shut so the room would stop spinning. Then, slowly, I felt that *feeling*. That floating surreal feeling that I craved because it made me feel light, instead of heavy under the burden of my misery. I didn't realize I was smiling until I felt lips touch mine, a tongue coaxing my mouth open as if seeking for some hidden treasure. My body suddenly felt enflamed and I returned the kiss, hungry for the desire that was consuming me. I was so out of it that I didn't even realize the lips felt entirely too soft, too feminine, too good.

Someone was carrying me to a room and suddenly, the music seemed to fade. Someone was touching me all over, I couldn't be sure who or where. I just knew my body was enjoying this attention and I welcomed every bit of it. I was too focused on this to even think about anything else but this sexual energy that had my body throbbing. And aching.

More soft lips, slick tongues, gentle caresses. How many? I had long since not bothered counting. Just lay naked and open, not wanting the feeling to end. I rode on this euphoria until I was brought to ecstasy and I lay spent in my own sweat and juices. And then, when I chanced opening my eyes and tried to adjust to the darkened room, I saw Barlow, completely clothed, his body silhouetted in a haze of his own smoke as two women, one of them in the skin-tight catsuit from earlier, tiptoed out the bedroom door.

I blinked, not really sure what I was seeing, or even if I had seen what I thought. Barlow reached in his pocket and pulled out a Ziploc bag, this time packed so tight with pills that it was nearly busting at the elastic, and tossed it on the bed beside me. It hit my leg and I eyed the medicine, almost desperately.

Not sure if I was so focused on the pills or if suddenly the music was louder. But I saw Barlow's mouth moving though I couldn't make out what he was saying. He smirked and I heard what sounded like him mumble something about a "crackhead ass" before he left the room, closing the door behind him and leaving me sitting there in the soaking sheets, the stench of sex surrounding me, naked. And alone. I didn't even know I was crying until I felt the tears sliding from my face to drip on my breasts. Yet still, I quietly reached for the pills. My relief, my sanity.

Chapter 8
Kimera

Maybe it was just me but I was finding this entire night significantly awkward. And we hadn't even arrived at the restaurant yet.

Leo had a white Hummer limo waiting outside of the house and he, Naomi, Kareem and I piled inside. Naomi, giddy like a kid in a candy store, immediately began pouring and serving us the champagne that was chilling in an ice bucket.

"A toast," she said, lifting her glass. "To new experiences, new love, and new romance. Even if it is all three of us together in one relationship." Because Leo seemed just as engaged in the pleasantries, I looked to Kareem to see his reaction. I almost laughed aloud to see his confused frown mirroring my own. At least I wasn't the only one finding all of this weird. I sipped my drink and turned my attention to the window.

Even behind the tinted glass, I felt freer than I had felt in a long time. It was as if the air out here smelled different, felt different. Like I had been breathing in nothing but lies and deceit in that stuffy mansion for the past few months.

"What is it?"

I turned, half-expecting to see Leo addressing me but he seemed to be so enthralled in sucking Naomi's face, he probably had forgotten I was even present.

To my surprise, it was Kareem who was acknowledging me. He watched me intently, waiting for my response.

"What is what?" I asked.

"What's on your mind?"

I sighed, struggling to keep from rolling my eyes. "You know, we don't have to do this."

"Do what?"

"This . . ." I gestured between us. "Little conversation thing like we're on some kind of date. It's not even like that."

"I know." He paused again, as if he were still waiting for an answer.

I hesitated a moment longer. A little attention did feel good. It wasn't like I would be getting it from Leo. We could keep it cordial to pass the time. I still didn't trust him. And I didn't have to like him to speak.

"Just glad to be out of the house," I admitted.

He nodded and looked past me to the streets sweeping by. "Yeah," he murmured. "Me too."

"You don't get it. You can come and go whenever you want. It's different."

"Nah, not really," Kareem said. His eyes focused on mine and even in the dark, I could see the intensity of his gaze, like he was trying to tell me something without words. But he didn't elaborate, and because Leo was so close in earshot, I didn't either. Still, his little comment had left me wondering.

The limo eased up to the curb of Abacus, a contemporary restaurant with global cuisine from the Mediterranean, Southwest, and Pacific Rim. I had never eaten there but Fernando, the chef, had raved so highly about the place and had even made a few of the restaurant's signature dishes at home, which had been absolutely delicious. Hell, as excited as I was to get out the house, Leo could've taken me to eat at McDonald's and I would have been just as content guzzling down a Happy Meal, elaborate gown and all.

We were shown inside to a private dining room that had been reserved for our little party of four. The round, spacious booth already had glasses of wine, bread, and what looked like some sushi rolls on the table, and a maître d stood waiting as we slid together onto the cream leather cushions, Leo between me and Naomi, Kareem on my left.

I'm not sure why that made me uncomfortable. Kareem had been all up and through my space for months, but this, this seemed like something more. Why was his leg bumping up against mine? We had more than enough room in the booth. Was that an accident, or intentional? Was that chemistry I was feeling? I reached for my glass of champagne and knocked it back. Damn, it was going to be a long night.

Naomi waited until we placed our order before turning to me. "So tell me more about this whole thing. How does all this work? I want to be sure I'm not getting in over my head." She laughed as if it were a joke but I wanted to tell her how right she was.

I looked to Leo to address her comment but he too was watching me, expectantly. The hell did he want me to say? The truth?

"What specifically do you want to know?" I stalled.

"Well, like, are y'all two legally married?"

"Yes."

"And what about us?" Now she did turn to Leo. "Do we get legally married?"

"It's just a ceremony, my world," Leo explained, gently. "It won't be a legal marriage but you'll be my wife in every other sense of the word. We'll act as husband and wife."

"So, basically, I'm just going to *play* like your wife," Naomi sat back as if she were deep in thought. "And then, like do we have to

share Leo? Get him on certain days? Or do we do stuff together?"

"A little of both. We do some things separate and some things
together." My mind flipped back to our honeymoon in Jamaica,
just me, him, and his two other wives. The thought suddenly had
me brightening. "So where are you thinking for the honeymoon?"

"Fiji," Naomi blurted, unable to contain her excitement. "If
not there, then a cruise. I've never been on a cruise. What do you
think, sweetie?"

"Whatever my world wants," Leo said. It was clear he was eating
this up. He probably felt as lonely as I did. I sure as hell hadn't
given him that kind of attention since we first got together, I know
Tina hadn't, nor had Leo's second wife Lena before she was killed.
His only source was Tyree, if that was even still going strong. Because from the looks of his face every time he came from one of
their visits, he was even more stressed. So, he certainly seemed in
happier spirits than he had been in a long time. I had to play on
this opportunity.

"I've never been to Fiji," I commented absently breaking apart
a piece of bread. "And a cruise, I don't think I've been since Leo
took me on Royal Caribbean when we first started dating. So I
think both of those should be nice."

Surprise had Naomi's eyes rounding. "Oh you're coming too?
Oh that would be so much fun!"

I smiled into my plate. There, I had planted the seed. So even if
Leo hadn't considered taking me, maybe my little new best friend
here could convince him otherwise. Baby steps to getting out of
here, but steps nonetheless.

"Oh yes," I went on. "We would have a ball. When we went on
our honeymoon, Leo's other wives and I did a lot of girl things together. Spa day, shopping, and just girl time. After all, if we are
going to be in this relationship together, I want us to be good
friends. I'm sure Leo is going to spend a lot of time with you so he

can get to know you better. I want to do that too." I smiled, proud of myself for laying it on so thick. Naomi's lips had dropped a degree and she looked to Leo, her eyebrows drawn together.

"Oh, Leo already knows all there is to know about me," Naomi grinned and nudged him with her shoulder, as if they had some secret code language. "I'm just a simple chick that likes nice things. And as long as Leo here can give me all of that, I'm happy."

They lingered on an intimate kiss. "I can give you all that and more," Leo whispered his promises against her lips. "You won't need or want for anything."

Except freedom.

"Sounds like a win-win," Naomi said. She then looked back at me, cocking her head to the side. The next question she uttered had my heart sinking to my stilettos. "Then why are you trying to leave, Saida?"

I swallowed hard, my heart damn near beating a hole in my chest. My head was already shaking, even as my mouth struggled to find the words to deflect my confession. I knew I couldn't trust her. "I didn't say that." And because I felt Leo's eyes piercing the side of my head, I added, "But speaking of leaving. I do need to use the restroom though, if that's okay. I've been holding it for a minute."

I turned away and finally looked at Kareem. Damn, I had forgotten he was there the entire time since he had been so quiet. And again, he was giving me that scrutinizing stare, like he could read every one of my thoughts. I nudged him.

"Excuse me, Kareem. Do you mind?"

To my disgust, Kareem first looked to Leo, who obviously gave him the go-ahead behind my head, because a few seconds later he shifted out of the booth to let me out.

"I'll come with you," Naomi said and I stifled a groan. *Can I even piss in private now?* Naomi bent to kiss Leo and I couldn't help but notice wistfully how she could just announce what she was going to do, no permission needed. "I'll miss you. But you know us women have to go to the bathroom in pairs. You can never be too careful."

"I agree, my world." He was talking to Naomi but still looking at me. I averted my eyes by pretending to adjust my dress as I rose to my feet. Had Naomi's little slip given everything away? I wish I knew what he was thinking but strategically, Leo kept his face completely blank. Still, I felt him looking as we walked off together. Maybe it was a good thing Naomi wanted to join me. That way I could put her in her place. I couldn't afford for her big-ass naïve mouth to mess up the plans I was trying to organize.

"Thank you so much for reminding me about the honeymoon, Saida," she was saying as we swung into the restroom. "I really need to start planning it. Or does Leo plan it?"

"Why did you tell him that Naomi?"

She blinked in surprise. "Tell who what?"

"What I told you. About leaving. Why would you repeat that?"

Naomi shrugged and side-stepped me to lean in the mirror. She absently began smoothing stray strands of hair that had escaped back into her little bun. "I honestly thought it was a joke when you said it," she said. "So I just brought it back up as a joke. Seems like you have the perfect life, so I knew you couldn't be serious about leaving."

I tossed a glance to the stalls behind me, satisfied when I saw they were empty. "Naomi listen," I started, lowering my voice. "This is serious. It's not a joke. I need you to help me, for real."

Naomi met my eyes in the mirror, but she didn't speak. Maybe she was listening. For real this time.

I was now talking barely above a whisper and I had to lean close to her ear so she could hear me. "My name is not Saida," I started. "It's Kimera. I've been kidnapped and I'm being held here against my will. I need your help, Naomi."

Stark fear had Naomi's eyes ballooning. She shook her head, as if denying my words. As if not listening would make them less true. "No, no, you shouldn't say that."

"I am saying it," I said, trying to keep from grabbing her by the arms and shaking some sense into her. "I'm saying it because it's true."

"No, stop Saida—"

"Listen to me," I pleaded, tears springing into my eyes. My voice carried even more urgency. "I live in Atlanta. Just please do a search and see if you can find my best friend Adria Davis or my brother Keon Davis. Just search my dad's church, Word of Truth Christian Center. It's a long and complicated story but I promise I will tell you everything if you—"

The door swung open, and we both gasped as Leo framed the doorway, looking straight at me. Beside me, Naomi stood just as frozen. How much had he heard?

"Naomi, leave us," Leo said, his voice calm.

Naomi spared me a quick, fearful glance before obediently, scurrying out the door and leaving me alone with this monster. The calm before the storm. I knew what that meant. I had experienced it too many times.

Leo moved closer to me and instinctively, I shifted closer to the open bathroom stall at my back. "Why do you make this so hard, Saida?" Another step forward, I took another step back. A tango between predator and prey.

"Leo," I was whispering, quietly judging the distance between him and the door. *Would I make it?*

"Don't I make you happy, Saida?" Another two-step.

I didn't answer. He paused a moment longer and I saw his move before he lunged at me. I screamed and ducked into the bathroom stall, quickly turning to try and close the door. But he was too fast, shifting his entire right side into the doorway between the stall and the wall so I couldn't close it completely.

I pushed the door, hoping, praying the pressure prompted him to pull his body out of the way. "Leo, please," I didn't even realize I was yelling or crying but I was doing both. "Just stop it. Leave me alone please."

He flailed his arm, grunting as I kept trying to push the door against him. At one point he grabbed hold of my wrist and turned it at such a painful angle that I couldn't do anything but yelp and let the door go. He pushed the door the rest of the way open, still gripping my wrist.

That first punch always hurt the worst. I once told myself if I could just get past that first one, it would make the rest all the more tolerable. Like that first punch was just a lot of built up energy and anger because he hadn't laid hands on me in a minute. I braced myself for the rest of the blows but he had me at a disadvantage. The stall was so tiny and I only had one hand free to block the strong force of his swings.

The familiar taste of blood hit my lip and when I pulled my hand away from my face, I saw blood had gathered underneath my nose. My face was sore and I could only sink to the toilet, exhausted from the pain. Then, I felt the hits stop and he let my arm go. I slithered to the cold bathroom floor and curled up in a fetal position, a mix of blood and tears pooling on the tile underneath my face.

I heard a set of footsteps storm away, then another set, this pair calmer, approach. I was afraid to move, in too much pain to risk doing anything other than lie there. Then, surprisingly gentle hands stooped down and gathered my head in a lap. Then I smelled that cologne, that delicious scent that had been invading my senses ever since he stepped foot in my room earlier.

I angled my head to look up and sure enough, Kareem was down on his knees with my upper body in his arms. He put a white, cloth napkin to my forehead and the chilled sensation immediately sent a shiver down my spine. "Hold this up here," he instructed, his voice gentle like he was nursing a baby bird back to health. I lifted my arm and did as I was told, holding the cloth in place against my head. Kareem then reached up and pulled off some tissue from the roll, taking care to gently pat around my nose to soak up the blood.

I was embarrassed and because I didn't know what to say; I kept my mouth shut as he cleaned me up. Yet still, I was grateful. At least someone cared.

Chapter 9
Adria

"Good evening, Mrs. Davis. This is Evelyn Waller. Listen, I had my assistant Mallory call you the last few days because you have cancelled two appointments with me and I am concerned. I'm not sure if you received our calls but please call me back as soon as you receive this so we can—"

I pulled my cell phone from my face and clicked the option to delete the message. Of course, I had received the calls. The three from her assistant and the two from Evelyn herself last week. Pretty soon I would have to block the number.

I wasn't trying to be mean. I actually liked Evelyn. She seemed like a nice person but I didn't see how the therapy sessions were helping me. It wasn't like my husband was joining me so I was basically making these meetings alone. And frankly, I was getting discouraged. It had been months and I was no better now than I was when I had made my first appointment.

But I certainly couldn't tell Evelyn that. She would find some way to convince me to come in and talk me out of my own thoughts. Frankly, her persistence was adding to my frustration, so rather than have that compounded on my misery, it was better to wash my hands of it altogether. Especially because I had Barlow for the medicine I needed, the medicine that was actually helping me. I loved my mother-in-law, but therapy had been her idea and what a shitty idea it was. Oh well.

Speaking of which, the next message was from her. Her voice did bring a slight smile to my face. "Hey, Adria, sweetie," Mama Davis said in the message. "You were on my mind and God told me to play this song for you. I think you need to hear this." The first few ballads of Mary Mary's *Can't Give Up Now* wafted through the speaker. Recognizing the message, I squeezed my eyes shut to keep the tears from springing free. Of course, God wanted me to hear it. Because every day, every hour, every second, I felt like giving up. Shit why was I even here anyway?

My finger hovered over the delete button but my heart wouldn't bring me to actually press it. So instead, I saved the message, promptly cutting off the breakdown melody before I had a nervous breakdown of my own. I was again enveloped in silence. Alone with the souls of my precious babies in this nursery.

I rocked in the chair, listening to the quiet. As damaging as it was, I loved when it was like this. Because if I listened closely, really closely, I could almost hear my children's laughter.

That was where Keon found me. I wasn't even sure how long I had been sitting in there, but judging from the darkened sky outside the window, it had been close to all day. I felt my husband looking at me but still, I didn't move. I couldn't bring myself out of that space, that little bit of gray area between conscious and unconscious where I often pushed myself because it was here I felt most alive. It was here I felt my girls.

Finally, "Adria, look at me."

Then slowly, the vision subsided, the feeling subsided, and I was once again descended back into that dark, sunken place, devoid of any emotion other than despair. Still, I turned my attention from the crib to Keon who hadn't so much as stepped a foot over the entryway into the room.

"You still in your pajamas," he said, his voice laced with pity.

I looked down and sure enough, the sweatpants and t-shirt I had gone to bed with the night before still clung to my body.

"You've been sitting here since this morning?"

"No." Not technically a lie. I didn't drag myself from the bed until about lunchtime anyway. What was the point? "How was work?"

"Sounds like you're just asking out of obligation."

I shrugged. Fuck it. I tried.

"You really need to come out of this room."

"Why? It's not like you come in," I snapped. "Like our children just . . . don't exist, right?"

"What the hell are you talking about?"

"Oh please, Keon. You don't even come visit them at the grave. You just go on about your little life like none of this happened."

"Yeah, I do. But it's not like you noticed because you have other visitors to entertain don't you."

Irritated, I pursed my lips and rolled my eyes. He hadn't brought up what he'd seen at the cemetery with me and Barlow so I had chalked it up to, maybe he hadn't seen anything at all. That had just been my paranoia kicking in, maybe a side effect of the meds. "Whatever," I mumbled.

"Oh now you don't want to talk." For the first time in a long time, Keon came in the room and stopped directly in front of me. "No, go ahead and say everything you got to say. Since I act like my kids don't exist. You sure have some pent up feelings towards me, so go ahead and say it all. Who was ole' dude at the cemetery Adria?"

I shrugged and tossed bored eyes back up at him. I wasn't about to entertain his foolishness. As much hell as he had put me through, was putting me through, I was entitled to my own little secrets. Just like him. Wasn't he meeting someone at the hotel and day spa? So I didn't respond, which I could tell only infuriated him more.

"You know what?" At my continued silence, Keon tossed up his hands. "I can't deal with this shit. I can't." He turned and stormed from the room.

Pride had me sitting right there as I heard him shuffle around. It wasn't until I heard drawers slamming and what sounded like bags being dragged around, that curiosity propelled me from the chair and into the master bedroom to see what was going on.

Shocked, I watched my husband's back as he busied himself with snatching clothes from his drawers and stuffing them into suitcases. The force of his abrupt gestures had perfume bottles and picture frames clattering to litter the carpeted floor. Even though he kept his head down, the clench of his temple and the crease of his forehead revealed his angry reflection in the dresser mirror.

Now, I was riding on stubbornness as I planted my feet and crossed my arms over my breasts. "I don't know what you're doing but you're not going any damn where," I said.

Keon paused long enough to give me a look that would have anyone questioning my sanity, before he resumed packing. This time when he spoke, he was surprisingly calm. "Adria, we just need some space," he said. "You're going through things in your own way, I'm going through things in my own way, and right now it's just not mixing with each other. All this fighting, all this anger and hostility."

"I said no."

"It's better if we take this little breather right now before we end up hating each other."

"I already hate you," I yelled, pissed when the tears started to pour. Of course, I hadn't meant that at all, but dammit I was hurt.

How could he leave me like this? Right when I needed him the most.

Keon lifted his hand in my direction as if to say I had proved his point exactly. "This isn't healthy," he went on. "I mean look at you. You get up and stay locked up in that nursery all day. You don't bathe, don't eat, don't do shit. You won't even go to church with me—"

"Fuck that, Keon. What has church done for me?"

My words seemed to be biting into him like blades and his face slacked a bit. "My father—"

"Your father is dead," I dug the knife in deeper. "Gone. Dead. Just like your daughters. So you keep on like life goes on. That's what folks do when they don't love anyone but themselves any damn way."

Keon turned from me then, but not before I saw his eyes gloss with what looked like a tear. Damn, I had never seen my husband cry. That stung my heart and I immediately ran to his side and threw my arms around his waist.

"I'm sorry babe," I sobbed into his back, my tears soaking his shirt. "I'm so sorry. I don't know what I'm saying. I didn't mean that. I love you and you know I loved your father."

Keon stood for a moment longer and just let me hold him. I felt his labored breathing and wanted to crumble when I felt his body tense before letting loose a little tremble. Then, slowly, he stepped from my arms and hoisted his bags on his arms. Never did he look at me again.

"I honestly don't know where we go from here," he said, quietly. "Or *if* we go somewhere from here." Stunned, I could only watch him drag the suitcase to the door, stopping only to pick up a duffel bag he had tossed there earlier. He didn't utter another word as he left and the slam of the door startled a gasp from my lips.

I stayed in place long after I heard the garage open and close.

Headlights flashed briefly through the window as he obviously backed his car out of the driveway. Then those too disappeared. My knees weakened and I crumbled to the floor. Biting back sobs, I crawled to my table and pulled my notebook from the drawer. I needed to write. I needed to keep my sanity.

I had never thought about poetry until Dr. Waller suggested it. Then remembering that was something Kimmy had picked up, it seemed only fitting that I tried it to see if it helped. I wasn't good at it at all. I didn't want to resort to cutting myself (something I had also tried before), but the way my depression was set up, it was liable to reignite the old wounds I was struggling to keep buried. So instead, I grabbed my pen and started scribbling, the ink so fierce across the paper that my words came out sloppy and illegible. But I knew what was in my heart:

What We Share

Forever my eyes shall grace your face
Forever my fingers should touch your skin
I now know not your heavenly embrace
Our heart will forever be as one
Your soul, one with mine deep within

My eyes are grateful to gaze on such a man
My love for you I can't ignore
These overwhelming emotions all so new to me
I know I can't go on without you
Time can only ignite what real love is for . . .

My eyes remained steady on the words staining my page and I sighed. My mind, and heart, was so cluttered, and this shit wasn't working. Frustrated, I tossed the paper to the side.

Completely numb, I willed my feet to move to the adjoining

bathroom. All I needed was my pills. That would make me feel better. I fumbled for the Ziploc baggie I had stashed underneath my sink. Blindly, I shook some into my hand and tossed them into my mouth. Then, another handful. And another. And once more until the empty bag fluttered from my limp fingers and the memory began to materialize.

For some reason, I felt dizzy. I blinked and my wavering gaze met Keon's. Our teenage bodies were still wrapped in the throngs of our youthful lovemaking but I was snatched out of bliss at the sickening feeling that was consuming me.

"You okay?" Keon asked.

"I think I just need to eat something," I said, my voice weak.

Keon glanced at his cell phone and jumped from the bed, beginning to put on his clothes. "That's cool because Jay is picking me up in a sec," he said, his movements brisk. "I got somewhere to be. Yeah maybe you should chill for a bit. You not looking so good."

"Gee thanks."

He rolled his eyes at my sarcasm. "You know what I mean. You got the flu or something?"

"I'm fine Keon." Then because he seemed suddenly in a hurry, suddenly much too eager to handle whatever "business" he was checking on his phone, I felt compelled to ask. "Keon, am I your girlfriend?"

Keon narrowed his eyes before readjusting his cap. "Why you asking me that?"

I shrugged. Because as young as I was, being sixteen didn't make me stupid. I saw the way he looked at other girls and I saw how quickly he would come over for a little quickie, only to be gone just as fast. But I didn't voice that. Just said, "Because I want to go out or something. We always sneaking around having sex but I want us to go on an actual date. What? You afraid Kimmy will find out?"

Keon rolled his eyes. "Girl, chill out. My sister ain't got nothing to do with this."

"Well, what is it then?" I pressed.

Keon's phone vibrated in his hand and he took a quick glance at the screen. "Hey I got to run. Jahmad is outside. I'll call you later." And he was gone in the midst of his lie. He wouldn't call later. He never did. Until he was horny again. Every time we got together, I always felt unbelievably stupid.

As soon as he left me alone, I climbed to my feet and tried my best to get dressed with what little strength I had. For some reason, I was feeling anxious. I would use the bathroom, maybe eat that nasty ass burger he had left on the table, and take a nap.

I was washing my hands when I felt it again. That nauseous feeling. I gagged a little and swallowed as my mouth watered. What had I eaten? I opened the cabinet to search for some medicine and paused when I saw the tampon box sitting on the shelf. I blinked on a frown. When was the last time I had a period? With everything going on, I hadn't even thought about it.

As if I would magically see blood in my panties, I pulled at the waist and eyed my crotch. Nothing. When was it supposed to come anyway? A nagging feeling was pulling at me as I eyed the tampon box once more. It was probably nothing. It would come on any minute, any day now, and erase all the doubts that were now trying to creep in. I probably shouldn't worry about it. I kept telling myself this, even as I crossed back into my bedroom to look for a pregnancy test.

Kimmy had bought me a box once and told me to keep them on the ready, because you never know when you would have a little scare. How right my best friend had been.

Sure enough, I pulled open the bottom drawer to my nightstand and there was the test box peeking from underneath a notebook, still wrapped in the grocery bag Kimmy had brought it over in. I opened the box and pulled one out. Trying not to think, I carried it *back into the bathroom with me. I needed to do this now or I would lose the nerve. This was for reassurance. I wasn't pregnant. Couldn't be.*

The positive symbol faded into the viewing screen before I had even finished peeing on the stick. My breath caught in my throat. Shit. Now what was I supposed to do? And when the hell did I get pregnant? My mind flipped backwards to my last sexual encounter. To be honest, it was too damn many to count. Me and Keon had been at each other for a while, sometimes with protection, sometimes without. It really just depended how horny we were feeling. Damn, I needed to call Keon.

I was halfway across the hall when I cursed. I couldn't tell this man I was pregnant. And I couldn't very well handle a baby now. Not when I was getting my own life in order. Neither one of us was ready for this responsibility. One day sure, but damn sure not today.

I stood in the middle of my room and tried to calm my increasing heart rate. I needed to think. I needed to calm down and think. The thought came to me as if Kimmy were there to place it in my mind herself.

I remembered when Kimmy had gotten an abortion. Well, did it herself in a sense. It was the previous summer, and Kimmy had insisted I spend the night. She had been a bawling mess saying what was she supposed to do and she was dead if anyone found out. I had assumed it was Jahmad's but she never said and I never asked. We had gone on the internet and stumbled across a YouTube video of some girl saying she aborted her baby using a hanger. I had been scared but Kimmy had been desperate.

So she had lain in the tub, naked from the waist down, her legs spread on the lip of the tub while I had used the hanger tip to poke and prod until a gush of blood poured out. I remembered Kimmy had been sore for a few days and other than bitching about not being able to have sex, she was fine. She took a test a week later and the negative results assured us the simulated abortion had been successful.

I opened my closet and grabbed one of the wire hangers. If it worked for Kimmy, it could work for me. I would probably have to explain the blood to Keon if he asked, but I could just tell him it was my period and be done with it.

I stripped naked from the waist down and laid back in the tub like Kimmy had done, putting one leg up on the faucet and one over the side of the tub. I stretched the hanger so the tip was as straight as I could get it. Then, without thinking, I inserted the hanger.

I expected pain but surprisingly, the hanger went in easily. I almost didn't feel it. I wasn't sure exactly where to position the hanger so I just began to poke against every fleshly barrier the hanger touched, grimacing at the pinches of the hanger's pricks. Uncomfortable more than anything but I remembered we had to poke hard to make the blood come out for Kimmy. So I did, crying out as the pain intensified. I used my foot to turn on the faucet. Maybe the water would muffle my screams.

Finally, I felt a piercing pain as the hanger made a hole in whatever I had stabbed inside. I felt the warm blood flow, bringing with it a burning sensation that had me snatching the hanger out and dropping it on the floor. The pain was excruciating as the blood poured to stain the clear water already pooling in the tub. My vision wavered and I prayed the abortion would finish before anyone came home. Of course we would have children, eventually. I had no doubt in my mind. But we had time for that, and when we were ready, I would give Keon all the babies he wanted. But today was not the day.

<hr>

My vision blurred, only for a moment, so I lowered my body to a sitting position at the base of the tub. My heart was quickening but I felt that calm feeling beginning to consume me, taking me to that place far from here, far from the heartache. Then I smiled as I heard them, my girls, their laughter like a harmonious song of angels roaring in my ears. With them, maybe, was the other child I had gotten rid of a long, long time ago. The child not even Keon knew about. And as the room went out of focus once more and began to blacken like a vignette around the edges of my vision, I relaxed in the comfort of peace. Finally.

Chapter 10
Kimera

Three days. It had been three days since Lupé had left out of the house and expressed she was going to the store to get some essentials. Three days since I'd tucked a little 'help me' note in her purse explaining as much as possible in as few words as possible and asking, no begging, her to mail the note to my family in Atlanta with my whereabouts so they could send help. Three days since I had been on pins and needles, watching the security monitors like a hawk and anxiously awaiting her return so I could see what happened. But as the sun set, yet again, on day three and rose on day four, still no Lupé. And I was beginning to lose all hope.

Every so often, I would ask Leo about her in hopes he would reveal something. But hell, he had been so tight-lipped with me ever since the restaurant fiasco with Naomi. Besides, he had beat my ass so bad that night that I was trying to stay out of his way as much as possible.

Still, I did muster up enough courage to ask one day at breakfast, and then again another time at dinner, since he appeared to be in such a good mood. Either way, his answer was always the same, 'still with her family.'

I had even tried to casually push the issue by suggesting we reach out to her. "I mean, she's like family to us," I reasoned, picking at the pot roast on my plate. "I miss her. The boys miss her. Maybe it'll be a nice gesture to call and send our love. Just so she knows we're thinking of her." Leo had simply said "no," and that was that. So, I had no choice but to sit back and just wait.

Obi's wives took turns coming over to help out with the boys. Well, I guess that's what they were doing. They never stayed long, never really played with them. Would just drop in, sit out by the pool for a couple hours, maybe pour the children some juice, and then they were gone. One of them, I don't even remember which one, actually went in the boys' room to get a diaper once. And that was to hand to me. So apparently, that was the extent of their childcare duties. Part of me felt that they were just extra eyes to keep tabs on me. But maybe that was my paranoia.

I don't know why the extra security because it wasn't like I planned to bother Naomi anymore. She had already shown she wasn't about to do anything to help and now, she was so wrapped up in planning her and Leo's ceremony she couldn't care less about what I had going on. So, I was really back at square one and didn't know what to do next.

After an extended period of time without Lupé, Leo brought home this new woman who didn't speak even a little bit of English, only Spanish. So even trying to communicate with her had been an epic failure. Once she started taking care of the boys, that allowed me more time to ponder my situation and try my best to strategize some other escape. Still, none of my ideas seemed like they'd be successful, or safe.

I woke up one day and was surprised to see the house nearly empty. Not even Kareem was at my door when I stepped from my bedroom. I glanced both ways and padded to the boys' room, noting the neatly made beds.

Fernando was in the kitchen, sitting at the bar area sipping on a mimosa with his face in a *Better Homes and Garden* magazine. He immediately sprang to his feet when I entered.

"Bonjour Mademoiselle," he greeted, rounding the counter to the refrigerator. "I was waiting for you to get up so I could make you some breakfast."

I accepted the glass of mimosa he poured for me and took his seat at the counter. "Where is everyone?"

"I believe Monsieur took everyone out shopping for the day."

Jealousy stung at the casual comment. Of course. Naomi and the boys could all go out with no questions asked. Meanwhile, I might as well have been dragging a ball and chain around this mansion.

"Did Kareem go too?" I didn't even know the question had been on my mind until it left my lips. What did I care? If he was, even better.

"I'm not sure."

Fernando was moving at lightning speed, rattling pans and sprinkling seasonings on whatever he had sizzling on the stove. Pretty soon, he was sliding a plate with two omelets and some chopped fruit in front of me, standing back to admire his work.

I thanked him as he handed me a fork but I paused before digging in. As delicious as it smelled, I had to admit this felt too good to be true. This was the first time I had been alone since I arrived. Maybe . . .

"Fernando, can I see your cell phone?" I asked, casually.

Fernando frowned. Clearly, he was waiting expectantly for me to enjoy his meal and I was prolonging the process. "Sorry, Mademoiselle, it's not on me at the moment."

"I have one."

I didn't even bother looking to the door. The man's voice was sickeningly familiar and no amount of time or distance could lessen the disgust.

I no longer had an appetite, but since Fernando was staring, I used my fork to cut off a corner of the omelet and took a bite. It smelled appetizing, but I couldn't taste a damn thing. Not with Tyree smirking at me from the kitchen doorway.

He inched towards me, dressed casually in some skinny jeans and a lime green tank top. His feet were bare and he carried the fresh scent of soap like he had just gotten out of the shower. I didn't care how many times the water hit him. After everything this man put me through, he would never be rid of the filth that followed him.

"I have a phone," Tyree repeated, and for emphasis, he held his cell phone in my direction. "Did you want to use it?"

Yeah, to knock it across his head, but of course, I couldn't say that. So I just sat and stared while he stared back, the phone held close enough to touch my arm, that glint of amusement in his eyes. I broke our little staring contest first, stabbing at one of the ripe strawberries. Damn him.

Tyree shrugged and stuffed the phone back in his back pocket. "Okay, suit yourself," he said. "But you can't say I didn't try."

"Monsieur, did you want me to fix you something?" Poor innocent Fernando, so oblivious to this torture.

"I'm good, thank you," Tyree answered, never taking his eyes off of me. "Fernando, why don't you run out for a little while? Get some fresh air. Just be back in time for dinner tonight."

Fernando nodded his appreciation and was gone within seconds. Now I was alone with Tyree, the man who had kidnapped my child, me, and Adria, the man who had killed Tina and had even threatened to kill me, the man who was on the down-low with Leo, and was so jealous that Leo had feelings for me. And, I shuddered at the last thought, the man who was only not slitting my throat at this very moment because of his love for Leo, and Leo's love for me.

Tyree leaned against the counter, a little too close to the chopping block I noticed, but he kept his movements fluid and casual. Like we were just two old besties catching up on a random morning.

"I haven't seen you in a minute," he said at my prolonged silence. "How you liking Texas?"

I pushed my half-eaten plate aside and rose. We weren't about to do this shit. Tyree caught my arm as I headed for the door, his grip tight on my wrist.

"Damn, you can't even speak, boo?" he said, feigning shock.

"I'm tired."

"Oh, I'm sure you get plenty of time to rest."

I snatched my arm but his fingers tightened. "What do you want?"

"We need to talk."

"No, we don't."

"You may want to hear what I have to say. I'm trying to help you."

I smacked my teeth. "You ain't trying to help shit. You're the one that got me in this mess in the first place, remember? Now I'm supposed to believe you have my best interest at heart?"

Tyree let my arm go and lifted his shoulder in a nonchalant shrug. "Well, Kimmy Boo, who else do you have?"

I started to respond but my eyes lifted at the movement on the security monitor. A car was pulling into the camera's lens at the driveway gate, and I damn near shitted a brick. Never had I ever been so thrilled to see Lupé's battered Ford Focus since she'd been hired.

"Excuse me," I said, not hiding the triumph in my voice. "I have to get the door for Lupé." I turned and headed to the front door, pulling it open as Lupé's car pulled to a stop near the six-car garage. I smiled and waved, surprised when she did not return the gesture. A few minutes passed and finally, she emerged looking completely exhausted. I remembered she told Leo she had been dealing with her sister in the hospital.

"Hey, Lupé," I said pulling her into a hug as she stepped onto the porch. "We missed you around here."

Lupé nodded and stepped past me into the house. She tossed a small smile at Tyree before turning to me, her eyes solemn. I hoped she wasn't going to talk about anything now. Not in front of him.

"Leo went out shopping with the kids," I volunteered so she wouldn't get any ideas. "But he should be back soon if you want to wait around. I know the boys missed you. How is your family?"

Lupé's nose crinkled in confusion. "My family, Señora?"

"Yes. Leo mentioned your sister was in the hospital."

Lupé shook her head slowly, as if she were trying to comprehend English. "I just came back to get my things," she said, turning and heading to her room.

I looked to Tyree who just stood there, watching us closely. I trotted behind Lupé to keep up. Hopefully this was just her way of giving us some privacy. Thankfully, Tyree did not follow.

Lupé's room was smaller than the regular bedrooms, just enough for a full-size bed. But the bed was on a platform with drawers underneath, which she immediately sank to her knees to begin pulling out. Her clothes were inside, folded neatly.

I approached her, lowering my voice. My anxiety was on an all-time ten but it was apparent Lupé had other more pressing things on her mind.

"Lupé," I whispered glancing over my shoulder. "Did you get my note?"

"Señora, please." She paused long enough to look at me, her eyes tearing up, her lips quivering. "I don't want any trouble. I love my family."

Confused, I kneeled down beside her as she burst into a fit of sobs. "Lupé what do you mean? What happened?"

She sniffed and pulled a used piece of tissue from the front pocket of her slacks. "I don't want any trouble. Just please let me be on my way."

"Are you really quitting? Why?"

"I can't have no parts of this, Señora." Lupé's eyes were filled with sadness as she looked to me once more. "Por favor, I just have to go. For my family. I can't help you."

I shook my head. No, this plan couldn't be failing. We were so close. "Lupé, do you still have the note?" My whispers were louder than I intended but I suddenly felt the urgency as Lupé resumed stacking her clothes on the bed. "If not, just let me write another one real quick—"

"He knows," Lupé hissed, shaking her head. "He will kill me. I have to go."

Her English was so broken and her accent had gotten thicker with her emotions so I knew I couldn't possibly have heard what I thought.

"Who knows?" I pushed, grabbing her shoulder. "Who, Lupé? Leo?"

"Señora, please," Lupé wailed.

"Lupé, what's wrong?" Kareem's voice had me snatching back and quickly standing to my feet. I'm sure I looked all kinds of guilty but still, I was in a frazzled panic. What was Lupé talking about? Who knew? How?

Lupé bent her head at Kareem's voice, her hair sweeping down to cover her tear-streaked face. "Lo siento, Señor," she murmured. "I am sorry. I am leaving."

Kareem looked from her to me, suspicion marring his face. He used his head to gesture towards the door. "Let's let Lupé pack, Saida," he said to me.

My feet felt dead as I wheeled them to move, out of the room and straight to the back of the house. I needed air. And vodka. But right now, air would do.

The smell of rain hung in the atmosphere and little drizzles caused ripples in the pool as I took a seat on the damp lounge chair. It actually felt good, the sprinkles of rain pelting my face, like a figurative cleanse. Washing away all of the disaster that had taken place. And it wasn't even noon yet.

Kareem sat on the lounger beside me and did me a favor by letting me enjoy the solitude. Thank God. It was the least he could do. I broke the silence first.

"Didn't know you were here. Thought you had gone with Leo and his 'family.'" I made sure to emphasize that last part.

Kareem chuckled. "Nah. I don't do shopping."

"You don't do much of anything," I countered. "Except watch me all day and night."

"Apparently Leo feels you're somebody that needs to be watched."

I snorted and didn't bother commenting. Of course he did.

A beat. Then, "I know what you gave Lupé."

The way he said it so casually, I had to flip back through my mind to make sure I had heard him correctly. He watched me for my reaction but I gave him none. Inside, I was scared shitless. What was he going to do? Was he going to tell Leo?

I didn't know what to say, so I remained quiet, hoping he would just reveal everything. How was he about to use this to his advantage?

"I told Lupé she had to go," he went on. "For your safety. The chick was ready to go running to tell Leo everything because she was so afraid."

Suddenly uncomfortable, I eased up into a sitting position, still eyeing him cautiously. "How do you know all of this?"

Kareem looked out at the water, watching the drizzles slowly pick up the pace. "Leo has cameras everywhere. He is watching you when you don't even know it."

Now I was afraid, and I'm sure every degree of fear was so expressly written all over my face. Damn, had I really been that stupid, that comfortable, that I hadn't even considered security cameras? Of course. No way he, Tyree and Kareem could keep eyes on me all the time.

"Did she tell?" My voice came out in a whisper and I held my breath waiting for his answer.

"I don't think so," Kareem said. "No way to be sure though."

I nodded and tried to convince myself that he was right. Because if Leo did know I was trying to escape, he wouldn't sit on that information, would he? I had to find comfort in knowing my ass was still alive, so that required his ignorance. At least for now.

"So," I pressed, my words coming out slow as I tried to make sense of everything. "You saw me on the cameras." Kareem nodded. "And Leo? Did he see me?"

"To be honest, I don't know."

Again, I had to believe he hadn't. Or I would be dead somewhere.

We were quiet again, both lost in our own thoughts. But all I could circle back to was, now what, now what, now what?

"I'm not going to tell," Kareem said as if reading my mind. "But you have got to be more careful around here."

He was right of course. "Wait," I thought suddenly panicked. "Are there cameras out here, too?"

"Yep." Again, Kareem kept his eyes forward. "But no audio so we're good. Just sit back and look like you chilling."

I did as I was told. The rain had let up and now a thin mist hung between us. A chill stung my arms and I shivered, or maybe it was just me. Now knowing that everything I did was being watched made me feel a little on edge. I take that back. A lotta on edge.

"Why are you doing this?" I asked, quietly. "Telling me all this? Helping me?".

Kareem glanced back to the house, probably confirming we were indeed alone, and rose to stand closer to the pool. I watched his body language, stiff for a while like he had retreated into his own world.

"I know a lot about what's going on around here," he admitted. "Leo's family. I'm his uncle. And I know all about you, Kimera."

Chapter 11
Adria

The headache woke me first. The shards of pain like nails grating across the length of my brain to the point tears stole from my lids and dribbled down my cheeks. I moaned and winced at the sting of raw tissue coating the inside of my throat. A chorus of beeps and buzzes echoed in the room and I blinked away the haze clouding my vision.

A hospital room. I should've known by the stench of antiseptic permeating among the pale blue walls. The realization of my whereabouts had my eyes darting around the room, mentally sighing in relief when I saw I was alone. But not for too long apparently. I spotted the rumpled sheets thrown across the lap of the dingy sleeper sofa. Keon probably hadn't strayed too far. I dreaded his return because I just couldn't bring myself to face him right now. What had I done?

The door opened and a man entered, adorned in a white lab coat and a pen tucked behind his ear to tangle in the graying edges of his hair. His eyes landed on me and his face creased into a smile.

"Well, glad to see you're awake," he said, lifting a clipboard from the file basket on the wall. "We've given you something for the nausea. How do you feel?"

I didn't even bother opening my mouth to respond. I knew the question was more of a courtesy than genuine concern. My smile was weak. I turned my head as he checked my IV, my monitors, and all the noise makers by my bedside. I guess everything seemed to be in order because he just murmured while nodding and scribbling something on his little clipboard.

"Vitals look good," he commented. "You seem to have hit your head and suffered a little nasty bump there. Do you need some medicine for the pain?"

Hell yes I needed something but right now, the thought of swallowing any more medicine was making me feel like I wanted to turn and splatter my insides on this pristine linoleum floor. So, instead I shook my head which only intensified the pain.

I let my eyelids flutter closed and tried my best to remember snatches of the events that led up to this moment. Nothing.

"What happened?" I asked. "Where is my husband?"

The doctor glanced up at the empty sofa bed as if he were just realizing its occupant was gone. "They were just here so probably downstairs to the cafeteria. I'm sure they'll be back soon. And as far as what happened—"

"Wait a minute," I said on a frown. "They? They who?"

"I'm not sure who was with your husband but, like I said I'm sure they'll be on their way back here shortly."

I nodded and weakly laid my head back on the pillow. "What happened?" I asked again, already dreading the answer. Being back here in this same hospital brought back way too many memories. Memories I wasn't prepared to handle.

"You overdosed." The doctor's voice broke through my mental anguish. "We found a great deal of prescription medication in your system, some things laced with . . . illegal substances . . ."

I tuned out as he continued on his little spiel to bring me up to speed, picking past the medical jargon to understand that I would indeed be okay but they'd had to pump my stomach and run a battery of tests to make sure there was no internal damage.

I heard the door open and what sounded like my husband's hushed voice speaking to the doctor about any of my changes during his absence.

I was too embarrassed about the situation so I didn't even bother to look over, just kept my eyes closed and feigned sleep. Maybe if I pretended long enough, it would eventually come. What would he think of me now, knowing I was on the verge of suicide?

It got quiet. So quiet that I risked lifting an eyelid. Not Keon like I had expected. Jahmad was seated right beside my bed his face filled with concern as he stared back at me. I sighed. *The hell was he doing here?*

Months hadn't aged Jahmad a bit. I had always thought he was handsome, of course he was no Keon, but decent enough I suppose. Kimmy thought the man was the black Adonis himself, that's for sure. He had cut his hair nearly bald and grown out a thick beard that looked good on him. To make matters worse, he looked clean, well-kept and doing good for himself in his jeans and polo shirt. Not at all like me. Not at all like he had been grieving the loss of Kimmy and Jamal. That thought alone pissed me off even more. And it pained me. Just another reminder that life goes on, with or without people in it.

Jahmad spoke first. "How are you feeling?"

I shrugged, not bothering to answer. I was sedated in a hospital bed, sore and sick from an apparent drug overdose. How did he think I was feeling?

"Where is Keon?"

"He was here all night," he answered. "I told him to go home, shower and get a change of clothes and I would keep an eye on you."

"Gee thanks." I didn't care the comment was dripping with sarcasm. I didn't ever want to be around this man, let alone right now. When he made no further move to speak, I decided to hurry him along. "I don't need you here looking after me. Don't you have a pregnant wife to get back home to?"

For a brief moment, irritation flickered across Jahmad's face. But it was gone just as fast. "I don't have a wife," he corrected, his voice calm. "And I've already talked to CeeCee so we're good. Didn't know you were so concerned." His turn to drop the sarcasm.

I rolled my eyes. "Of course. Why wouldn't I be? My friend hasn't been in the ground but a few months and you have already moved on to your happily ever after with little Miss CeeCee. You're probably wishing she had died and gotten out of your way quicker, huh?"

Jahmad got up and started to the door. Good riddance. To my surprise, he stopped, his hand on the knob. On a sigh, he turned around and faced me once more. "Just get it all out, Adria," he said. "Here. Everything on the table."

I squinted my eyes against the tears threatening to erupt. Not here. Not now. Not with him. "What difference does it make now, huh?" I asked. "Kimmy and Jamal died. They don't have tomorrow to look forward to. You're not grieving. Hell, you don't even seem upset. Don't seem to care. It's like, you just replaced her. And I guess because Jamal wasn't yours, his little life doesn't even affect you either. Especially because you have your new baby on the way. I don't even see how you ever claimed to love her. I don't see . . ."

I clamped my mouth shut when I saw the first few tears glisten on Jahmad's face. He didn't speak, didn't even acknowledge them and if it wasn't for the angle of the light, I would have missed the outward display of emotion completely. The sight cracked my little tough exterior and as if they were just looking for permission, my own tears began to fall.

"I get it," Jahmad said finally after we both had cried silently for a moment. "But let me just say this Adria. I haven't always been perfect. Other than Kimmy and Key, you've known me long enough. Do I strive to be a better man? Hell yeah, all the time. Do I fail? Hell yeah, all the time. But one thing I can say, is that I loved Kimmy with everything in me. That girl was my life. So when I found out about Jamal not being mine . . ." His voice cracked and he cleared it before powering on. "That shit cut a nigga deep. I didn't even know anyone could hurt me like that. Did I handle the situation the best with her? Probably not. But like I said, I'm not perfect. Folks think men are soft and shit for having feelings but hell, we get hurt, pissed, and fucked up in the head just like women. So yeah, I was acting out of anger rather than actually being rational. Shit has been eating at me ever since."

Jahmad stepped forward and resumed his seat next to my bed. He was again, looking at me but his eyes had wandered somewhere else. Somewhere far from me. "Me and CeeCee had a one-time thing. She was there when I was going through the shit I was going through with Kimmy and yeah, we did some things we shouldn't have. I have a lot of regrets about that. But still, she's pregnant now, that's my child, and I'm going to do what I need to do as a man and a father. Because I *owed* that to Kimmy and Jay-Jay and I didn't give *them* that. And it's because of them I want to be a better me. That's all I can do, Adria."

I sighed, digesting the information. My heart ached for him because where I couldn't see it before, it was more than obvious, Jahmad was grieving in his own way. I lifted my arms and he leaned in to give me a hug and my body relaxed into his.

That's how Keon found us when he pushed open the door moments later. He looked between us and we smiled at each other, that silent exchange of mutual understanding. Keon didn't say anything, nor did he interrupt. Just let us have our little moment of healing.

"I'm gone run home for a bit," Jahmad announced. "You need anything, Sis?"

The familiar name warmed my soul. "I'm good Jahmad. Thanks."

"Cool." The men exchanged a quick fist bump before Jahmad left us alone. Keon crossed to put down the overnight bag he had in his hand before coming to sit next to me in the chair Jahmad had just left vacant.

When the silence stretched longer between us, I said the only thing that seemed appropriate in this situation. "I'm sorry." My voice cracked with the weight of the words and I saw Keon blink back tears.

"Dria," his voice was soft, compassionate and filled with so much loving fear that I almost sobbed out loud. "How could you do that? Why didn't you tell me?"

"I didn't mean to. I just . . . wanted to get rid of the pain."

"You didn't even tell me you were on any medication for all of that."

"You stopped going to therapy with me," I murmured.

Realization had Keon dropping his eyes to where his hands lay absently on the bed, mere inches from me. Yet still, he didn't move. I wondered if I reached out to touch him, would he flinch, would he pull away? Was he now disgusted by me?

"I guess I didn't think—" he cut himself off, shaking his head. "It doesn't matter. I'm sorry, Dria. For not being there when you needed me."

Now I did chance it, gingerly placing my hand on his. He was trembling and my heart wept.

"I came back," he said, almost as if he was talking to himself, reliving everything that he was speaking. "I forgot something and came back home. I found you in the bathroom, and I couldn't do anything to save you."

I shuddered at the image. Keon coming back to find me unconscious. But even worse, what if he hadn't come back? I would have still been back home, dead.

"I'm sorry," I said again. "I love you Key. You know I would never do anything to hurt you."

Keon looked at me, as if he was trying to believe that. "We need to get you help," he said.

"I'll start going back to the therapist."

"No, I was thinking like psychiatric care. Maybe here or for a few weeks at a mental health hospital."

I sat up with all the strength I could muster. *What the hell?* "No," I said. "That's bullshit and you know it. I told you this was an accident—"

"And how do I know there won't be any more accidents, Adria?" Pissed, Keon got to his feet and began to pace in front of me. "They got your ass in here under suicide watch. We get out of here, how am I supposed to make sure you're okay? That you're safe and won't try this shit again?"

"What do you mean, how? You'll be home with me. We'll get through this together."

Keon shook his head, "You make it sound so simple. Shit ain't simple. You damn near died."

I started to cross my arms in defiance, then realized the IV needle in my arm was keeping me from lifting it too much. Instead I just rolled my eyes and looked away. "Ain't happening," I said.

Keon nodded and pulled his phone from his back pocket. I narrowed my eyes, watching him dial some numbers. "Who you calling?"

Keon placed the phone to his ear. "Dr. Waller."

My eyes ballooned. "Wait, why?"

"Because you're going to this hospital whether you want to or not. And I'm pretty sure she'll draw up some papers that force you to go after I tell her how you tried to commit suicide on the medicine *she* prescribed."

Shit. I couldn't let that happen. My prescription ran out for those pills a long time ago and Dr. Waller would know something was up because she sure as hell didn't prescribe the dosages I had in my possession. And if she told Keon, then shit would hit the fan about Barlow, the drugs, the affair, hell every damn thing.

"Fine," I agreed, my panic subsiding when he pulled the phone away from his ear.

"I'm only doing this because I love you." Keon's voice was disgustingly reassuring and I began to feel my anger boiling under the surface. How could he do this to me? "And after rehab, we can go back to working on us."

I didn't respond. Okay, I would have to play by his little rules for now. But he had shown his true colors. He wanted to lock me up in some psych ward, didn't even trust his own wife. And for what? For him to go back to sleeping with everything in a skirt? Here I was, battling my own issues and my husband wasn't concerned about me, about my welfare. He was trying to do everything under the sun to show me he was done with me. Hell, hadn't he just packed his shit and moved out? Why was I hanging on so desperately? Was it really him, or the memories we shared I was clinging to? Hell, was this marriage even salvageable?

My heart cracked under the weight of my own range of emotions. Anger, yes, that one was clear. But also fear. Anxiety. Hurt. I didn't know how we could go on without each other. But I didn't see how we could go on with each other either.

Chapter 12
Kimera

"Leo's father, my brother, is very powerful in Côte d'Ivoire," Kareem explained. "He's involved in some heavy-duty shit. And I don't mean just drugs. I mean drugs, firearms, human trafficking, you name it and Obi has his hands in it. Being this kind of man, this kingpin, he has also gained a lot of enemies. However, with his alliances and the law enforcement on his side, he is basically untouchable."

I tried to steady my breathing as I listened intently. I felt like I was tumbling deeper down the Alice in Wonderland rabbit hole and I was nearly salivating in anxiety to hear it all. I had always wondered more about Leo's father. I sure as hell didn't expect any of this.

"There are a lot of people Obi has fucked over to build his empire," Kareem went on. "But for every one enemy, he has four allies. So no one would dare touch him."

Kareem paused for a moment too long and my eagerness got the best of me. "So how did you get mixed up in all of this?"

Kareem returned to his seat on the lounge chair, almost as if what he was about to reveal required too much strength. "I was greedy," he admitted. "I let money cloud my judgment. Make me turn my back on my family. I got involved with some people who wanted to take down my brother. So, I became an . . . informant."

Nice way to say a snitch but I didn't voice that. Just let him keep talking. "I began filtering information to them and helped them to rob Obi. Also, some sabotaging to make sure we were destroying his whole operation. Of course, shit went south. Obi found out about all them niggas that was in on it and had everyone killed. And," he added, looking me in the eye. "Just to show you how ruthless he is. Not only had them killed, but one immediate member of their family."

I gasped. "So, children too?"

Kareem shrugged. "Children, grandparents, mothers, he doesn't care about that. That's what I'm telling you."

I was still in shock so all I could do was acknowledge I was listening with a nod. "But you . . ."

"Yeah," he knew exactly what I meant. *Why was he still alive?* "Obi didn't know I was involved. I had kept my shit clean and nothing could be traced back to me. Plus, everyone that knew was dead so . . ." Kareem shrugged and looked again to the house. "At least I thought so until ole' boy."

I frowned in confusion as my eyes followed him to the house. "Tyree?" I asked. "But how?"

"I didn't know it at the time, but his brother was one of the ones killed during the takedown. They probably talked, so Tyree knew shit I didn't even know. He one-upped me. He approached me with evidence proving I was involved. So now, I'm basically being blackmailed."

"Yeah," I mumbled. "I know that feeling." I was floored by the information. Not only was Kareem actually a nice guy but he was in the same predicament as me. We were both prisoners and the key was in Tyree's hand. Funny how life throws people in your path, and you don't really even know why.

"Just remember," he went on. "There are cameras everywhere and the phones are bugged." I remembered Tyree offering me his cell phone and wondered if it had been tapped too.

"What about your cell phone?"

"Yeah, that too," he said. "Don't ever use my cell unless you want to get caught. I'm working on getting another one."

Just for good measure, I asked cautiously, "So you know all about Tyree and . . . Leo?"

Kareem's face wrinkled. "Yeah the whole situation is messed up. The way I see it, if you gone be gay, be gay. Don't bring other folks into your situation because you don't want anyone to know you like dudes."

"Agreed." We lapsed back into silence, the echo of our conversation thickening the air around us. Then, the idea crystallized, slowly at first. Fuzzy as it tried to piece itself together. Then more and more clear, until I was nearly bursting with excitement.

I sat up. "Wait. Of course Leo doesn't want anyone to know about Tyree."

"Of course."

"But *we* know."

Kareem nodded, trying to follow. "Yeah . . ."

"And what if Leo's father found out?" I barreled on as the idea seemed more and more brilliant. "In Atlanta, right before he took me, Leo told me that he needed me because we had to keep up the image of husband and wife. Because under no circumstances could his father find out he was gay, let alone that he had been having a whole 'nother relationship with a man. Obi would disown him and he would be in some kind of danger."

"I believe it. Obi don't play that shit."

I sprang to my feet then and Kareem gestured for me to calm down. "Cameras," he reminded me simply.

I nodded, lowering myself back to the chair but that didn't stop the sheer joy radiating from my face. I felt like if I smiled any harder, my lips would split.

"This could work," I said. "We just need to tell Obi everything next time we see him."

I noticed Kareem wasn't sharing my excitement and it calmed me down, a little. Now, he was giving me that look as if I belonged on the short bus.

"With what proof?" he reasoned. "Seriously, Kimmy, you think you can bring those kinds of accusations to Obi about his son, his one and only heir, and he's just going to believe you? That nigga will slit your throat before the words make it out." Kareem shook his head.

I tried not to let his words discourage me. There just *had* to be a way. Hell, after the Lupé disaster, I was running out of ideas.

"Kareem, this can work," I pleaded. "We just have to find something so he believes us."

"Believe me, I've thought of that," Kareem said. "It's going to be hard to prove, for one. And for two . . ." His sigh was labored. "I'm walking a thin line here. Even with you. If I fuck this up and shit comes out before we have time to tell Obi, I'm dead. Not just me, my family."

"But—"

"I have a daughter," Kareem snapped before dropping his head in his hands. He seemed to be breaking right in front of me and my first instinct was to go console him. But the cameras. So I stayed put and let him gather himself.

"How old is she?" I asked, gently.

"She'll be nine next month. I haven't seen her in three years."

"Where is she?"

"In Nigeria, with her mother. I had to send them there after . . . for their safety." Kareem sighed and then, more composed, lifted his eyes back to mine. "One of the dudes I worked with before, cool guy. He did surveillance. Kind of a nerd but he was smart as hell. Could hack into any camera anywhere. Never hurt a soul. I don't even think dude cussed." Kareem grinned at the memory.

Then just as quickly, his smile fell and his eyes darkened. "When the whole takedown happened, they killed him, raped his pregnant girlfriend, and set her and their daughter on fire. She was three."

I felt the ache work its way up from the pit of my stomach to my heart. Immediately I glanced up to the window at the boys' room. What kind of demon would do something like that?

"I had to watch," Kareem went on. "Watch them be tied up and gagged. Watch those dudes pour gasoline on them, laughing and acting like the shit was hilarious while the little girl cried and the mom begged. And then we stood across the street while the house went up in flames. Do you know what that feels like?"

I shook my head. I wouldn't have any shred of my mind left. I could almost feel the fire warming my cheeks and it sickened me and depressed me at the same time.

"I watched grandmothers shot execution-style, at point blank range. Mothers dismembered limb by limb. These dudes are gutta. Ruthless. You see what I mean? I can't gamble with her life. Not again." I could tell this conversation was taking him back to a bad place. Hell I felt like I was suffocating.

My face was wet from what I thought was rain but putting my fingers to my skin, I felt the hot tears.

Neither one of us spoke anymore. I think enough had been said. Somewhere, a door chimed, signaling Leo was back. As if I wasn't torn already about Kareem's story, I heard Leo Jr.'s giggles riding high as he squealed from whatever delight. I couldn't imagine. How much was I willing to gamble for freedom?

Chapter 13
Adria

The squeaks of the hinges echoed off the empty walls as I shifted and twisted, searching for some remote form of comfort on the flat mattress. It didn't help that my wrist was handcuffed to the iron bed. Defeated, I sat up, resting my bare feet on the cold linoleum. The gray sweat suit did nothing to protect my skin from the chill in the room. With a smack of my lips, I pulled at the cuffs, hissing as the metal bit into my tender flesh.

Bastards called themselves punishing me for my latest outburst. I had hauled off and attacked one of the nurses after the chick tried to shove some medicine down my throat. To be honest, I was just pissed I was confined to this damn mental hospital. Keon had stuck to his word and I hadn't been released from the hospital for more than twelve hours before we were pulling up to Atlanta Regional and Rehabilitation.

If I had to be honest, between the group therapy and counseling sessions that they required daily, it hadn't been that bad. The rooms were somewhat decent and everyone pretty much kept to themselves. With the exception of the occasional schizo bashing her head against the windows or stripping in the middle of the recreation room, it was tolerable. But damn I was just pissed that I had to be here, that my husband felt this was necessary. And not to mention embarrassed.

Bad thing was, I was having to adjust to not having my pain pills. That kind of withdrawal would make a sane person go crazy. For the longest time, those had been my only lifeline, my mode of survival. They had made my grief that much more bearable by numbing the ache and temporarily filling the void that left me an empty shell of myself. But now, I was having to face my fears of life without my daughters, my friend, and my nephew. Face the realities of the torture I had been subjected to. And the shit was eating me up inside.

Every night I closed my eyes and a nightmare would invade my unconscious. In the daytime, I would hear Kimera's voice, so vivid and clear I often had to look around to make sure she wasn't there. It was scary and often left me wondering. Hell, maybe I was crazy. Maybe that medicine I was taking had done nothing but keep all my craziness at bay. Now it could manifest full throttle, no inhibitions, what had been bubbling under the surface all along. That's why the nurse had claimed to be trying to give me some medicine, something to help me sleep. But no, I didn't want to sleep. I didn't want to be awake. I was afraid of my own psyche.

This wasn't my first time tripping out. The last time, one of the other patients had approached me on some Looney Tune shit in the recreational room and I felt compelled to defend myself. I ended up spending three days being closely monitored. I wasn't allowed to join the other patients and I had to go to twice as many therapy sessions, plus an anger management class. The shit was nerve-racking, wasting away in there while I had no contact with the outside world. And it wasn't like I could keep up with what was going on. We weren't allowed to watch the news. Instead, they kept movies and music on repeat. Like we were in a bubble. I could easily see how even if people weren't crazy going in, they damn sure went crazy while in there.

The footsteps coming towards my room had me stretching my stiffened muscles. I glanced towards the barred window, noting the beautiful orange sky signaling the transition to morning. "Assholes," I murmured angrily through clenched teeth. They had left me in here all night. I swallowed the stream of curses already itching on my tongue. It wasn't much but I had become accustomed to the small conveniences of the center so I knew I needed to be on my best behavior to get through the rest of my time here. It had been ten days, so I only had four left. Keon told me two weeks, tops. I was holding strong to that. I turned to the approaching steps and waited patiently as the locks were clicked out of place.

The nurse entered, a petite little thing with a patient smile and kind eyes. Much nicer seeming than the one I had gotten into it with earlier.

"Adria," she greeted. I noted she stayed at the door, making sure to keep her distance from me. "How are we feeling?"

To reassure her, I gave her a smile of my own. "Thank you so much for coming to get me," I said.

"Well we think you're much calmer now," the nurse said. "And good news. You have a visitor." She chanced taking a step towards me and I did my best to remain as still as possible. Didn't want her changing her mind about releasing me. It wasn't like I was really excited to see Keon. Hell, he came every other day like clockwork. Truth be told, I still had some ill feelings about him putting me here in the first place. But I put on my best pleasant face as the nurse leaned down to undo my handcuffs. If seeing him meant a little moment of freedom, I would take it.

I showered, changed into a fresh sweat suit, and inhaled a quick breakfast of pancakes and fruit. Then, I joined the other patients in the lounge and settled into one of the reclining chairs to wait.

This area was used for what they called 'recreational therapy.'

It was set up like a living room, complete with numerous sofas and chairs and throw pillows that clashed horribly with the dated floral upholstery. A boarded-up fireplace served more as a decoration but it added minor charm to the quaint space. The only modern convenience was the flat screen TV mounted to the wall above the mantle. Now, scenes from an old movie danced on the screen, but no one paid attention. Though it was meant for interaction, everyone kept to themselves in here and that was why I loved it.

"Adria Davis?" The nurse's authoritative tone had me freezing just a bit. Damn, was I in trouble again? Then, I remembered I did have a visitor and I sighed in relief. "You're ready," the nurse said, and I rose to be led down the hallway.

I was escorted to the sunroom. Wicker furniture with plush cushions adorned the area with potted plants giving the air the smell of a garden. Floor-to-ceiling windows exposed the overcast sky outside and as I took a seat on the sofa, a few droplets of rain splattered on the glass and harmonized with the soft jazz wafting through the speakers in the ceiling.

My husband entered the sunroom shortly after I had sat down. I put on my best smile and rose to greet him. To my surprise he appeared to be upset. He stopped in the doorway and didn't move any closer to me.

"What's wrong?" I asked.

He was quiet for a few more moments before he spoke up. "Do you have something you want to tell me?"

My heart quickened. *What the hell was he talking about?* I had been here for the past couple weeks so I hadn't done anything to tell him about. He seemed to be waiting for me to answer so I shrugged. "Babe what do you mean? What are you looking for me to tell you?"

"Where did you get those pills, Adria?"

The direct question had my eyes rounding and the best response I could muster was to counter with another question to stall for a moment. "Where do you come off asking me that? You know I go to therapy. Or you *would* know if you ever showed up to therapy and you would see that my doctor thinks I need them."

Keon just nodded but I could not tell if he actually believed me. Then he opened his mouth again and I knew for a fact he didn't believe me. "Out of all this time, I would have never thought you would lie to me. All this bullshit you feed me about communication and trust in our relationship, never did I think you were the one being deceptive."

Keon took a step into the room and, at the same time, held out a cell phone in my direction. My cell phone, I could tell right off the bat. Shit had he found it? I mentally flipped through my pictures and text messages trying to pinpoint what he could be talking about. Then I remembered Barlow. But we had not been stupid enough to text about the fact that we met in person. So maybe it was something else and I just wasn't thinking at the moment.

I took the phone from him and looked at the black screen. For some reason, I could not bring myself to power it on. I looked up, my anxiety riding so high I felt like it would strangle me. "Keon," I said. "Just tell me what it is you're talking about."

Keon did the honors, taking the phone back from me and turning it on. We both waited while the start-up screen brightened to life, our breathing the only sound in the room.

"I called Dr. Evelyn," he said simply. That was enough.

My knees weakened and I sank back to the sofa, keeping my eyes on him. "I thought you said you wouldn't." I didn't even know I was whispering the words.

"Well, I thought it would be a good idea to make an appointment," he said, now clicking the touch screen. "I thought to myself, let me prove to my wife I'm trying to be better. Let me take the initiative and schedule a follow-up appointment for her so we BOTH can discuss our grief and our marriage."

I shook my head, already dreading his next few words. He had found out. Of course it would've been too easy for him not to call, I get out of here and we move on. I saw his lips moving, but my mind was already working in overdrive to prepare for when he revealed what I knew was coming.

"Imagine my surprise when I spoke directly to Dr. Evelyn and she said, 'oh thank God. It had been so long I was starting to get worried about y'all.' Now I'm thinking, how is that possible it had been so long? You claimed you had an appointment with her earlier this month. So of course I assumed she meant both of us together."

Keon held out the phone again and though I didn't look, I could tell my message inbox was flashing up on the screen. Still, I refused to take it.

"To make a long story short," he went on, his voice rising an octave. "You haven't been going to Dr. Evelyn and she sure as hell didn't prescribe all the medications they found in your system. So I decide, 'you know, she must be seeing another doctor' . . ."

No, no, no.

"That's a logical explanation. I just hate she didn't feel like she could tell me . . ."

Oh God, please no.

"So I go through your phone looking for this other doctor's contact information. And lo and behold, I don't find it but I damn sure find something else."

Keon closed the distance between us and dropped the phone on the cushion beside me. "Who is Barlow, Adria?"

I had remained silent up until that point, waiting for this moment when I could lash back in anger, confusion, or even just plead for forgiveness. I had been caught, and as solid as his logic was, I still had no answer for him. And that infuriated him.

"I'll tell you who he is." Keon was yelling now as his eyes darted around the room. Probably looking to punch a wall or something. "That nigga is a known drug dealer and MY wife has his number saved in her phone. That's the muthafucka you were meeting at the cemetery, wasn't it?" He rushed on not even bothering to wait for an answer. "Yeah that's the nigga. I couldn't get a good look at him but thinking back on it, hell yeah."

I clutched my hands together letting Keon rant. I still had no words, and better to let him run off his steam than make matters worse with a lie or even the truth right now. I was silently wishing I had something to take the edge off but I was sure the shit would've looked real bad if I had snatched up my phone and called Barlow right then and there.

"You ain't got nothing to say?" It was as if Keon was just now noticing I had not uttered a single word since his revelation.

I dropped my head to stare at my hands, the tan line from my wedding ring a stark contrast to my brown finger. For 'safety' reasons, they'd made me take off the ring and leave it behind when I was admitted. Now it was as if the gesture had been symbolic.

"I'm sorry," I murmured. "I didn't see anything wrong at the time."

"You didn't see anything wrong at the time?" He tossed my words back at me, clearly trying to show how ridiculous they sounded. "This is some bullshit Adria. But you know what is even worse? Look at the message."

I didn't have to. I already knew what I would find. But because he was looking and waiting, I picked up my phone and looked down at the screen.

I had taken the naked picture lying down in bed angled up from between my legs with a clear enough view to see both my goods and my grinning face. One of several I had sent to Barlow.

The phone trembled in my fingers before slipping free and making a gentle thump on the rug at my feet.

"You fucked him, didn't you, Adria?"

A lie doesn't care who tells it. Mrs. Davis used to always tell us that when me and Kimmy had gotten caught in some deceit or another. And as much as I wanted my lips to form the truth, I pursed them together and shook my head instead. This time when I did look back up, the tears were already spilling over.

"Just pictures, Key," I said. "That's it."

He looked doubtful as he turned, putting his hands to his head. His pacing took up the little space in front of me as he looked more and more like a caged tiger.

"How could you do this?"

"I'm sick, Keon. I mean look at me!" I gestured wildly to the sunroom in the mental health facility I was currently residing in, as if it wasn't obvious. "I came because you were right. I can't do anything but apologize. I'm so sorry."

I rose to my feet on shaky legs, pausing only to see if Keon would step back at my advance. He didn't so I crossed to him to put my arms around him. Now I was full on sobbing, a mess and I realized how much I desperately needed him.

"I'm sorry," I murmured against his shoulder. "Please, babe." I thought for a moment, then added, "I was only doing it to get back at you."

That confession prompted him to whirl around, his face twisted in confused angst. "What the hell are you talking about, get back at me?"

Maybe, just maybe, I could weasel out of this. "I saw you," I said, "at the hotel next to Spa Jadore. I followed you and I saw you get out to meet someone there."

Keon shook his head, clearly baffled by my words. "And how do you figure I was meeting someone?" he asked, his eyes accusatory. "Did you see someone?"

"No."

"So you just assumed I was out cheating and you thought it would be fitting to retaliate, right?" Keon scoffed at the absurdity of his own comment. "That's some low-class hoe shit right there Adria. I really didn't think you would stoop that low."

Damn his words were piercing my heart. Still, I couldn't be

angry. He had caught me red-handed. "Then what were you doing?" I asked instead.

Keon stared at me a moment longer before reaching in his pocket and pulling out a receipt. He tossed the flimsy piece of paper in my direction and I watched it flutter to the floor, the print side up, displaying two gift certificates he had purchased. The date matched up with the date I had followed him.

"I figured you would assume some shit," he said, the utter disappointment evident in his tone. "So I brought this along just to show you. I was getting CeeCee and Jahmad a gift. I didn't realize that would have been an issue for you. And certainly not an issue to go cheat on me for."

I shook my head, refusing to believe the evidence lying in front of me. "But the late nights," I went on. "Always working late, never paying me any attention. I thought . . ."

"Come on Adria, look at us." Keon gestured to us and then to the room we were in. "We got too much shit to be worried about for me to be sitting up here cheating on you. But instead of sneaking around, why the hell didn't you just say something?"

He was right and I had no comeback. I had really let everything spiral out of control and now, I was grasping at straws trying to reel it all back in. No use. It was clear I had crossed the line.

After a moment of silence, I spoke again, the only words that seemed to be a reflection of me. "I'm sorry." I still clung to him, needing him to feel me, to understand my heart. This man was my everything. Didn't he recognize me enough to know when I wasn't even myself? Surely he couldn't fault me for my actions when dealing with my mental issues.

Keon stayed in the embrace for a few seconds before he put his hands on my forearm and nudged me back. No longer propped, I sank to my knees. If anyone walked by, they probably would have thought I was praying.

I didn't hear him leave but I did catch his feet moving to the door, stopping only briefly before he disappeared altogether. I cried alone from the depths of my soul.

My phone lit at my side with a new notification that startled me. I wasn't allowed phones but he'd mistakenly left mine. I picked it up to look at the screen. A new voicemail message. Well, to be honest I couldn't tell if it was new or old since the icon had been there since Keon handed me the phone.

I looked around and not seeing anyone, I quickly logged into my mailbox to listen.

Some junk messages but the very last one was from Ms. Davis. I would have hung up, resolving to speak to her another time, if it wasn't for the concern in her voice that stopped me. To be sure, I had heard what I had heard, I played the message again. Sure enough, it was the same. "Adria please call me when you get this sweetie. I wanted to talk to you without getting Keon involved just in case this was someone playing a cruel practical joke. But I got this strange letter in the mail today . . ."

Chapter 14
Kimera

One thing I could say, I was sick and tired of weddings, that's for damn sure. The whole ordeal was becoming more and more nauseating and it was becoming harder to keep up the song and dance, feigning like I was happy. My wedding was the same way, déjà vu reincarnated.

Freddie Jackson's *You Are My Lady* wafted through the overhead speakers. Tulle draped from the ceiling in a canopy effect that drew attention to the altar. Two pillars stood on either side with silk wedding flowers weaved around each pole. An aisle runner covered the length of space from the door to the altar which had been customized: *Naomi and Leo. And the two shall become one.* A little tacky in my opinion, and not to mention deceiving given there were three of us.

Of course Adria's wedding had been different. The thought immediately saddened me as I reflected on that day. My brother, my best friend, my father officiating, that was genuine, real love. And Jahmad, I didn't allow my mind to crowd too often with thoughts of Jahmad, because it would thrust me into an even deeper depression. He was the one I was supposed to be with. I'd taken him through so much that no longer did I even feel deserving of him. He was much too good of a man for that.

I brought my attention back to the bride and groom standing beside me. Leo was, again, professing his love for yet another woman, and Naomi was eating that shit up like it was Thanksgiving dinner. Pathetic. Could I really blame her though? I had been the exact same way. I'm sure if I looked in her face now I would see huge dollar signs. Because at the end of the day that was all that mattered.

Much like Tina and Lena had done in my wedding, I stood next to Naomi at the altar, my wedding dress a little subtler than the elaborate gown she wore. The white, A-line dress I wore was light and airy in the satin material, but this white birdcage was itching my face, plus these heels were killing me. I was counting down the minutes until I could retreat back to my bedroom. At least because it was the wedding night, I could sleep in peace knowing Leo wouldn't bother me. Naomi could have all of that, all the time, if she so chose.

I looked out into the audience, saw Obi with his wives. I shuddered, still thinking about the stuff Kareem had revealed to me. I saw the man now in a whole new light. To be honest, I saw him in a whole new light when Leo stuffed my ass in the dog crate, claiming his father said he needed to get me under control. And even though Leo hadn't gone to that extreme since, memories of that kind of torture humbled my ass with a quickness. And that Obi, smiling in my face like the dutiful father-in-law, had suggested that shit.

Obi turned and tossed a little wink in my direction, his smile spreading like a proud father. I let a little smile of my own hit my lips before shifting my gaze elsewhere. The man was some next level devil. And here I was sleeping with the enemy.

Kareem was standing off to one side of the room, his eyes trained on the couple as if he were waiting for something, anything, to rear its ugly head. He looked good in his suit and it only took me back to when we all went out to dinner and the man had every part of me melting. And after our discussion and me realizing I could put my guard down and trust him, well let's just say he was beginning to invade my senses. I was beginning to notice everything about Kareem. The way he licked his lips, that subtle lazy stare when he was listening to me talk, the casual touches of my arm or hand. Shit was becoming intoxicating. He was awakening things in me I had long since buried, long since forgotten even existed. Now the question was, what the hell was I going to do about it?

As if Kareem knew he was all up and through my thoughts, he turned and locked eyes with me. I couldn't bring myself to turn away. I was yearning for this man. I caught the corner of Kareem's lip turn up, silent recognition, and he winked. *Damn.*

"I promise to love you," Naomi said bringing me back to reality. "Honor you. Give you everything you could need and want. Leo, you are my one true love and I vow to spend the rest of my life showing you that."

It took everything in me to keep from rolling my eyes. That probably wouldn't have looked so polite given the circumstances.

Because this wasn't an official marriage, the ceremony just consisted of some music, exchanging vows and rings, a kiss and then it was over. The audience cheered in delight as Leo turned and held out his hand to me. I accepted it and he kissed me as well as the claps intensified.

He turned to the audience. "Family, I give you my two wives, Saida and Naomi Owusu."

More claps, more hollers, more congrats as Leo turned to first

Naomi to kiss her again, and then me. I tried not to wince at the public display of affection. His intimacy with me was revolting.

Hand-in-hand, we walked up the aisle, the three of us, our heads ducked under the rain of rice that was thrown in our recessional. Thank God that part was over.

The photographer took some pictures and again, I had to fake happiness I didn't feel. As soon as the band started, I pulled Leo to the side.

"What's wrong, my love?"

I wrapped my arm around my stomach and leaned forward for emphasis. "Sweetie I think I ate something that didn't agree with me," I said on a moan. "I just really need to lie down. Please."

Leo didn't bother hiding his disappointment. "My love, I need you here."

"I know—"

"Babe, I thought we were dancing." Naomi flounced up and threw her arms around Leo's neck. She placed a firm kiss on his lips before looking to me, her face crinkling in concern. "Saida, what's wrong? You don't look too good."

I turned my act on to Naomi. Maybe she could work in my favor. "My stomach is just killing me. But don't worry about me. I don't want to ruin your wedding, Naomi."

"Oh no. Go lie down, Saida. I don't want you here if you're not feeling good."

I cast pleading eyes to Leo who, to my relief, nodded in agreement. Damn he was eating out of the palm of Naomi's hand. And I loved it.

"One hour," Leo instructed. "Get yourself together and then come back downstairs."

I bit back my disappointment.

"Want me to get Fernando to send you up some soup or something?" Naomi asked and I shook my head as I backed away.

"Maybe later. I just need to use the restroom and lie down for now. Thank you. And congratulations. Welcome to the family."

Because I knew they were probably still looking, I trudged my way up the stairs, even stopped a few times to double over as if my stomach pain was excruciating. That was just for dramatic effect. At that point I really didn't care if Leo believed me or not. Just as long as he let me leave.

The door hadn't even closed all the way before I was stripping from the dress and kicking off my shoes. A bubble bath was calling my name.

I had just run my water and submerged myself in the scalding hot liquid when I heard the bedroom door open. I groaned inwardly. Of course Leo would come in to check on me.

I heard him approach and stop short at the doorway. When he made no move to speak, I sighed and let my eyes close. "What is it Leo?"

"I was just checking on you."

My eyes snapped open and I sat up so quick that water sloshed over the lip of the tub. Kareem hadn't taken his eyes off me and though the water was high enough to cover everything, I suddenly felt myself blushing.

"Thank you," I said. "I'm feeling okay. Just wanted to rest for a moment."

He moved slow and I saw his gaze drop down to the top of the water, right where the bubbles met my breasts. I squeezed my legs together under the water.

"Well, do you need anything else?" he asked.

I turned the loaded question over and over in my mind and the naughty thoughts played like some kind of porno. It was erotic. Oh, he knew what he was doing, that was for damn sure.

He knelt down at the tub and dipped his arm in the water. It came up to his elbow and drenched the sleeve of his shirt but he didn't seem to care as he fumbled for something. At one point, I shuddered when I felt his fingers graze my thigh but he didn't linger, just kept on. Then he pulled my washcloth from the water and used his other hand to grab the liquid soap from the side of the tub. I let out a staggering sigh and he grinned.

"Turn around," he instructed.

I did as I was told.

He was gentle as he washed my back, so gentle that one would almost think my body was overreacting. I mean it had been a long time, but still, if I was just yearning for sex I wouldn't be withholding it from Leo.

"Kimmy," Kareem said to get my attention.

"Huh?"

He chuckled. "You heard me?"

Not a damn word. Now it was my turn to laugh. "I'm sorry I wasn't paying attention."

"I said what did you think of the ceremony."

"Oh," I tossed up a hand. "You forget I've been down this road with him before. Shit is fake as fake can be. I'm just going through the motions." I paused remembering Obi while I stood up at the altar. Watching me, a little too closely. "I'm not sure, but I think they're planning something."

Kareem's hand stilled. "Yeah, I think so too."

"Leo mentioned taking me back home."

"He said that? When?"

I turned back to face Kareem. "You didn't know? You always know what's going on."

Kareem seemed to settle into his own thoughts but obviously, he found that just as strange. "I may have a way I can get you what you need," he said suddenly. "I just don't know how far I can go with you though because if Obi finds out—"

"Yeah, I know." I was dead that was for sure. But then what?

What about the kids? "Do you think I should go through with it, Kareem? Honestly?"

Kareem sighed and leaned back. "Sometimes you have to do what you have to do. That's a choice for you to make. But just know either way, I'm here for you."

There it was. That tenderness. That compassion. Hell, in so many ways, Kareem reminded me of Jahmad. Rough, rugged exterior. But when he opened up, his heart was a complex work of art that beckoned me like a coy finger. A distraction. That's what I used to tell myself about him. But now, a welcome distraction, no less.

The tension between us had thickened and now, both of us were taking long shallow breaths, as if even inhaling oxygen was a chore. I snapped out of it first and averted my eyes. What was I doing? What were *we* doing? Leo would kill both of us, that much was certain. Why were we even flirting with the danger? But then, hadn't we been doing that all along?

Kareem rose and I was sure it was to create some much-needed distance between us. But to my surprise he reached for my hand and guided me up out of the water. I stood there completely naked as the suds drizzled down the curves of my breasts and hips, my whole body heating under his stare as his eyes wandered down, then back up, appreciating the view.

Again, he tugged on my arm, prompting me to step out and over the lip of the bathtub, the water now dripping down my slender legs to dampen the plush bathroom rug at my feet. I didn't speak but I knew my face was doing the talking, screaming, no *begging* him to take all of me. But he seemed to be relishing in drawing out this agony, all the while looking like he wanted to devour me right then and there.

He lifted his hands and cupped my breasts, and I was surprised at how tender his fingers felt on my flesh. I tried my best to grapple the edges of my sanity as I looked to the bathroom door, half-expecting someone to catch us. Muffled music could be heard through the walls, but other than that, nothing, no one there to catch us in our forbidden tryst.

"Cameras?" I whispered and though my mouth formed the word, I almost didn't give a damn. Let them see.

"Turned them off," Kareem said and he leaned forward, taking one of my nipples in his lips until it ripened like a provocative gemstone against his tongue. That was all it took. I opened for him, wrapping my arms around his neck, urging him to continue. I moaned as he propped my foot up on the tub and used his tongue and hands to guide his head down. He closed the distance, his tongue moving expertly to drink in all my flavor. My head fell back and the way he was working that mouth on me, I thought my knees were going to give out. It wouldn't take long, I could already feel the orgasm building. I had gone without for so long, I had almost forgotten what ecstasy felt like. But Kareem was sure to use all of the tips and tricks to remind me just how much my body had been craving.

I gasped and tried to catch my breath. *Too much, too much.* I felt like I would explode. I gripped his head as he used his tongue to trace each neat, pink fold. My thighs clenched his face and the orgasm left me shaking.

When he came up, my wetness soaking his beard, he gave me a soft kiss and I tasted my own juices. "Come in the bed with me," he said simply.

I didn't know why the simple statement sent my heart racing. The insinuation was clear, the bulge in his pants was even more so, but still, I was nervous. I sat my hand in his and let him lead me to the adjoining bedroom.

I stood in the middle of the room, the air prickling anxious goose bumps along my arm. He circled me, my body shuddering as he stroked my back, then neck, with his fingertips. "Ask me what I'm doing?" His voice was as soft and silky as his caress.

I opened my mouth, let out a shaky breath. "What are you doing?" I whispered.

He placed his hand over my eyes, using his fingertips to motion for me to close them. I obeyed, but I could still feel his eyes on me, casually taking in my body inch by agonizing inch. I felt him ease closer, felt his cheek against mine, his breath stroking my ear.

"I want to make love to you."

I was surprised I moistened at the comment. Make love? Hell had I ever made love to anyone besides Jahmad? Leave it to him to make me feel like a shy virgin with a whisper and a touch.

I felt his large arms circle underneath my legs and around my neck to hoist me into the air. I kept my eyes closed, felt myself being lowered to the sheets. The bed sank under his weight as he straddled me, and my breath caught as I felt all of his package rubbing against my leg. I braced, but he merely leaned forward and replaced his hands with his tongue. Thick, wet, and gentle as he slowly caressed my skin. I felt the pool of cream dampen my thighs and I moaned, unable to control the pleasure coursing through my body. "Kareem," I whispered. This entire sensation was so foreign, I didn't know what to expect. But damn, I was loving it.

He sucked each breast tenderly, his tongue tracing the outline of my nipple before inserting it whole into his mouth. He didn't move until he'd paid the same amount of attention to each breast and slowly began working his way down. I felt his tongue flicking over my sensitive skin and the sudden burst of the first burst of pleasure had me nearly screaming out loud. I felt his lips curve, heard him take a deep whiff as if he were savoring his favorite dessert.

"Please." My voice came out in a desperate whisper and I wasn't sure what the hell I was begging for. More? Mercy? Gratitude? But I continued to moan, "please, please, please" like some sort of mantra as he began to send me climbing again.

Then, he pulled away, gave me just a second to catch my breath as he put on the condom he grabbed from his pants pocket. He slid in, gentle and deep. A pinch of pain had me tightening but he worked me open until the elation overrode and I felt like I was in Heaven. I gasped at the thickness, my breath catching again as he slowly inched his way in, loosening me up until I swallowed him whole, the bunch of the sheets balled in my fists. I bucked and arched my back against him and when he started stroking like an expert masseuse, I knew it wouldn't take too much longer. I felt my muscles clenching to catch the wave and I gripped his body, yanking him to me.

"Yes," he huffed in my ear as he quickened his pace. I heard mumbling, didn't realize it was my own voice. I felt him swelling with the impending euphoria but I was already riding on the recesses of my own. I whimpered and my legs began to tremble as the flood ruptured free and sent me careening over the edge in a glorious stupor.

We didn't lie together for long before I remembered the timetable Leo had put me on. Shit, had it already been an hour? I jumped up, my body immediately chilling outside of the warmth of the sheets.

"What's wrong?" Kareem watched as I fumbled for the wedding dress.

"I have to go," I said. "Leo told me I needed to be back in an hour."

Kareem waited until I was fully dressed before he folded me into his arms and kissed me senseless. My legs turned to jelly. As much as it pained me, I pulled back and stepped out of his embrace.

"We can't keep doing this," I whispered, not knowing who the hell I was trying to convince. "Leo . . ."

Kareem licked his lips and I felt the heat rise between my

thighs at the memory of just what he was doing with that mouth a moment ago.

"You're right," he agreed.

I turned around and struggled to the door on still shaky legs. That had been too easy. And I already knew we both had a feeling it wasn't about to be that easy.

Chapter 15
Adria

The satin sheets tangled around my bare legs as I turned over. Fresh tears dampened my pillow as I gazed over at the digital clock on the nightstand. 2:24 PM. For days, I had been in and out of consciousness, floating on auto-pilot like some post-apocalyptic zombie. I had called Keon too many times to count and had clogged up his voicemail and text messages with an abundance of pleas and apologies. Apparently, he hadn't been running from me but towards something because he seemed well and content with not acknowledging me. Now here it was day four of his mysterious disappearance, and he hadn't so much as called to make sure I was still alive. His apathy was what hurt the most when my heart was drowning in emotional turmoil. The least he could do was care.

I dragged myself out of bed and began getting ready. It had been a few days since I'd been released, and I had promised myself I would make it over to see my mother-in-law.

I had to admit, part of me put it off because I was nervous. I did not know what to expect from this visit. She had left a message talking about some kind of note from Texas, and I tried my best not to get my hopes up. I knew my mother-in-law had been in and out of her right mind given everything that had happened. Shit, she was not the only one. Keon had told me before that she was exhibiting early stages of dementia. Looking at her you couldn't tell it, or maybe her being the only mother I really ever had, her mental deterioration was something I was not ready to accept. Still to satisfy my curiosity and to humor her, I promised I would make the trip.

I had gone back and forth with whether to tell Keon about her call and had decided against it. It wasn't like he was talking to me anyway, as evidenced by the lack of contact. Because it had been four days since I had been released from the hospital, a total of eight since I had last spoken with him when he stormed out after revealing his discovery, and yet here and still I had no idea where he was or who he was with (though I assumed it was Jahmad). He hadn't even picked me up upon my release, which spoke volumes. Maybe that had really been the last straw. I had tried not to harp on how hurtful that was. Because if I let myself get back to that place I was liable not to come out alive this time. Those last few days in the mental health facility I had devoted to doing better. I knew I had to because I did not want to rely on that crutch of those prescriptions. I did not like that woman. I did not *know* that woman. And as much as it pained me to admit it, I was broken and needed to fix myself. It was my sunken grief and depression that had me backsliding in the first place.

Something one of my counselors asked me during a session was enough to force a change. I remember I was sitting across from her desk, she looked me straight in the eye and asked, would my daughters still be proud of me if they were alive? I had sat there at a complete loss for words. The fact that I couldn't answer that seemingly simple question scared the hell out of me. She then went on to assure me though there wasn't anything I could do about the past; God had given me another chance, and thankfully, I still had a future.

I took that to heart and had even started going to the facility's church service. It was no Word of Truth Christian Center, but it did edify my spirit and remind me of what, or rather who, was important in my life. I imagined my father-in-law not being very happy with me, especially with how I was treating his son. But still, I prayed for forgiveness and opened my heart to receive. That was all I could do.

I felt renewed and, though still sore from the grief and now my situation with Keon, I felt better than I had in months.

I knocked on the door to Mrs. Davis's unit and waited patiently for her to buzz me in. I was surprised when the door swung open and a nurse stood opposite me. I panicked, immediately pushing my way in.

"Where's my mother?"

"It's okay, she's fine," the woman said calmly. "We just had a little scare. You are?" She held out her hand and I shook it.

"Adria. Where is Nancy, her nurse?"

"Nancy had a family emergency and will be on extended medical leave. I'm Jackie."

"Why didn't you call?"

"We did. Several times actually to a Mr. Davis. Her son. We had no luck reaching him."

Join the club.

"I'm sorry to have to ask, but may I see your ID please?" I nodded and pulled my wallet from my purse as Jackie swiped through some kind of hand-held device. Once she matched my ID with her records, she seemed satisfied.

"Thank you, Mrs. Davis."

I craned my neck to look towards the bedroom. "Is she awake? May I see her?"

"Yes, of course. Just please keep it short okay? She needs rest."

Jackie followed me to the room and I lowered my voice. "What did you say happened again?"

"Just had a little fall," she answered. "We've had the doctor come take a look but it's just a few minor scrapes and cuts. She was complaining of a headache so we gave her a little medicine for the pain."

Ms. Davis lay on the full-sized bed, her eyes closed. She looked thinner but still had her vibrant melanin color and her breathing was steady so my panic subsided. She looked as if she had dozed off so I lifted my finger to my lips and indicated to Jackie I would just sit here with her for a while.

"I'll be out here," Jackie said and left me alone.

There was a small vanity against the wall, and I took a seat on the bench. For a moment, I just sat in silence and watched the First Lady, remembering how she used to be compared to now. Life really had a way of building you up and tearing you down that's for sure. Once the pastor died, Ms. Davis was never the same and I couldn't blame her. They had been together for over thirty years so it was as if a piece of her had died with him.

"Where have you been?"

The question startled me and I looked over to see Mama Davis still lying down but her eyes now open, looking pointedly at me. "Mama I thought you were sleep."

"I was just pretending so Jackie could leave," Ms. Davis shifted to sit up. "That girl knows she can talk."

I couldn't help but laugh. At least she hadn't completely lost herself. "Jackie said you fell. What were you doing?"

She paused, her face furrowing in confusion. "To be honest I really don't remember."

I smiled gently. "Well it doesn't matter. I'm just glad you didn't hurt yourself."

"Where is that son of mine? Tell him he needs to come see me."

Keon and I both agreed we wouldn't tell Mama what was happening between us, nor that I was in a mental health hospital. It was just easier not to worry her. But as much as Keon was avoiding me, I knew he wouldn't NOT come see his mother. No way. He probably had been there on Tuesday for his usual visit. More than likely her lack of memory was just another consequence of her ailing condition.

"Mama you called me," I started getting to the reason for my visit. "Do you remember? It was last weekend."

Ms. Davis pursed her lips and I could tell she was thinking back. Slowly, she shook her head. "When did I call you, sweetie?"

"Last weekend," I repeated. "You left me a message mentioning something about a letter from Texas in Kimmy's handwriting but you really didn't elaborate too much."

Ms. Davis seemed suddenly overcome with emotion and she dropped her eyes. "I miss her. So much."

I moved from the bench to sit beside her on the bed, taking her hands in mine. "I know, Mama. I do too."

Jackie told me to keep the visit brief so I kissed her on the cheek and stood to go. Mama closed her eyes and relaxed into the pillows.

"Don't go sweetie," she murmured.

"I'll be back," I said. "I'm just going to run out for a bit, and I'll check on you later." She seemed satisfied with that and I headed to the door, dimming the light on my way out.

Jackie was seated at the dining room table, pecking away on a laptop amidst folders and papers scattered around her. She looked up when I entered the kitchen.

"She's asleep," I announced. "Just wanted to drop in and check on her."

"Aw that's so sweet." Jackie put her hand to her chest in some sort of dramatic gesture. "I swear it's the children like you that just make my heart so happy. Do you know I've worked for this place for three years, and I have some patients who haven't had not one visit this entire time?" She shook her head. "Absolutely, pathetic if you ask me."

I opened the refrigerator on a laugh. Mama did say the woman could talk.

Jackie rambled on about something and I tuned her out as she took a stroll down memory lane. I took a glass down and began pouring some lemonade. As I stood at the counter taking leisurely sips with the occasional grunts of acknowledgment to appease Jackie, I noticed Mama's opened mail fanned out in front of me. The envelope on top was what piqued my interest.

It looked like it had been forwarded from her old address, but, more than that, the Dallas, Texas hastily scribbled in the upper right hand corner had me reaching for it. I flipped it over and removed the single sheet of paper inside. And nearly screamed out loud.

I could recognize Kimmy's handwriting anywhere. She had written many an essay for me, signed many a form for our *Melanin Mystique* business. She had always written in elaborate cursive that looked way too sloppy.

I looked at the date. Exactly two weeks ago to the day.

Unfolding the letter, I leaned on the counter and began reading.

Family,

I am hoping and praying this letter finds you. I'm taking a huge risk by even sending it so if and when you do read this, I hope I am still alive.

First off, let me say I am sorry for everything. I know it may or may not matter now but it matters to me that you know my feelings.

Jamal and I did not die in the fire. I have been kidnapped by Leo and Tyree and I'm somewhere in Dallas, Texas, though I'm sorry I can't be sure where. I'm in some kind of mansion and I'm not allowed to speak to anyone, nor am I allowed to go outside so though I wish I had more information to help you, I'm sorry I don't. We have new identities. I'm going by the name Saida Owusu now. Leo's father is also here so if you find him, I'm not too far away. His name is Obi Owusu and his women are Amora, Natasha, and Yana. Please just send help. I don't trust the police here because Leo has a lot of connections so please be careful. But just know that for now I am alive, my baby and I are well but we need you to come find us. I love you with all my heart and soul.

—*Kimera (Kimmy) Davis*

Chapter 16
Kimera

The conversation was low, so low it was nearly inaudible. I had to take a moment and pause just to be sure I was hearing real voices and not just some craziness in my head. Hell, with my confinement in this house, I wouldn't have been surprised at the latter. At this point, even a trip to the damned mailbox would have been considered a luxury.

Still, I paused near the stairs and craned my neck to make out the words that were coming out in hushed whispers from upstairs.

The first one was obviously Tyree. No matter how the man tried to disguise it, his voice I could pick out in a crowd because it always brought about this sickening feeling of disgust whether he knew it or not.

"We had a deal," he said, at least that's what it sounded like. Now my interest was piqued because maybe this was something Kareem and I could use. Some kind of sneaky deal between him and Leo had to be worth something.

"Don't fuck this up," Tyree went on. "Don't forget I know

some shit about you too that could get your ass killed. And I know that's not what you want."

A pause, and I held my breath waiting for Leo's response. My chest felt like it was going to explode with anxiousness. Come on. Fuck what up? Say something Leo, I was silently praying.

"Nah." One word. One word and that's all it took. Not Leo. I damn near fell out. No, in that little half-assed response, I recognized him as if he had been talking right to me. Kareem.

"Then you need to get your shit together," Tyree went on. "It seems like you're playing, but we had a deal. When are y'all going to have this little fling?"

"Soon," was Kareem's response and that was all I needed to hear. I turned and nearly ran back to my room.

My soul felt shattered. I had trusted this man. Here I was thinking that he was actually trying to help me. His little sob story had been so believable, and I felt like an idiot. To think all this time, he was really working with Tyree? So all that stuff he told me about his past and his stake in this plan, was nothing but a lie? Just to get me in bed with him? Why?

I didn't know, but hell, it's not like it really mattered anyway. What mattered was there was absolutely no one I could trust and the reality was enough to have tears springing to my eyes. How could I have been so stupid? Now back to square one.

I shut my door and climbed back in the bed. It was the middle of the day but it was overcast outside which shed a dark shadow over my room. One would think it was almost nighttime anyway and it wasn't like I had anywhere to go. My days had become so routine the hours seemed to blend together to the point I didn't know where one ended and the other began.

I hadn't realized that I had dozed off until a knock startled me awake. I sat up, my eyes on the door. I didn't bother responding. Whoever my little unexpected visitor was would end up just coming in anyway.

Sure enough, the door opened, and Kareem poked his head in. I scowled. "Yeah?"

He seemed a bit taken aback by my icy tone but still, he stepped in the room and closed the door behind him. "Hey I was just checking on you," he said.

"I don't need checking on."

He frowned. "What's up? You okay?"

"Never better." It was a lie of course, saturated with sarcasm, but it wasn't like I was trying to hide my attitude. Not after what I had just heard. Hell, I was surprised he was bold enough to even come to see me right after his little conversation with Tyree. The gesture showed his ignorance or lack of care. I don't know which hurt more.

Kareem walked in further and stood in the middle of the room. He shoved his hands in his pockets and seemed to be waiting for something.

I crossed my arms over my chest. "I'm trying to rest," I said, hoping that would prompt him to leave. It didn't.

"For real," he said. "Stop with the shit. What is supposed to be your problem? Did something happen?"

"You tell me." I paused and when he made no further move to speak, I went on. "So, when is your deadline?"

"What deadline? What are you talking about?"

I rolled my eyes. So that's how he was going to play it? Dumb? How insulting. "Heard your little talk with Tyree. It's pretty clear what deadline I'm talking about."

That had him freezing, and I could tell my statement had caught him off guard. He sighed and took another step towards my bed.

"Stop," I said. "I don't trust you."

"Kimmy," Kareem's voice was gentle. "It's not what you think. I swear."

"You sure about that?" I asked. "Because what I am thinking

came from what I heard. So, tell me the truth Kareem. Are you and Tyree really trying to set me up to have an affair with you?"

Another pause, and his lack of an answer was answer enough. I shook my head. Pafuckingthetic. "Get out," I said.

"Not until you hear what I have to say."

"Oh, believe me. I've heard enough."

Kareem ignored me, instead walking closer while holding out a tablet. I didn't want to look, but curiosity compelled my eyes to fall to the screen when he just stood there waiting patiently.

The image was slightly fuzzy and disoriented, but I could make out what looked to be a bedroom. And looking closer, a man moving around the room while on his cell phone. My eyebrows drew together, and I looked up at Kareem. "Is that Tyree?" I asked though I already knew the answer. Just like I knew his voice, I knew that man's walk anywhere.

"Yeah," Kareem answered. "I'm trying to explain to you that I needed to find a way to put a camera in his room. He didn't have one in there and hopefully now we can catch him with Leo."

I looked closer as Tyree stepped out of his shoes and continued pacing the room, his cell phone to his ear.

"What is this I'm looking at?" I asked. "Is this like a live feed? You have access to the security cameras?"

"Something like that," Kareem said. "A friend of mine taught me how to tap into the feed so I can see the same footage from the cameras."

Now I was confused. In one breath, it looked as if he was helping me but what about what I had just heard? "So, what's this thing you were talking about with Tyree?"

Kareem sighed. "Yeah, about that." A pause. "It's a little complicated, but to make a long story short, yes, Tyree approached me about setting you up to have an affair with me, so he could tape it and show it to Leo. He's trying to push you out of his life. And it's obvious he's just tolerating you because of Leo."

"But still," I shook my head trying to make it make sense. "You agreed to do it? Why?"

"Tyree had a point. Not sure if you heard but remember I told you he knows some things that could get me in a lot of trouble. Whether I was going to go through with it or not, I needed to agree to it to keep myself alive for the time being."

For some reason, Kareem's rationale seemed believable. In addition, I was having a hard time understanding this man trying to hurt and help me at the same damn time. So far, he had been so helpful, and part of me did not want to believe it had all been a lie.

"Kimmy." Kareem stooped down until he was eye level with me. "You can trust me. I promise I got you."

And I believed him. His words broke through my tough exterior and touched me in a reassuring way. I felt his sincerity and I nodded my understanding. At least I wasn't completely by myself in this. When he inched closer, we both heard my quick intake of breath.

"Look at you, Kimmy." He fingered the dangerously low neckline on the T-shirt I wore, smiled when he felt my reflexive shudder in response to the absent brush of his knuckle against my skin. Damn, my body was responding to him without my permission. "Lying here in bed. Picking a fight. Most people would say you were flirting." I felt his fingers graze my bare shoulder and kept my eyes level with his.

"Is that what you want Kareem?" We both knew the simple question had been a dare, and I would be damned if he would continue to taunt me. It was just a test, I assured myself. I would like nothing better than to prove him wrong. He didn't have that control over me like he thought. I let my eyes fall to his lips before grabbing his collar and dragging him to meet mine.

Peppermint. I relished in the flavor on his tongue, used my own to caress the roof of his mouth and swallow his moan in response. His grip tightened on my arm, seemingly urging me for more, or demanding it, I wasn't sure. But, he seemed to be not only reigniting that passion I had long since buried, but coaxing it, propelling it, until it was erupting into new sensations that made me feel like a stranger in my own body. He sucked on my bottom lip, and I quivered. His body hummed against mine. I felt the power I had over him as much as I was weakened by the power he had over me.

It was Kareem who broke contact first, pulling his face back to rest his forehead on mine. We remained quiet for a minute, our jagged breaths in perfect unison as we struggled to slow them down and eventually, even out.

"Now what?" I spoke up first, letting the simple, yet complicated question hang in the air between us. I saw Kareem shut his eyes, his face reflecting the clear confusion that I felt. After the first time, we had promised we wouldn't scx each other again. It was too dangerous. Too risky. Too complicated given the circumstances. But, it was more than obvious neither of us would be able to resist the temptation.

"Sooner or later, we may have to go for another round," he answered finally. I noticed he had yet to remove his hand from cupping my heated cheek, just as I realized mine was still at his neck, his bunched collar still clutched in my fist.

"And now?" I asked, lifting my face to read his expression. He drew in a shaky breath.

"Now, I think we need to check out this video," he said on a laugh.

I relaxed into a chuckle, torn between relief and flattery at his statement. "Fair enough," I agreed. I released his shirt and made a weak attempt to smooth out the wrinkles. I didn't know why I felt suddenly embarrassed. We were both adults. We had made our boundaries perfectly clear. To avoid the inevitable would only heighten the tension between us and complicate our relationship since we continued to leave issues unexplored, right? A little friendly . . . what was it between us? Fling? Well, that wouldn't hurt, would it? It was better to tackle it all now instead of letting it fester, hoping it would fizzle and die out. That would surely not be the case. We just had to make sure we didn't get caught.

When I was sure we had both calmed down, I gestured to his tablet. "So, what else can you do on that thing? Send emails?"

Kareem tossed me a sarcastic glance. "Yeah, I would love to. Let me just ask ole' boy for the Wi-Fi code. And try to make sure he doesn't see this thing connected to it."

I nodded. Worth a shot.

"It's pretty basic," Kareem went on. "I have some e-books on it for reading. That's about it."

Now it was my turn to give him a doubtful look. "Really? Reading? You?"

"Yeah. It's an outlet. Some of us simple, *educated* brothers do exist. You can borrow it if you ever want to check out some of my stuff."

I eyed him a moment longer, decided he was completely serious. "I used to write," I revealed after a brief moment of silence. "I actually picked it up from Leo's second wife, Lena. She used to write the most beautiful poetry. My stuff never came out like hers, but that was my outlet."

"Why did you stop?"

My sigh was heavy. I didn't know enough words in the English language to describe the turmoil I had been feeling since I left Atlanta. And putting pen to paper sure as hell didn't make me feel better, nor did it make my circumstances any more tolerable. What was the point? But instead of spiraling deeper into my sorrows, I just shrugged.

"Show me this footage you were talking about," I said, changing the subject. It was obvious Kareem wanted to push the issue, but thankfully he didn't apply pressure. He just tapped a few buttons on the tablet's touchscreen in silence and held it between us so we could view the image together.

The position of the camera looked like it was from a dresser.

Tyree's room was huge and though the camera didn't capture every inch of it, it did a great job of keeping most of it in view.

Tyree was now perched at his desk on a laptop. By the angle of his screen, we could make out a woman's face. It seemed like he was talking to someone via video chat. Interesting. I didn't even know Tyree had any friends, or anyone for that matter, outside of Leo. To be honest though, I didn't know a damn thing about the man at all.

"Is there some kind of audio?" I asked.

"Yeah, one sec." Kareem began punching the touchscreen buttons, fiddling with this and that until Tyree's voice seeped through the phone's speaker. It was very low and nearly muffled by static in the background, but still I nodded, thankful to be able to hear something as opposed to silence.

"This is as loud as it can go," Kareem said, which to be honest wasn't very loud but still it was something. He held the device closer to us and we both angled our ear to the speaker.

". . . not supposed to be like this," Tyree was saying. "I mean, damn, how long am I supposed to give him before he gets himself together Gina?"

"You made the bed," the woman he called Gina answered. "You told him you were okay with all this. So now you're not?"

"Hell no, I'm not okay with it." Anger was evident in his voice. "I've put up with a lot of shit from him. And it's not fair to me. Don't I deserve better?"

"I've been told you that."

We continued to watch as Tyree began pacing in front of the desk. "I do what he asks, I don't say anything, and I still get the shitty end of the stick. While he continues to play between me, that Kimmy bitch, and now Naomi."

Gina sighed. "Why do you put up with it Tyree?" she asked. "Why don't you just leave?"

The question had Tyree stopping in his tracks and he shook his head. With his next comment, the anger was gone. Now replaced with angst and sorrow. "I can't Sis," he said softly. "I love him too much."

Sis? Kareem and I glanced at each other, both of us clearly surprised by the established relationship. Since when did Tyree have a sister?

"You're wasting your time on Leo," Gina said. "And I get it. When you love, you love hard. That's always been your blessing and your curse. You love so deep you become obsessive."

I had to agree, thinking back to all the events that had transpired with this man. All in the name of "love." Shit was crazy.

"Didn't those months in rehab teach you anything?" She went on, and I had to take a breath at how right on the money I had been. She seemed to be speaking my own thoughts but when I actually digested this man and his actions, his underlying mental issues were more than evident. His behavior almost irrational. Spending time in a mental health facility was right up his alley. But it wasn't like it helped, that's for damn sure.

"You told me what you had done," Gina said at his continued silence. "About the kidnapping, the whole thing with Kimmy's friend. And Tina. Does all of that seem like a sane person?"

"You think I'm crazy?"

"Yeah. Crazy in love," she clarified and I had to shake my head in disagreement. Nah. Ole boy was just crazy-crazy. Period.

"I just love and care about you so much and I hate to see what this is doing to you. You're not even the brother I know anymore."

Tyree sank back down into the chair and placed his head in his hands. "Do you feel different about me, sis?" he asked. His tone was almost pleading. "After . . . everything?"

"Of course not. I'm just worried. When mom died, she told us to take care of each other because we're all we got left. I failed our brother. When he died, I beat myself up for a long time, wondering what I could have done to get him out of that lifestyle."

I glanced at Kareem's profile, wondering what he was thinking. I remember he mentioned that Tyree's brother had been killed in the whole operation to takedown Obi. Did he feel guilty about it? Or, was he so used to killing that it didn't even faze him anymore? Kareem kept his eyes trained forward and I looked back to the phone.

"I just want to take care of you," Gina was saying.

"Then what should I do?"

"Give all of that shit up," Gina said quickly. "Give Leo up. Just walk away and leave it all behind you. You've already spent nearly twelve years of your life invested in this man. Don't waste anymore."

I held my breath, listening and waiting for Tyree's response. He didn't answer her directly. Just said he loved her and would reach out to her later before clicking off the computer.

I began to pray that Gina's words took effect and he did what she suggested. Maybe if he was gone, Leo would have no need to keep me. He would no longer have anything to hide. But of course, I never knew what to expect with either of them. That would've seemed too much like right. Too logical of a thought process. And both men had made it more than clear they weren't logical. So, Tyree leaving, would it help my cause? Or hurt it?

Chapter 17
Adria

The police station was abuzz with activity that whirled by with such urgency and chaos I felt like I was in a circus. The place made me nervous because it seemed like no good ever came from here. Not to mention with the rapid increase of cops killing our innocent black youth, being in the same atmosphere seemed almost hypocritical on the heels of the Black Lives Matter movement. But, as much as I hated to admit it, I needed their help, specifically one cop in particular. So, I bit the bullet and stepped up the brick staircase leading me right into the pit of it all.

The lobby reeked of sweat and cigarette smoke. All around, officers shuffled along either escorting prisoners in handcuffs or clustered in groups chatting about some business or another. I made my way to the front desk, waiting patiently for the receptionist to finish her call. When she did, she eyed me wearily and turned to her computer. "May I help you?"

"Yes, I need to speak to Detective Terry, please." As I spoke her name, the woman from the prior year's investigation came straight to mind. The blond-haired, badge-wearing chick whom

Kimera and I had agreed looked more like a cheerleader than an officer.

"Is she expecting you?" the receptionist went on.

"No, but I have some information on a missing person."

The woman didn't break stride, leaning over to snatch a form from her files and placing it down in front of me. "You need to fill out a Missing Person's report," she said. "It can take an average of—"

"I really need to speak with Detective Terry," I reiterated, almost pleading. "She is familiar with my case as she was investigating a murder that happened with my family."

The receptionist seemed completely unimpressed. "I'll let her know you're here. What's your name?"

"Adria Davis."

I waited while she dialed a few times before she spoke briefly into the phone receiver and hung up. "She'll be right out."

The lobby was full, people scattered in the pastel blue plastic chairs, each looking like they were trapped in their own little world of sorrows. I don't think anything could be pleasant from being in a police station so the atmosphere was definitely weighted with tension.

I was able to snag a seat between a woman who looked like she'd had a number of rounds with Mayweather, and a woman who looked like she was so burdened with stress she was going to have a stroke right there in the center of the floor. I turned my attention to the reason for my visit.

Kimmy's words were still fresh in my mind. For some reason, in my heart of hearts, I knew it was completely true. But knowing that, I feared for my friend and her circumstances. Hell, the letter had been dated a few weeks ago, what if he had already gotten to her? I shook the thought from my mind as quickly as it came. I couldn't afford to think like that. I had to hold on to that hope that my friend and her son were alive and I would do everything in my power to bring them home safely.

I hadn't bothered telling Mama Davis how right she was about the note. The added worry was not what she needed to be focused on right now. Nor had I told Keon yet, but that was partially because he still was not answering my calls. I had debated if I wanted to call Jahmad and let him read it for himself, see what we needed to do next. But, given the severity of the circumstances, I needed to see what Detective Terry said first. And though the case had gone cold, she knew what had gone down with the murder of my father-in-law and everything that had happened to me. She had to realize this was no coincidence.

"Mrs. Davis?"

I rose to greet Detective Terry as she strolled up and offered me her hand to shake. She hadn't changed much at all with the exception of chopping her hair off. I guess she figured it gave her more of a "grown-up" look.

"Thank you so much for meeting me on such short notice," I said taking her hand.

"My pleasure. I have to admit, I was surprised to hear from you. I'm sorry for your loss."

I nodded my appreciation, not really knowing or caring how she even knew that information. I was just eager to get to the matter at hand.

We entered her cramped office with its oversized desk, wall plaques, and tiny window displaying a view of the parking lot. Boxes were stacked everywhere, and Detective Terry had to move a few just to give me a place to sit.

"Forgive the mess," she said, rounding the desk to plop down in her own seat. "We are currently in the process of moving to another, larger building." She sat back, picking up a mug and lifting it to her lips. When she finished her sips, she smiled in my direction. "Now, how can I help you?"

I removed the envelope from my purse and passed it in her direction. "My mother-in-law got this strange letter," I started, watching her unfold the paper. "I wanted you to take a look at it and tell me what you think."

"What? Some kind of threatening note?"

"No, not that. It's . . . just please read it."

Detective Terry sat back, her eyes quickly glossing over the words in front of her. She remained quiet as she read, and I watched intently for any kind of reaction that would let me know how she was receiving the information. She was good. Not even a tensed jaw or furrowed brow or any kind of outward display of her thoughts.

When she was done, Detective Terry sat the paper on her desk and looked at me again, as if she were waiting for more.

"Well?" I prompted.

Detective Terry lifted a hand in the air. "Well, it's interesting that's for sure. But I'm not quite sure I follow what you want me to do."

"What do you mean 'what do I want you to do?' Help her. She's in trouble."

"Whoa, whoa let's hold up a minute." Detective Terry held up her fingers as she counted. "Number one, we don't have jurisdiction anywhere in Texas so we can't very well just go stomping around in someone else's backyard. Number two, what makes you think this note is actually for real?"

"Why would anybody send a fake letter asking for help?"

"Money, revenge, attention." Detective Terry said it like it was obvious. There could be a multitude of reasons."

I shook my head, doubtful. "No, there wouldn't be any reason for anyone to do this to First Lady Davis," I said gesturing to the paper. "Everyone around here knows what she has been through. She's like a pillar of this community because of the Word of Truth Christian Center."

Detective Terry sighed and leaned on the desk. For the briefest of moments, her eyes flickered back to the letter before focusing on me again.

"What I'm saying," she tried again, this time her voice a little gentler, "is that there is really no reason for someone to play some kind of cruel prank. Sometimes it's just self-gratification. I just don't want you or Ms. Davis to get your hopes up about this. It just seems really suspect."

No, that wasn't true. Couldn't be. I knew for a fact she was wrong.

"Have you told anyone else about this?" she asked. "Your husband? Other friends?"

I don't think it was the right time or place to assure her I had no other friends. So, I just shook my head in response. "No. I haven't told anyone. I wanted to bring this to your attention first because it's so serious."

"Okay." Detective Terry's smile was warm as she reached down and slid the paper back in my direction. "Well I do appreciate you showing me this and again I wish there was more I could do—"

"Detective Terry, please." I tried again, refusing to pick up that paper. Picking up that paper meant what? I was going to just stuff it in the trash? Ignore it? Pretend it never arrived? I at least had to try. "Can you just . . . take a look into it? I don't know if you have any friends in Dallas or anything that can maybe look around up there or something."

"What exactly are they looking for here?"

"My friend." My voice cracked under the healing grief. "My *best* friend. She isn't perfect, by no means. And she's not without fault in this whole mess. But still, she doesn't deserve this." I picked up the paper, my fingers trembling over the words. *Please help.* My eyes squeezed shut against the threat of tears. She was in trouble. And her life was hanging in the balance. "Even if you think with all your heart and soul that it's not her, would it really hurt to just . . . make some calls so someone can look and see for sure?"

When I paused again, my eyes met Detective Terry's who seemed to have softened under my words. Still, she said nothing as if she were really contemplating my request. But, the little shred of hesitancy was etched on her face and her fingers drummed the armrest of her chair.

Suddenly remembering, I reached into my purse and fished out my wallet. "Wait, before you say anything," I said, fumbling through the folds of black leather for something in particular. "Just please take a look at one more thing."

Finding what I needed, I held the wallet out to her so she could see the photo for herself.

His picture was in one of the plastic sleeves, by no means a professional, but still intimate enough to capture the moment. I hadn't been back long from my honeymoon when I took the picture. I believe it may have just been a random day I was babysitting for Kimmy, but Jamal had been looking too angelic in his little swing, sucking on his closed fist, his eyes large and curious at the 'wondrous' sight of low-hanging plastic toys in his face while music billowed from the speakers in a relaxing lullaby. It seemed the shutter had captured the sheer innocence, youth, joy, and miracle of this little boy's birth and often looking at it to this day made my soul cry.

"This is Jamal," I said, sadly as Detective Terry peered at the image in my outstretched hand. "He's only a baby. I'm his Auntie and Godmother. I look at him and I feel that special love people have for children. No, I don't have my own here anymore, but if this little boy is alive and in some kind of danger, he deserves a chance. Even if you don't do it for Kimmy. Please, Detective, just do it for Jamal."

We shared an aching moment of silence and I had just about given up hope that I had moved the woman still perching quietly at her desk. Until, slowly, she nodded her head, and her smile was one of sympathy and understanding.

"I'll make some calls," she agreed, and I sighed in relief. "But," she held up a finger to stop my inner celebration. "I can't make *any* promises. You understand? I usually don't deal with cases like this."

"I understand. Thank you so much." Remembering the letter again, I added, "Can you please keep this as quiet as possible? Kimmy says not to trust the Dallas police because she thinks they're in Leo's back pocket."

Detective Terry gave me a little thumbs-up. "Got it."

———※◦◦———

I maneuvered my car through a stop sign as I eyed the familiar brick stone houses peppering the street. I should've prepared myself. A feeling of nostalgia settled on me like a stale blanket. I remembered how I had loved the neighborhood with its manicured lawns and family-oriented charm that looked like something out of *Pleasantville*. Even now, I rolled past a group of preschoolers scampering across the rubber mulch of the neighborhood playground; their shrill screams of joy dancing in the autumn breeze. It was as if time had stood still. I was tempted to squint through the mist of tears and search for my own children among the grinning faces.

Sunlight spilled through the windshield and sent a welcoming stream of light across my downcast face as I eased into the cul-de-sac. Everything felt familiar. Down to the cluster of shirtless teenagers jostling through a friendly game of basketball. They paused to let me pass through. I didn't bother meeting their curious gazes.

It was once a nice area with rows of neat houses and safe streets. An ideal little suburb in which to bring up children and build plans for the future. The place offered the promise of hope to the working families who moved in during the seventies and eighties. Each house was more or less the same and had its own miniscule frontage that passed for a garden, which was lovingly tended to add a picture book quaintness. I smiled, remembering the different scenes that had become part of my childhood. During the week, the lady of the corner lot home pruned and watered; on weekends her husband got out the lawnmower and tidied the grass while the kids pitched in and did their bit to keep up the image the family wished to present. Seduced by the assurance of a good life, the residents worked hard and dreamed their dreams. Neighbors knew one another and cheery smiles, friendly waves, and cordial greetings were the normal exchange whenever they met. Children went to school, studied, played and grew up together, all striving to uphold their parents' expectations of excellence. Happiness and laughter were woven into the fabric of the neighborhood and its progress was small but evident.

Unfortunately, the good start did not guarantee continued advancement. Life happened in large doses, affecting most of the population. Somewhere along the way, families were afflicted by misfortune and sadness. Jobs were lost or a spouse took off. Perhaps it was an illness, bereavement, or an addiction that caused the downfall of families, extinguishing all hope.

Children eventually left dysfunctional homes in pursuit of their own dreams. What remained could not sustain a vestige of its former radiance. The neighborhood was now old and run down, much like its habitants. Once a picture of optimism, it was now a portrait of despair. Derailed prospects and broken dreams eroded the landscape. Rot set in, spreading its malevolent tentacles throughout the place. Unkempt residences reflected their habitants' disinterest in their surroundings, advertising the fact that they were past caring. The low crime rate merely implied that even criminals knew there was nothing to take from this community.

One of these derelict houses had belonged to my family, or

what was left of it. There was a time when things were perfect, before my father left, unable to bear the household responsibilities while keeping his little side chick satisfied. Before my mother had to work in a demeaning, exhausting job that wrung out whatever little piece of woman remained in her. Before I began spending so much time at my Aunt Pam's, and then later, at Kimmy's house, I spent time trying to force myself to forget my own broken existence.

<hr />

As I approached the house, I noticed the bits of paper caught in a frantic dance with the overgrown grasses and shrubs. Even nature had succumbed to the pressure of inertia that bullied the neighborhood into submission. Uneasiness gripped me the moment I climbed my front steps. I saw my mother through the half-open window walking about the room with a cigarette in her hand and a scowl on her face. The paint on the porch was peeling. The entrance door had long since lost one of its hinges and it needed a special knack to get it open. Turn the handle, lift and a solid push. It also needed a good wash to remove the accumulation of grime from all the many years of passage. I fumbled for my key and let myself in.

The cluttered entrance had cardboard boxes and large plastic containers everywhere. Packages had always inhabited our space and more had been added over the years. These boxes did not indicate movement; rather, they represented a sort of permanence. Unlabeled and uncatalogued receptacles for junk; anything and everything found its way into these containers stacked in piles about the place. Long since unopened, their jumbled contents were forgotten. It would have been quite a feat to find anything, so it was lucky that occasion never arose.

It wasn't a hoarder's house. If someone came and cleared the debris, nothing would be missed. It was just too much for my mother to tackle alone, but, hell, it wasn't like she had ever really considered it.

The neglect in the house was tangible; its presence was evident everywhere, permeating every nook and cranny, touching each item, ingrained in the grubby walls, faded drapery, and stained, frayed upholstery. It was obvious no one gave a damn about the disorder, well no one except me of course. Carelessly misplaced items of clothing and magazines were scattered about and overfilled ashtrays were forced to disgorge their contents, adding to the litter of already messy surfaces. The smell of stale cigarette smoke hung about the fetid air. Dirty dishes lay on the dining table and filled the kitchen sink, begging for attention as did the rest of the untidy house.

"That you, Adria?" my mother yelled out.

I didn't answer and began to walk up the stairs to my room. The fridge door slammed shut and my mother came out holding a glass of wine in her hand. I didn't bother looking at her as I climbed the stairs, but out of my peripheral, I saw her standing there in her ill-fitting, faded polka-dot robe, and bedraggled bedroom slippers. Since my dad left us, she had been so different. I didn't even recognize this woman anymore.

I made it to my room and closed my door, tossing myself on my bed. I was mentally and physically drained. Plus, I knew it was the calm before the storm. But I wouldn't be long anyway. I was going over to the Davises' home. Kimera had invited me to dinner and I often looked forward to the refuge. Not to mention, her brother Keon was fine as hell, not that he ever paid any attention to me. The sudden thought of Kimmy brought a smile to my face. What would life have been like if my best friend wasn't there for me? Hell, my own father had a new family and hadn't bothered to see how I was. Granted it was hard to deal with my hostile mother when he tried to visit once or twice in the beginning so to be honest, could I really blame him for his absence?

Kimmy and I were damn near inseparable, how we were together whenever possible, whether we stayed at the mall hanging out in the food court, or sneaking in the movie theater to catch every show on one child's ticket. What kept me entertained was that Kimmy was a PK, or preacher's kid, as she was known in school. Not that she cared. She probably was the most rebellious be-tween us, as if she was on a mission to prove how "cool" she was. When we got in trouble (which was pretty often), chances are it was because of her. Nevertheless, that was my girl and I loved her for it.

"My sister for life," I had promised, *to which Kimmy pledged the same.*

"I'll always be with you."

———✦———

Keon was the very last person I had expected to see at the cemetery. I was still mentally exhausted from my little quick trip down memory lane so I could only really sit in the car and watch him through the windshield.

His head was bent down and his lips were moving, but I couldn't tell if he was talking to the girls, or praying. He had a bouquet of sunflowers in his hand though he had not placed them on the grave just yet.

I wasn't sure how long he had been there, nor could I be sure how long he was going to stay. As much as I didn't want to inter-rupt his private visit, I stepped from the car and made my way across the stone walkway.

He heard me approaching, I'm sure, but still, he did not look up to acknowledge me. Without thinking, I joined his side, not standing too close as to accidently touch him but close enough our presence was undeniably as one. Not that it mattered, but to our girls we were a united front. Even in the midst of our discord.

"I feel them," he said quietly.

"They're always here."

"I don't understand how you have the strength to come."

"I don't," I admitted. "But my heart is here so I have to."

"I feel like, I didn't come like I should have because part of me was embarrassed."

"Embarrassed? Why?"

Keon shrugged. "I couldn't save them. I failed them. And I failed you, Adria."

I still kept my eyes on the gravesite at our feet but I felt his eyes turn to look at my profile. I wished like hell I knew what he was thinking.

"You're looking better," he observed. "I'm glad the hospital helped."

I nodded. "Me too." And because I felt so compelled to, I murmured, "Key. I am so sorry."

Keon shook his head against my apology. "No, I'm sorry. I was wrong. I don't think I could ever understand what you must have been going through because I was too busy going through my own shit dealing with this." He reached into his pocket and held a business card in my direction.

I looked down, instantly recognizing the pale blue design of Dr. Evelyn Waller's practice.

"I've been going to sessions," he affirmed with a hesitant smile. "Never thought I would need to do anything like this and to be honest, I didn't really see the benefit. But, she convinced me to come talk to her for a few hours. Well those few hours turned into every other day."

My heart swelled. "I'm very happy for you," I said with a smile. "Seriously. I don't know what I would have done without Dr. Evelyn. I hate that I talked myself out of going. I guess I was just trying not to face my own demons."

Again, we eased into comfortable silence. "I want us to go together," Keon said. "And, I want us to start going back to church. We have to do this, for us. For our girls, Dria."

More silence. I was so engrossed in everything we had been through, I couldn't help but wonder was there even hope for us? We had gotten to a bad place and me, well I was damaged, utterly and completely damaged. Could I ever be enough for him when I wasn't even enough for myself?

Then, I felt Keon shift and dip his hand into my pocket to find my fingers. Lacing his with mine, we just stood there for a moment longer, as if relishing the silent reassurance.

"I have to tell you something," I started, turning to look at him. "Your mother got a note."

"A note?" He was clearly not following where this sudden statement came from. Or why.

I nodded. "Yes. From your sister."

Chapter 18
Kimera

"Do you have any regrets?"

I turned to look at Kareem directly. We had just finished another quickie, this time standing up in my closet. We had gotten dressed and lay across my bed, me at the head and he at the foot. It felt nice, Kareem's companionship. I think I had been so focused on getting out that I hadn't noticed I was craving someone to talk to. Kareem was easily filling every one of those voids.

On top of that, the man was a pure protector. I needed that too. He had spoken with Leo and apparently, someone had smashed a brick through the back-patio door and shattered the glass the other day. Shit had startled all of us because we didn't even realize someone was able to get on the property. But Kareem had sprung into action, trying to make sure me and the boys were safe. Though a few days had passed and they still hadn't found out who had done it, Kareem was around me more than ever, just to make sure. And that comforted me.

I rested my head on my hand, reflecting on the question he had just asked. "Do I have any regrets? That's kind of obvious, right? I mean doesn't everyone have regrets?"

Kareem nodded. "Right. I guess I should rephrase and ask what are some of your regrets then."

"Well how much do you really know about me?"

"I want to hear it from you," he countered. "Not what Obi and Leo have said about you."

I sat up. Fair enough. "We have more in common than you think. I was blinded by greed too. At the time, money looked so good to me that I would do anything for it. Even sell my soul. A long time ago, I dated a man and all I saw was what he could do for me. I had been hurt before, so I wasn't looking for love. I didn't believe in that shit anymore. So, this man promised me the world in exchange for my freedom. And me being me, I agreed. I didn't realize this agreement would cost me pretty much everything. So, talking about regrets, I'm still living in the regret of mistakes I made a while ago. And my life will never be the same." Hearing it all out loud prompted the beginning of tears to sting my eyes.

"Tell me something about you," Kareem said breaking through my despair. "Something good."

I had to smile at him trying to lighten the mood by changing the subject. "Like?"

"Like . . . what are you good at?"

My grin was wicked and prompted him to moan in response. "Besides sex," he clarified on a chuckle. "What else are you good at?"

I relaxed into the now positive direction of this conversation. "Makeup," I answered with a wistful sigh. "My best friend, well sister-in-law now since she married my brother, and I had always wanted to open a cosmetic store called Melanin Mystique."

"Catchy name."

I laughed. "Yeah, we came up with that when we were like fourteen, and it just stuck."

"Well, I'm sure you'll get that store one day."

A shadow suddenly fell in the room, that memory like a ghost. "We did," I said. "Tyree burned it to the ground." I unfolded my legs and rose, suddenly needing to move. "Just like I had a father. Tyree got rid of him, too."

"Damn."

"Right." I looked out the window. Naomi was doing laps in the pool, her taut body glistening in the sun as she pierced through like butter, sleek and agile in her tiny, yellow bikini. I was once like that. Nothing to worry about but what fun I was going to get into next and how much of Leo's money I was going to spend during the next shopping excursion.

At one point, Naomi stopped on the side, resting a bit before lifting her body out of the water and strolling to one of the lounge chairs to grab a towel.

"I don't even know what's going on at home," I murmured. I was looking at Naomi but my mind was far from the backyard pool. "I don't know if my best friend is alive, dead. My mother. She was already dealing with my father's death and now this." I buried my face in my hands, now letting the tears flow freely. Thankfully, Kareem didn't speak, didn't move, just let me self-console and I needed this cleansing more than I realized.

After I was sure I was calm enough, I sighed and turned to face him. Kareem patted the space on the bed beside him and I obeyed, sitting down next to him. "We're going to get you out of this," he said, resting his hand on mine. I nodded, holding that assurance close and allowing it to bring me comfort.

The sound of a chime had us both looking at each other. Kareem grinned and sat up quickly, reaching for a gym bag at the foot of the bed. He fumbled through some basketball shorts and a t-shirt before pulling his tablet into view. I could feel his eagerness and I sat up, alert. "What is it?" I asked.

Kareem looked at his tablet, punching buttons and swiping the screen to get to something apparently. "Security cameras, remember?" he said. "I'm able to tap into them shut them on and off as needed. A little something my boy taught me. He continued clicking buttons as he spoke, his fingers flying over the keys. Whatever it was, was definitely pressing. "Remember when you heard me talking to Tyree and I told you I put the camera in his room?"

"Yeah."

"Well, I just got an alert of some activity up there." He glanced up with a wink. "And we may want to check it out."

Anxious, I scooted closer and peered over his shoulder, watching the images play across his screen. The image was slightly distorted and pixilated, definitely not the best quality. But, I recognized Tyree clear as if he had been standing in front of me. And the other, well I had seen that body too many times to count so I would've been able to identify him in my sleep. Even though it had been a moment, it was unmistakably him.

The more the scene unfolded, the happier I became. Maybe, just maybe, I would be out of here sooner than later.

<hr />

"Christmas just ain't Christmas without the one you love."

I frowned as the O'Jays crooned through the house's built-in intercom system. *What the hell?* My eyes slid to the bedside table to read the digits on the clock. 9:37 AM. Not sure whose bright idea it was to play Christmas ballads this time of morning. Or at all for that matter. The music already felt like it would throw me into an even deeper depression. *"Now I'm staying home alone, And my house is not a home . . ."*

I sighed tossing the sheets off. If that wasn't the damn truth. This time last year, I was home with my family and my friends. Everyone had gathered at my parents' house for dinner and to exchange presents. Of course, we couldn't pull the men from in front of the TV for whatever NBA game was playing (I never could keep up but I knew it was usually Lebron James and friends). Then, we would go down to my dad's church, the Word of Truth Christian Center, to open our doors to serve meals to those who needed it and (if it was a Sunday) have service. It was never big or extravagant but it was our little Davis family tradition. One that I didn't realize how much I appreciated until now because it was a celebration stemming from pure love.

I continued sitting on the edge of the bed, not being able to bring myself to get up and face the reality. That there was nothing on the other side of that door for me. With the exception of my children, this would be the first year devoid of that family and love I had grown to cherish. My mind wandered to my mom and I had to squeeze my eyes shut to keep the tears from falling, even as music continued to echo around me. *"Last year this time, goin' shopping with friends together . . ."* This would be my mom's first Christmas without my dad. And the idea that I couldn't be there for her in her time of need sickened me to my core.

The song ended and Boyz II Men's "Let it Snow" began to play in its place. I was still settling in confusion. Leo did not strike me as the kind of person to celebrate, well anything outside of himself, let alone Christmas. I shoved my feet in my slippers, belted a robe around my pastel pink negligee, and opened my door.

My room was situated near the banister overlooking the grand living room below. It was here I could see a huge white Christmas tree adorned with red and gold baubles, garland, and lights that blinked in rotating sequence, though they weren't really necessary since every light was on in the house and daylight streamed through the open blinds. Lights, wreaths, and red bow ribbons hung on walls and wrapped around columns to add festive color and charm. Leo sat on the couch while Jamal and Leo Jr. played with some unwrapped toys at his feet. Well, Leo Jr. played with the toys. Jamal was enthralled with the cardboard box and eating the Santa Claus wrapping paper. More wrapped boxes and holidays bags were cluttered underneath the Christmas tree and at the fireplace, Naomi, in her little skimpy hot pink short set, looked to be hanging stockings, each with our names carefully embroidered in huge cursive font. Any other time and any other place, this would've looked, I don't know. Like a regular family.

Satisfied, Naomi stood back, admiring her work while swaying her hips and mouthing the words to the music. My first instinct was to just go back in my room and crawl back in the covers. The last thing I wanted to do was pretend to be in the Christmas spirit here when I felt everything but merry. But, as if Leo knew I was watching and contemplating, his eyes lifted up to meet mine and his smile spread. He rose, extending his arm in my direction like some pseudo Romeo move.

"My love," he called over the music. "Come. Join us."

I wanted desperately to make up something, anything, to not have to be bothered. But it was just easier to go with it. The 'sick' excuse was only going to work so many times. So, I sighed and descended the stairs.

"Mommy, I miss you," Leo Jr. said, and whereas usually he would've jumped up and run into my arms, he stayed put, his head bent down to his train set. Jamal was just as occupied, but I stooped down anyway and gave them both a kiss.

"Saida, I'm so glad you're here." Naomi turned, resting her hand on her hip. "I need a woman's opinion because you know Leo says it's fine. What do you think about the tree over here? Or should we move it over there?" She gestured across the room to an empty space closer to the window. I'm glad she wasn't looking at me because she would've seen me frowning. Did she really think I gave a damn about the placement of that tacky ass tree? If it were up to me, it would have been in the trash.

Still, I nodded and took a seat on the couch, folding my legs underneath me. "It looks good right there," I commented absently.

Naomi turned her head from one side to the other, as if she were in deep thought about the decision. I half-expected a bead of sweat to pearl on her forehead. Oh, if life were that simple. When my deepest concern was where I wanted to put a Christmas tree.

"You're right," she said finally, a wide smile on her face. "I like it there. I just wanted our first Christmas here to be perfect."

"I didn't know we were doing anything for Christmas," I said to Leo, and he shrugged.

"Naomi's idea," he said. "But I kind of like it. Really makes the house feel like a home, don't you think?"

No. But better than say that, I just kept quiet.

I glanced around, not trying to make my search look obvious. Apparently, Kareem hadn't gotten back yet. He had told me last night he was going first thing in the morning to get the security footage transferred to a DVD or something we could show on the screen. I was anxious, yet still in disbelief that we actually had something we could use. And even more afraid for when it was time to show Leo's father.

I felt someone's eyes on me and glanced over to see Leo had been watching my profile. His face held suspicion, that much was obvious but to ease the tension, I tossed him a pleasant smile, or at least as pleasant as I could muster. "What is it?" I asked.

"What's on your mind, my love?"

Taking your ass down like Scarface. I shook my head. "Nothing much. Just taking in everything."

"Yeah this wasn't really something I wanted to do," he admitted. "This was Naomi's idea. But I figured it would be nice to do one last thing before we leave."

"Leave?"

"Yeah, I told you we were moving."

I felt my panic start to rise, but still, I kept my voice even. "I know you mentioned it. But you didn't say when."

"Well, probably tomorrow night."

Christmas Day? Yeah, something was definitely up. Hell, Leo even looked uneasy.

"So soon? I haven't packed or anything."

Leo was now staring off in the distance, his face furrowed with what looked like thoughts weighing heavy on his mind. Around us the festivities continued to play out, Naomi prancing around (she had moved on to hanging lights around the bay window), the boys had begun to fight over tissue paper, and Leo seemed oblivious to it all. I swallowed the last bit of my anxiety. Maybe he was just talking. He couldn't seriously be thinking about moving us to Africa, just like that.

A sudden vibration had Leo snapping from his daze and fumbling through his pocket. Whatever, or whoever's number he read on his caller ID of his cell phone couldn't have been good because he quickly rose and half-jogged from the room. I wondered who that was and what the hell was going on that had Leo so damn jumpy?

Could've just been my own paranoia. They say when you're up to something it was as if everyone's eyes were on you. Every conversation was about you. I had to remind myself there was no way Leo knew anything about what Kareem and I had been up to. We had been careful, too careful. Since Kareem now had access to the security system, he could turn the camera feeds on and off as needed. Plus, he knew where the blind spots were, the little nooks and crannies so we could openly converse about our plan without fear of getting caught or recorded. Or we could sneak a little quickie here and there, which lately, truth be told, it seemed we had been doing more sexing and less talking.

Which was why I was thrilled when we had finally caught Leo and Tyree, because now we were full steam ahead. The two were strategic about their little intimate moments, but Kareem had been right. It was only a matter of time before they slipped up.

Now, we just had to get Obi over here and sing like a couple of canaries. Well, first Kareem had to come back home with the evidence. The hell was taking him so long anyway?

"I am loving the way this looks." Naomi was sickeningly excited as she plopped down beside me on the couch. She looped her arm through mine and to my surprise, laid her head on my shoulder. "I hope you don't mind all of this," she went on. "But Christmas is my favorite holiday. I can never just NOT celebrate it."

I wished I could feel the same spirit she was so clearly engulfed in. Maybe then, I would be able to handle the depression that was beginning to settle in my heart.

"So, what are you wearing tonight?" Naomi said turning to me eagerly. "I was thinking of a little red number Leo got for me. It's like lace—"

"What's going on tonight?"

Naomi's face reflected the confusion I felt. "Leo's father is coming over. Not sure what's going on, but apparently they have to discuss some things with us. Something important."

"Is it about moving?" I asked.

Naomi's frown deepened. "Who's moving?"

"Leo said we were," I explained. "He told me a while back and I didn't really think much of it. But he just mentioned it again."

She shook her head. "Leo hasn't told me anything. When? Where?"

"Tomorrow night," I said. "To his home in Ivory Coast."

Naomi's eyes widened in shock and just as quickly, she tore her gaze from me and looked to the Christmas tree, as if she were deep in thought. The movement was so quick I wasn't sure if I had seen anything at all. I stared at her profile, watching the sequence of lights dance on the grimace that marred her face.

Finally, she murmured almost to herself. "Africa." The one-word was more of a statement than a question. "He didn't say anything to me about it." *Why?* Was all I could think. Were we leaving and not taking his new bride? That didn't make any sense. And that was completely uncharacteristic of Leo. So why, then, did she not know? Was that really what Obi wanted to discuss with us tonight? If so, why would Leo care to give me any type of heads-up? It's not like I actually *liked* the idea of moving. No, not moving. That sounded too consensual. Being kidnapped *again* sounded more appropriate.

"That's what he told me," I said. I, too, didn't like the news, if it were even true. I was hoping and praying another solution would present itself long before we boarded a plane to the motherland. And by solution, I meant Kareem. But while I was somewhat anxious about the abrupt decision and the urgency with which it seemed we were having to relocate, Naomi seemed even more unsettled. I couldn't help but wonder why. She said she had no family here, nor a home to go to. What was the big deal for her whether she was physically in Texas, Ivory Coast, or Jupiter? She made it clear what her intentions were with Leo, and that entailed going wherever he decided to go. While I, on the other hand, had a reason to be upset, what was Naomi's?

She rose then, nodding her head towards her room. "I need to see what shoes match this dress," was all she said before strolling off. It was a weak attempt at an escape and one that was completely useless. Hell, it wasn't like I was going to stop her. I was too busy worrying about myself and how all of this was going to play out.

The front door chimed with a visitor, and I looked over, jumping up eagerly when I realized it was Kareem. He looked at me and shook his head, silently communicating for me not to speak. He then subtly shifted his eyes to a vase resting on top of the fireplace. I had always thought the brown-and-gold piece was completely hideous and did not match the décor at all. But Kareem had let me know the tacky thing was yet another security camera.

I nodded my understanding and lowered myself back to the couch, watching him out of the corner of my eye. He moved to his room, a doorway behind the grand staircase, and closed the door behind him without muttering so much as one word. Now I was even more confused.

Kareem supposedly went out this morning to get footage. I half-expected some sort of underlying excitement once he got back. Obviously, we still had to play it cool. Discretion was key, but Kareem hadn't acted at all like we were sitting on the key to our freedom. Which meant, to my horror, something was wrong. But what?

"Mama. Juice." Leo Jr. brought my attention back to him. Damn, I had forgotten the kids were still playing quietly at my feet.

He looked at me, half-pleading, half-demanding and the innocent look brought a small smile to my face. Almost habitually, I looked around expecting to see someone, Fernando, Leo, hell someone, and, to my surprise, I was alone. It seemed too good to be true.

I shifted on the couch so I could look around the room and sure enough, it was completely empty. Had that ever happened outside of my bedroom?

I looked to the door, just a few feet away. Then my eyes dropped to the children at my feet. Would I be able to scoop them and make it to the door before anyone came back? I wasn't wearing much of anything but a robe, not even any shoes and the kids were still dressed in Marvel pajamas themselves. I could make it to the door, couldn't I? Shit then what? It was a good drive to the front gate. Let alone hiking it by foot. Naked. With two kids. Hella risky. My chances of making it even to the edge of the yard were slim. Too damned slim. And when, not *if* but *when* I was caught, what would Leo do to me? Would that be something I could lie or fake my way out of? "Oh, it's not what it looks like sweetie I was just taking the kids out for some air." Not suspicious at all. But still . . .

Thirty seconds, I concluded. Thirty seconds is all it would take me to get across the room and to the door. How much time had I already wasted just sitting here thinking about it? *Ten seconds, fifteen? Tick, tick, tick, Kimmy.*

Slowly, I rose to my feet, my eyes darting to all the doors in sight. The kitchen, Leo's office, Naomi's room, Kareem's room. Damn, Kareem. For a moment, I just stared at his closed door as if I could see right through to his bedroom. What was he doing? What had he found? He had risked so much so that we *both* could get out together, and, here I was, plotting to just up and leave without him. What would happen to him? Moreover, I couldn't forget, he had footage with him. Valuable footage that would be the solution to both of our unanswered prayers. Was I willing to take an impulsive chance and make a run for it when we had a better plan in place?

I refused to look, but I remembered the vase's security camera pointing right at me. One of many, I knew because Kareem had subtly pointed them out to me once. I was open, in the clear, but for how long? Someone was watching. I could almost feel it in my spirit. Eyes trained on me, watching my every move. A test maybe. Yes, this was probably a test. But in my heart of hearts, I knew I wouldn't be able to swallow not seizing this opportunity.

I gently picked up Leo Jr. and nuzzled his neck, letting the fresh smell of soap and baby lotion relax my tension. Then, I stooped to pick up Jamal in my left arm and casually carried them both in the kitchen. "You want some juice?" I asked, putting on my best smile and Leo Jr. clapped his hands appreciatively. Yeah, I wouldn't be able to live with the fact that I didn't try to make that dash for the door. But hopefully, I wouldn't have too much longer to dwell on it. As soon as Kareem was able to talk, I had to know we were set to go. For my own sake.

⸻

The pool had become our little unofficial meeting place. When we weren't letting off our much-needed sexual tension that is. So, I sat poolside, a thin cotton sundress letting the sun tan my skin, and waited for Kareem.

I hadn't seen Naomi since this morning when she left so quickly after I dropped the bomb about this mysterious move to Africa. Now that a few hours had passed, Leo had commented she was getting ready for tonight's Christmas Eve get-together with Obi.

The French door slid open, footsteps, and then closed on a quiet click. Kareem's shadow draped over me, suddenly shielding the sun and cloaking me in a slight dimness. For a moment, he just stood there as if trying to find the words to speak. Restless, I looked up to him and watched him stare out at the water.

"It's not there," he said finally.

"What?" The word was reflexive even though, unfortunately, I had heard loud and clear what he just said. But that didn't help with my clarification.

"I checked last night," Kareem went on, shoving his hands in the front pockets of his jeans. "It wasn't there. I figured I had just messed up the settings, got something mixed up but it was still salvageable."

"But . . ." My mouth hung open. Not true. This couldn't be true. Not when we were this close. "You went to the store today. The security place, right?"

"I went to some IT guys I know," Kareem clarified. "I couldn't risk going to the company who services these cameras and have

Leo or Obi find out. I hoped and prayed they could find the footage we had seen. But it was nowhere."

"I don't understand. How is that possible?"

"Someone must have erased the source file," Kareem said. "From the actual camera. My thing was just a feeder that duplicated what was being seen on the cameras. It hacked into the footage, but it can only broadcast what's there. So, if there is nothing there . . ."

He trailed off and I mentally filled in the blank. He was right. If there was nothing there, there was nothing to see. Shit, now what?

I tried my best to keep the disappointed panic out of my voice. There just had to be another way. "And they said there was no way to get the footage back?" I said, almost pleading.

"He said he may be able to retrieve the data from the original camera," Kareem said.

"The original camera?"

"In Tyree's room," he clarified. "If we had that camera, I could take it to him and let him look at it."

The idea seemed hopeless and it took everything in me not to bust out in tears. It felt like everything was slipping right through my fingers. Again, I remembered my opportunity earlier to make a run for it. Damn if I wasn't regretting it now more than ever.

"We don't have that kind of time," I murmured, shutting my eyes and taking a deep breath.

"What do you mean?"

"I'm moving, remember?"

"Yeah, but none of that shit is finalized," Kareem assured me, and I could only shake my head. Now, the first few tears did sting my eyelids and trail down my cheeks. *I should've run when I had the chance.*

"Leo told me we're leaving tomorrow night," I said, lifting wet eyes to finally look at Kareem's bewildered face.

He was in denial, shaking his head against my words. "No, that can't be right."

I shrugged, helplessly. "That's what he said unless he's lying."

"When did he tell you this?"

"This morning while you were out."

Kareem began to pace behind me but as far as I was concerned, it was no use.

"Well fuck it, we won't worry about my IT friend," he said, his voice carrying the urgency of his brisk movements. "I just got to get my hands on that camera."

"And do what?"

"We need evidence," Kareem said. "Without that camera, we have nothing. Then what?" He was right, then what? I had been asking myself that since I'd gotten here. There was nothing, no end goal, no final count. As far as I could see, this nightmare just kept going, sequel after sequel, with no foreseeable future. And the only thing that was foreseeable was the realization that Leo was about to pack my ass up and ship me off to Ivory Coast. I was as good as dead anyway because banking on someone to find me was becoming more and more farfetched. Let alone if I was living 10,000 miles away under a phony name with no contact to the outside world.

"How are we going to get it?" I asked.

"Have you seen Tyree at all today?"

I shook my head. "I hardly ever see him," I admitted. "Leo told him to stay in his room upstairs basically."

When we first moved in, I had overheard the conversation and Tyree definitely had something to say about the arrangement. There were some stairs that led to a finished walk-in attic, the staircase nearly so discreet you would almost miss it. Tyree had been instructed to remain in there at all times, unless otherwise specified. Him, well he had showed his entire flamboyant ass with that request. Me, I felt like gloating. He was in no better position than I was, a prisoner. Confined to this luxurious 12,000 square foot cell. If I hadn't been so sure about what was going on, I could almost swear there was no such thing as a Tyree.

"So, he should be up there then?" Kareem said.

I nodded. "I would guess, yeah."

Kareem moved to the door and the gesture brought me to my feet. "I'm coming with you," I said before even realizing I had even wanted to.

Kareem shook his head. "Nah. We can't afford to have things go wrong."

"I know. That's why I want to go." I thought for a moment, then added, "And besides. Aren't you going to need some kind of lookout? What if Leo comes up to see him?"

"True. But what are you going to do?"

I shrugged. "Not sure. But I won't let you get caught." That seemed to comfort him and after another moment, Kareem nodded and gestured for me to follow him.

I had never ventured up here. It had always seemed like some forbidden Nazareth-type territory I shouldn't dare explore. But having Kareem by my side certainly helped calm my scattered nerves.

We climbed the last few stairs towards the third floor and stopped in front of the closed door. Tyree's door. He had always been so close, just quietly hovering in the shadows. Shit made my flesh crawl. Kareem lifted his fist to knock but paused with his knuckles a breath away from the wood.

"What is it?" I whispered, watching him put his ear to the door. He held up one finger to his lips signaling for me to be quiet. Panic started to set in and I took a step back towards the stairs. Maybe this wasn't a good idea. What if Leo were in there? What would he say?

"I don't think he's in there," Kareem murmured almost to himself. "It's too quiet."

I let out a gentle sigh of relief. "That's a good thing, right? We can get the camera and get out of there before he comes back."

"Yeah," Kareem seemed to agree, but for some reason, his apprehension was louder than his words. He glanced both ways down the empty hall and turned the knob to push the door open. "Stay here and stand guard," he instructed.

"No, please don't leave me out here," I whispered. "What if he comes back?" The thought alone had me shook. How the hell could I explain my presence up here? *Oh sorry, Leo I was just looking out while Kareem rummaged through Tyree's things.* Yeah, that was sure to end well.

Kareem paused, considering my fears before stepping to the side and letting me enter first. Grateful, I stepped over the threshold into the dark room, my hand feeling against the wall for a light switch.

"Kareem, I can't see anything," I said flicking on the light. Instantly, the area lit up in a haze of yellow. I turned to the room and screamed.

I couldn't stop screaming. Even when Kareem stepped in behind me on a muffled curse and folded me in to his arms, shifting his body to block my sordid view. But even now that he stood in front of me, I still saw Tyree dangling from the ceiling fan, an overturned chair below his suspended bare feet, his body swaying like a gentle pendulum from the extension cord connecting his neck to the railing. Trickles of blood colored the neckline of the blue t-shirt he wore and I was thankful his back was to me. I wouldn't have been able to bear it if I actually saw the death in the man's expression.

Kareem ushered me back into the hall and I took a deep pull on the brisk air and bent over to the banister. I coughed, squinting my eyes shut against the fresh image, and dissolved into sobs.

I felt his lips touch my temple, and I lifted my face, my vision blurry with tears. I watched him study my face as if I had an answer, and, defeated, he rested his forehead against mine wearily. "I'm sorry," he murmured, and I couldn't help but wonder what he was apologizing for but hell, those may have been the words I needed to hear. I let out a shaky breath and listened to the distant haze of voices and footsteps.

Chapter 19
Kimera

It was as if life just went on. Like there wasn't even a suicide that had taken place only hours before.

I was still in shock and spent the better half of the afternoon throwing up my sorrows and regrets. Tyree's lifeless body hanging there was all I kept seeing, and it played over and over again in my subconscious like some sick, perverted movie. None of it seemed real.

Even after Kareem had pulled me screaming back into the hallway and tried to shield my view, it just seemed like a bad dream.

I sank to the floor next to the toilet, weak from exhaustion and sickness. Bad dream my ass. As if my guts in the toilet didn't validate what I'd seen, my sore throat damn sure did. I was trembling, and I felt bile simmering in the pit of my stomach and threatening to rise up and onto these newly waxed floors. The anxiety was causing a massive headache, and I had to rest my head on the wall just to keep the room from spinning.

Suicide? How? Why? None of it made sense. Not after everything Tyree had put me through. To commit suicide seemed too much like a welcome relief. Hell, too much like perfect timing. And it just didn't sit right with me for some reason. Tyree committing suicide on Christmas Eve, right when we were about to expose him and blow the lid off all this shit. The night before we were set to move to Africa. How much of a coincidence was that?

My mind was urging me to take his death for the blessing it was. My gut, which was making more sense of this at the moment, was telling me something else was there. What, I didn't know. And that's what was sending me into the beginnings of a panic attack.

Even more perplexing was the way this little Christmas Eve get-together was still taking place downstairs. Nothing elaborate but food was being prepared, cheerful music was being played, and the general 'holiday cheer' was in the air as if life just went on and a suicide was a simple hiccup. Like burning the macaroni and cheese. *Oh no worries. Throw it out, we'll make a new batch or eat something else. Who needs a drink?* And me, being around so much death in such a short period of time, shit was never that simple or quick to get over.

I gathered the beaded hunter green gown I wore and bracing against the wall, rose to shaky legs. Thankfully, I hadn't even bothered with my shoes when I'd come running into the bathroom to throw up for the fourth time. Even barefoot, I felt like I was unstable and wouldn't have been able to keep them on anyway.

My makeup, well what little I had bothered with, was smeared so I made my way to the sink to wash it off completely. Nude face it was tonight. I ran quivering fingers through my hair and let out a shuddering breath.

I had been so distracted with the suicide that I hadn't even considered the fact that Kareem and I were still in a shitty mess. In the midst of the confusion, he said he had tried to look for the camera to no avail. It was nowhere to be found. Which meant someone had moved it. Had Tyree found it and erased the feed first? None of it was making sense and at that point, I wasn't trying to sift through the problem. I needed a solution. Because Obi was downstairs and we had nothing. No proof. No nothing. And now, by some crazy happenstance, the primary culprit in all of this was gone as if he never existed. I was out of ideas. And by the knock on my door, out of time too. That thought alone had a fresh wave of nausea simmering in my stomach.

Leo stood on the other side of my door and a grave smile spread when he saw me. The way he looked so pale (which was not easy for a man with his rich, dark complexion) and his eyes nearly sunken and rounded taking up a lot of his face, he looked like he was here in body only. His mind was clearly elsewhere. If I didn't know any better, I could almost feel his ache surrounding him like a thick cloud.

"My love," he murmured and more of an unconscious habit, he kissed my palm. "Ready?"

I touched his arm, halting his movements. "Leo," I said, my voice barely above a whisper. "We need to talk about . . . about what happened with Tyree."

Leo hesitated for the briefest of moments before his eyebrows drew together in feigned confusion. "I don't know who you're talking about," he said, his tone dismissive. "Let's go. My dad is anxious to see you." And that was the end of it.

So, I guess that's how we were going to play this. As if this man, this gay man that had killed my father, kidnapped me and my friend, and held us hostage in a storage closet, who had been living in our attic for months, had never even existed. Was that the best he could do?

I let Leo lead me down the stairs and into the huge dining room with its teardrop chandeliers and expansive glass table that easily seated twenty guests. Someone had decorated in here as well so white garland was draped from the walls and windows in a last-minute attempt to be festive.

Fernando had done the most, as usual, with a turkey and southern-style soul food sides laid out in the center of the table, surrounded by candles, wine, and elegant, Christmas-themed chinaware. An instrumental song played somewhere over the intercom and Obi, his wives, Naomi, and Kareem were all already seated and waiting, dressed in their various formal wear of reds, greens, and blacks.

Leo pulled out a chair next to Kareem, and I sank down into it, grateful for the reprieve. No one even bothered to notice I didn't have on shoes, thank God. Leo sat to my right, between me and Naomi and directly across from his father.

"Great now that my son and his lovely wife have arrived," Obi began with a huge grin. "We can enjoy this feast."

On cue, one-by-one, Fernando and his wait staff entered from the kitchen, carrying plates of salads and appetizers. They placed everything in front of us and my stomach balled tighter in knots. How could anyone eat after what happened earlier? I glanced around, and, sure enough, I looked to be the only one stalled. Even Naomi, who this morning had seemed on edge, had appeared to have calmed down and was even smiling and giggling with one of Obi's wives. Of course, she wouldn't have been affected. She hadn't witnessed what I had. I wasn't even sure she had known what had taken place. Come to think of it, had she even known about Tyree at all?

I turned to Kareem and gestured for him to pass the salt and pepper. It was more of an excuse to see how he was holding up because I hadn't even sampled the salad on my plate to see if it needed dressing. Without looking at me, Kareem sat the shakers in front of me and resumed eating quietly, his head bent to avoid eye contact. I was pretty sure he was thinking exactly what I had been mulling over since this afternoon. What were we going to do?

"So, since we're all here I might as well share the news," Obi started, clasping his hands together. He looked to Leo as if to prepare him before he spoke again. "Business has been good. Better than I could have expected actually. So, it's time for all of us to go home."

Leo's wives were the only ones who seemed to squeal in delight. The rest of us were silent. So, it had been true. Part of me was hoping Leo had just been talking. Obviously wishful thinking.

"Oh Obi, that's so exciting," Natasha threw her arms around him. "I've missed home. It's just not the same here."

"When do we leave?" Yana asked.

"Tonight."

I felt like I had swallowed a rock. Did he say tonight? No that couldn't have been right. Leo had said tomorrow. Which was really no better but hell at least I had another twenty-four hours to come up with something. Anything, to keep from going.

"Right after dinner," Obi continued at the silence. "I already have the plane ready, and they're throwing us a huge holiday celebration at home."

"Why so soon?" I was surprised to hear Naomi's voice. Her question came out tiny, voicing what I myself wanted to ask.

Obi didn't seem fazed by the question. "Business wrapped up early," was all he said as if that was enough explanation.

Naomi remained quiet, and I swallowed hard. I couldn't let this happen. "I like it here sweetie," I said turning my attention to Leo to hopefully appeal to his emotions.

Leo slid a quick glance at his father before taking my hand and kissing my palm. "You'll love it much better in the Ivory Coast," he said. "It's beautiful and a great place to raise our children."

"No." The word stabbed the air sharply and I didn't realize it had actually left my lips until everyone's eyes turned to me with various expressions. My heart thumped against my chest as I waited for what seemed like an eternity for someone to break the tension. I heard erratic breathing bellowing in my ear and realized it was my own. *Shit.*

It was Obi who spoke up first, his words slow and meticulous. "What did you say, Saida?"

I opened my mouth but no sound came out. Abruptly I closed it again and squeezed my eyes shut as if to block out everything. Fear strangled my voice as I, again, opened my mouth, and I wasn't even sure what was going to come out until, one-by-one, the words fell from my lips and stung my ears.

"Leo is gay."

Chapter 20
Kimera

I now completely understood the phrase "time stood still." Because that's exactly how it felt. For a moment, everyone, down to Fernando and his crew just froze in place as if someone had put the world on pause. I took slow, labored breaths and waited for the explosion that was sure to come.

Leo didn't even blink as he continued to stare at me. Then, finally, movement. Slowly and steadily, he placed his fork down beside his plate and picked up his glass of wine.

I couldn't bring myself to look at Leo but I felt his eyes on me and I already knew if looks could kill I probably would've been laid out on the floor in a pool of my own blood. *What had I done?* Of course, I hadn't been thinking before I had just blurted that out. Especially with not a stitch of evidence. Yeah, I was clearly asking for that death sentence.

"Ladies." Obi's tone was surprisingly calm. Too calm and every danger sign, red flag, bell, whistle and warning alarm went off in my head. "Take Naomi upstairs please."

His wives moved in-sync, all of them rising together and placing kisses on Obi's cheek one-by-one. The one, I believe Natasha, circled the table and taking Naomi by the hand, guided her to her feet. I looked to Naomi whose eyes flickered between all of us, clearly confused by everything that was going on. But, she obediently rose to her feet and allowed herself to be led away.

"Fernando," Obi continued simply, and, understanding his cue, Fernando and his crew left the room as well.

Now it was just us, me, Kareem, Leo, and Obi. I got a little sense of *The Godfather*, the way Obi sat on his side of the table alone and the rest of us on the opposite side, watching and waiting. I half-expected him to reach under the table and come up wielding machine guns.

Obi sat back and clasped his hands together, putting them on the table in front of him. "Sorry about that," Obi said but he sounded anything but. "Now. Please, Saida. Continue. You were saying?"

Don't do it, Kimmy. It was a clear trap. But what was I supposed to do? Just play it off and go back to the way things were? The normal in this prison? Move to Africa with all of the Owusus tonight and suffer through my "happily ever after"? Or what Leo had told me my happily ever after should be with him?

I swallowed hard and lowered my eyes to my uneaten salad. What was the point of holding it in? I was dead in this situation anyway. What was worse than this?

"Sir," I started, my voice coming out in a squeak. "I have been kidnapped and held against my will. Leo forced me to marry him because he doesn't want you to find out the truth."

Obi nodded, his lips pursed together tightly. "The truth, huh? And what is that my dear?" The bait. But I had to take it.

"That he's gay," I repeated my earlier statement.

Obi narrowed his eyes and I noticed he not once looked at Leo but kept his eyes focused on me during this little confession.

"And," his words continued slow and meticulous as if he seemed to be reflecting on everything. "Do you have any proof of these allegations? If so, I would absolutely love to see."

I shut my eyes remembering first the images we had seen play out on Kareem's phone. Then him admitting that he'd gone to his IT friend and there wasn't anything left.

"Well?" Obi prompted. "Let me see."

"I don't have it," I admitted. "But, Mr. Owusu, you have to believe me. I wouldn't lie about something like this."

Now Obi finally turned his attention to his son, his eyes narrowing. "Son, is any of this true?"

I took another heavy breath, afraid to look at the man sitting next to me. Then his next words chilled me to my core. "No Sir," he said. "None of it is true. She is lying."

Obi seemed satisfied and nodded, now turning his death stare back to me.

"Sir," I rushed on. "Please understand. You remember me as Kimera Davis. Not Saida. You remember when I was in Atlanta. Now, all of a sudden, we're in Dallas and I have a new name. Don't you see?"

I turned pleading eyes to Kareem. "Please tell him. I know this isn't the way we said we would do this but please. We have no other way. No other choice."

Kareem's expression was blank and he didn't bother looking at me as I continued to beg him to cosign my story. *Please, not now Kareem. Don't leave me in this alone.*

"So, you knew about this too?" Obi's question was more of an accusation.

"She's right," Kareem murmured, almost regretfully. I sent my gratitude to God for allowing this man to be on my side. With two of us, maybe Obi would see the truth. Evidence or not.

Obi cleared his throat and I held my breath as his finger "casually" grazed the blade end of the steak knife in front of him. "Saida, do you know who I am?"

Was that a trick question? I decided it was rhetorical and didn't bother answering. Obi continued. "I am a very wealthy, very powerful man. But I'm sure you already knew that. Which was why you decided it was a wise idea to bring this type of reproach against my family, correct?"

I shook my head. "I just wanted you to know the truth."

"Oh, the truth? Whose truth? Yours? Because it's certainly not my family's truth."

I couldn't stop the tears as I slowly felt this spiraling out of control. "Mr. Owusu, please. We had footage and someone erased it. I swear."

"And where is he, huh?" Obi pressed. "This alleged man my son is gay with. Where is Tyree?"

The horrible image of Tyree's body dangling from the ceiling fan only hours before made me nauseous. But then, something began to fit together, and I felt the color drain from my face in horror. "How did you know?" I whispered.

"What?"

"His name. I never said his name."

Obi's smirk gave it all away and my heart crumbled at the realization. All this was for nothing. Because Obi already knew.

"Told you this girl was too smart for her own good," he murmured nodding towards Leo. "The moment you first said you had picked her, I knew it was a mistake. Even still, I welcomed you into my family. Gave you my name and a piece of us. Only for you to try and bring down and tarnish Leo's legacy, MY legacy, and destroy what has taken me years to build."

I shook my head. This couldn't be. This was supposed to fix everything. "Of course, I know Leo is gay," Obi continued. "I know him better than you. I saw the signs even from a young age. But I knew damn well we weren't having that. So yeah, he needed a cover. You're right, Kimmy, is it?"

I shuddered, and yet still even hearing it, I couldn't get over it. He knew. He knew all along.

"I guess your secret is out, son," Obi teased and gave a light laugh. "Oh my, now what are we going to do about this?"

Obi rose, and, for the first time, my blood chilled at the sight of the gun in his waistband. It was almost inconspicuous against the black of his slacks, but the piece was very much real and very much there. And I was very much afraid.

"Son," Obi addressed Leo again who rose to his feet. I had never seen him look so pitiful, so damn defeated but not even he was a match, I guess, to Obi Owusu. "You need to handle her like I told you to do a long time ago. Now, I was going to let you wait until we took her back to Côte d'Ivoire, but it seems everything is out now. It's time you prove your loyalty to me." Obi placed his hand on Leo's shoulder, looking at him dead in the eye. "No one," he said slowly, "is going to destroy my reputation. Understood?"

Leo nodded. "Yes, sir."

The exchange was smooth. Obi took the gun from his waistband, popped open the chamber to check the bullets, and snapped it shut on a satisfied grin. He then handed it to Leo. "You started all of this mess," Obi went on. "You can finish it." Now he looked at me again, then Kareem. "They both have to go."

I reacted on instinct, remembering Kareem's daughter and I threw my arm out in front of him. Like my little limb would really stop a bullet.

"Wait," I cried, desperately. "You don't have to do this."

"Kimmy," Kareem nudged my hand to the side and tossed me a reassuring smile. "It's okay. I promise I got you."

He stood, lifting his hands palms up in the air. "Brother, it's not her you want," he said. "It's me."

I shook my head fiercely as Leo lifted the gun. No, Kareem couldn't go out like this. Not after risking his neck for me.

"Nephew," Kareem turned his attention to Leo. "I'm not sure if you know but the penalty for killing a cop is capital punishment."

My head whipped up to Kareem in shocked confusion. *What did he say? A cop?*

Chapter 21
Kimera

I had to shake my head to make sure I had heard Kareem correctly. No, he did not say he was a cop. Couldn't be. This entire time? That just didn't make sense.

Leo now had the gun aimed at Kareem's chest, the piece nice and steady as if he were used to holding something so lethal, so deadly. I guess with a father like his, he had to be.

To my relief, Obi lifted his hand in front of Leo to halt his movement, and, though Leo did not put the gun down, he took his finger off the trigger.

"What did you say?" Obi said, his own voice carrying disbelief.

Kareem didn't blink, didn't waver. "You heard me, *Brother*," he said. "I don't think hearing it a second time will make it any less true."

Damn, he was bold. Did that explain how he had all these connections? His IT guy? The security feed? Was he undercover this entire time? My brain sifted through all of the stories he had told me trying to decipher between what was fact and fiction. He called Leo his nephew and Obi his brother so perhaps that much was true. But, as far as the rest, hell, I didn't know who this man was.

"I suggest you think long and hard about your next moves, *Brother*," Obi said mimicking Kareem's emphasis on the word. The word that obviously meant absolutely nothing between these two. "You have known me for a long time and you, of all people, know what I am capable of."

"Oh, I know," Kareem nodded. "I've seen it for myself."

Obi waved his indiscretions as easily as he would a pesky fly. I remembered Kareem had explained this man's roots and dealings so of course he wouldn't let something as irrelevant as a life get in his way. "This is bigger than Tyree," Obi went on.

"Your empire."

"My legacy," Obi corrected. "Do you think I could sit on my throne and let my son's *confusion* ruin my life? His life? We have come too far in this family. You, of all people, should know that. That's why I don't believe a word you're saying."

"What? That I'm an officer?" Kareem shrugged, a silent dare. "Well, there is only one way to find out. I guess we'll see after Leo shoots and this house is surrounded by FBI and Dallas SWAT units. Or when your son is sitting on trial with a capital murder charge."

Obi tossed his head back and his laugh was so loud and jovial, I had to replay the previous comment to see what the hell was so funny. I still sat there in stunned silence, my eyes not moving from the pistol Leo still gripped in his hand. I didn't know what Kareem was doing. Was this his plan? Was he stalling? What if Leo called his bluff? Then I would be next, and who the hell would save me?

Leo finished his little amused break and shook his head. "I know you're lying," he said. "You know how I know? Because Tyree told me all about you and your little setup."

I watched Kareem's jaw clench. That obviously was not what he wanted to hear. He remained quiet as Obi went on. "Oh yeah, he told me everything. Told me all about how you worked for the cartel and y'all had a plan to set me up and take me down. Ain't that something?"

"Tyree was lying."

"Was he? Because he sure as hell seemed to be telling the truth when he thought he could bargain his way out of his imprisonment." Obi lifted an eyebrow. "Yeah I think we know who the liar is. And I should've gotten rid of your ass a long time ago. I knew you weren't loyal but I ignored my gut and kept you around. Why? Because we were family. And look how you did your family."

Obi shook his head and continued his statuesque stance alongside Leo who, to my surprise, still hadn't uttered a word. Obi nudged Leo's arm, shifting the aim of the gun from Kareem to me. My eyes rounded and my heart dropped to the floor. *Please God, no.*

I held up my hands in surrender, my vision clouding and my head reeling. "Don't do this," I pleaded, my eyes on Leo. "Baby. I thought you loved me."

"I think we know who the main problem is here," Obi said, his finger wagging in my direction. "And here I thought a change of scenery would fix you. Make you appreciate all what we've done for you. Isn't this what you wanted, Kimmy?"

I shook my head, no longer caring how pitiful or desperate I looked. "No," I said. "I didn't want any of this. This whole thing ruined my life and I am so sorry I ever got involved."

"Ruined your life?" Obi scoffed. "*Your* life? What about Leo's life? Did you think for one moment how your little selfishness affected my son, the one you loved?"

"I lost my father," I cried. I wasn't sure what they wanted to hear. What was going to crack the tough wall these Owusus had put up? "I was taken from my family and everyone."

"Don't you deserve it?" This time, it was Leo who spoke and I shifted my pleading eyes back to him, unsure how to respond. "When you got involved with me, wasn't that what you wanted?

A business arrangement? Trading your morals, your family, hell even your freedom, for a quick come up?"

Had I asked for this? Was this my own karma? Sure, I had done that, but did that warrant every subsequent consequence that came barreling in my life? Jail? Murder? Jahmad? The kidnapping? Adria?

"One question," Leo said. Now, he did put his finger back on the trigger and my heart thumped so fast and so hard it was like one single beat that threatened to erupt from my chest.

"Leo, please. I'm sorry for all of this," I tried a different tactic. "Don't you see? I came here with you to Dallas because I wanted to please you. Doesn't that mean something, anything to you?"

"One question," he repeated, obviously not moved by my sobs. "Did you ever love me, my love?"

"Of course I did," I shrieked. I didn't care that it was a lie. I didn't care how I sounded. I just needed to say whatever he needed to hear to spare my life. "Leo, yes. I've always loved you."

Leo lowered his head briefly, only briefly before shaking it and lifting his gaze to meet mine once more. "All this time," he mumbled. "I thought you would at least tell me the truth."

"Leo—"

"Because I've always loved you."

As I watched his finger stroke the trigger, I let my heavy lids drift closed. Kareem's words echoed in my ear. *"I promise, I got you."* I didn't know what he had been lying about but that much was true wasn't it? He would save me, wouldn't he? These were all just dreams.

I saw myself with Jahmad. I was on my back, my arms clasped around his neck, my legs wrapped around his waist as he ran across the sandy Bahamas beach. He murmured something inaudible before spinning me around. I laughed. When was the last time I had laughed? My laugh echoed in harmony with the crash of waves at our backs and I kissed him. Love.

Then a new vision. This time of my parents, Keon, and me situated around the dining room table. We couldn't have been any more than teenagers but the love that filled our home was so steeped in richness. Completely priceless. Keon shoved me as I snatched a biscuit off his plate. That was real. That was family. That was love.

And last, Adria. We sat together, our heads bowed over some plans for our makeup store. Even at sixteen, we had dreams bigger than ourselves and blood couldn't have made us any closer. That bond that had only strengthened with time. My best friend, my sister. My entire heart. I clung to the sensation with everything in my power. Leo had never known true love and thus, had never shown it to me. No matter how warped his sense of reality was, I knew love. I had felt it, grown up with it.

When I opened my eyes, I saw Leo's face, but, slowly, as if I was watching a movie, the face transposed until it was my own face. Starring back with that malicious grin and pointed gun. I watched the lips move, my lips, even though it was Leo's voice that came out.

"Goodbye, my love," he said.

I couldn't die. I couldn't give up. Not yet. I wanted to go to Paris. I wanted to get married. For real. I wanted to have a normal life with my kids. Not like this. I had so many reasons and I needed to live.

My eyes were still closed, but I heard the gunshot so close and so loud that it sent my own body convulsing. It popped like a firecracker, the hollow explosion echoing off the empty walls. One single shot. That was all it took.

Chapter 22
Kimera

The smell of blood was strong and sickening. Whose blood? I moaned and tried to move, wincing at the pinch of fractured glass against the side of my face. *Where was everyone? What happened?* I couldn't hear anything with the exception of a crisp ringing in my ear. Slowly, I lifted my eyes and tried to get my vision to clear. Just as I suspected, I was lying face down on the ground among tiny pieces of glass. I saw the crimson pool of blood but I couldn't be sure where, or who, it was coming from. My entire body was on fire and throbbed with varying degrees of pain that startled a cry from my lips and left me paralyzed with the aching.

The noise was louder now. Not ringing. Sirens. Thank God. My vision waned again but relief coursed through my body when I saw the sequence of blue and red lights flashing through the living room window to blend with the lights from the Christmas tree. Never had I been so grateful for those sirens.

Then I saw it. A body. The face was positioned away from me but I could clearly tell who it was by the outfit and the body's frame as it he lay limply a few feet away. *Oh God Kareem!* I couldn't tell if he was conscious but he was certainly way too still. And was that blood seeping from under his chest?

I mustered all of my energy to lift my head first, pausing only briefly to let the dizziness subside. Then my upper half. But that was as far as I could get. The pain was just too intense and I was just too weak.

Someone had shot someone. I couldn't remember much but that much I did. *Had Leo fired his gun and killed Kareem? Where was he?* Then a swell of fear and exhaustion had me collapsing back to the floor, ignoring the glass that nicked the flesh of my arms and hands. Shit, what if he was still around? Should I play dead?

A shadow fell across the floor. Then legs moved quickly across the room, sexy legs I recognized stuffed into sneakers. She moved first to Kareem, stooping to his body to touch his neck, then his back. Just as quickly, she had come to me and bent in my face. My eyes were open as I could only stare at Naomi's beautiful face as her lips moved though no sound came out. Was she talking to me? Her eyes certainly looked fearful as she kept her face close to mine and her intoxicating perfume tangled with the raw stench of death that thickened the air.

I felt my lids getting heavy but was able to make out the other footsteps rushing in and lifting Naomi out of the way to get to me. Hands moved and shifted me though I couldn't feel anything. Nothing but darkness and numbness.

"Baby girl."

I didn't see who was talking, but I definitely recognized that voice. It sent a sudden wave of comfort throughout my body that enveloped me. Damn, I hadn't heard that voice in so long, the sound prompted tears.

"Daddy?"

"It's okay, baby girl. You can come home now." I didn't even re-

alize I was smiling, reveling in the pastor's voice and encourage-
ment. Welcoming the end. Home.

———◦•◦———

A dull ache had me moaning, my heavy lids ignoring my brain
and willing them to lift. My head was tight with wrapped ban-
dages. Every stiff muscle, every bone, every cell in my body felt as
if it was being squeezed with pliers and saturated in scalding hot
water.

Disoriented, I managed to open my eyes into narrow slits, the
room blurry at first before slowly coming into focus. I saw the
stale, blue couch, heard the beep and hum of various machines,
saw the needles embedded in my arm as it rested lifeless on the
starched white sheet. I didn't bother trying to move; I just lay
there waiting for what felt like death to take over.

The door opened, and I couldn't even muster the energy to ex-
press my confusion when I saw Naomi ease through, an elaborate
flower arrangement in her arms.

"I was hoping to get back before you woke up." She spoke in a
hushed voice walking over to the bedside. "The nurse said you
were kind of in and out." Naomi sat the bouquet on the table and
rubbed her arm. "How are you feeling?" I groaned in response,
and Naomi nodded in understanding. "I'm sure you are a little
weak. Here." She grabbed a plastic cup from the counter and angled the bendy straw to my lips.

I took an appreciative sip, the warm water almost stinging as it
dribbled down my raw throat.

"Better?"

I nodded. The pain was excruciating. Almost numbing all over
my body.

"Well, you certainly gave us all a scare," Naomi teased. My lips
twitched with the humor but I didn't even have the strength to
smile.

"How . . . ?" The word came out in a raspy gush of forced air and I could only breathe at the intense energy it took for just that. The subsequent pain had me closing my eyes. I felt Naomi's reassuring pat.

"I understand. It's a lot and you're a little dazed because of what happened. Well for starters, we took care of Leo."

Now I did lift my eyes and I know my face carried sheer and utter confusion. That was when I actually noticed Naomi. She looked, different. Her hair was pinned in a neat bun at her neck, gone was all that elaborate weave she used to wear. And she didn't have on all of the scant clothing showing off her voluptuous body. In its place was a crisp, white collared shirt and some navy slacks. Not to mention a police badge around her neck.

Naomi noticed me staring and she glanced down, fingering her badge on a slight chuckle. "Yeah, I know, right? Weird huh?"

"You . . . ?"

"A cop? Yep." Her grin was proud but I still sat in amazement. Never would I have guessed.

"And Kareem?"

Naomi chuckled. "He likes to *think* he's a cop and we just let him go with it. He is more of an informant. He helps us out a lot." She touched my arm gingerly. "And he certainly helped with your case, Kimera."

I started to lift my head from the pillow, didn't even bother. For the first time in a while, I felt completely safe and relaxed even in the midst of confusion.

"We had been working the Leo Owusu case for years and never really had an 'in.' Kareem was feeding us what we needed but the Owusus are very tight-lipped about their operation. So, we needed something else. I decided to go in undercover. I felt so sorry for you Kimmy, and I wanted to help you as best I could but I knew those cameras were rolling and until we were able to get control of that security footage, I knew we really couldn't do much talking in the house. Hell, even I was bugged." Naomi rolled her eyes. "Not by the police. By Leo. He suspected you were up to something. Therefore, I couldn't really say or do too much around you without him being on to you. I knew you and Kareem had a plan going too. So basically, we were all on the same side, trying to work from different angles."

"But how did you know about me?" I asked.

Naomi grinned. "Funny story. I got a little call from a Detective Terry in Atlanta, Georgia. She said your friend Adria came to see her. I guess a little birdy must have told her."

I was so happy I wanted to cry. So, my note did make it. And Adria, thank God Adria was okay. I was speechless.

"How is she?" I asked. "And my brother? My mother?"

Naomi patted my arm. "Everyone is fine. Don't worry. You will see them soon enough."

"And my boys?"

"Fine, I promise. And Leo, I shot him but it wasn't fatal. He'll live but he and his father are going to jail for a very long time."

So, the gunshot was from Naomi, not Leo. I remembered blacking out but I certainly thought it was because I was as good as dead.

"Thank you." Overwhelmed, all I could muster now was a whisper and another quiet prayer. I released a sigh, my chest tightening from the gesture. Damn. Talk about a crazy turn of events.

I felt Naomi's gentle fingers on the side of my head, above my ear. "No damage other than a few bumps and bruises. You took a pretty nasty fall when you passed out and hit your head on the table, so you may have headaches and feel yucky for a while." Naomi leaned down and, much to my surprise, planted a comforting kiss on my forehead. "I know that's not really 'police-y' of me," she said with a bright laugh. "But after all this time of being your sister wife, I think we've gotten pretty close, right?" I couldn't do anything but share in her joy. "But, seriously," she said, changing her tone. "I'm just glad you're all right."

I smiled to myself. Yes, I would be all right. I was safe. My family and kids were safe. And I was finally free.

"The hospital told me to make calls to your family," Naomi went on. "I didn't know how you felt about that, so I said I would wait until you woke up to ask you. Do you want me to call anyone and tell them what happened?"

I sighed once more as everyone flashed through my mind one-by-one. Keon, my sweet baby brother who had become a pseudo father-figure to me, so protective. My mother, who was still so damaged, I was sure, from the whole ordeal, especially considering it resulted in my father's death. Adria, my best friend who I had gotten tangled in my shit. And Jahmad. Poor Jahmad, who I had hurt beyond measure and I loved enough to leave alone because I knew he deserved better.

Sure, I could tell them now and they would be on the first thing smoking out of Atlanta, too. Cards and flowers, sympathy and regret. It might even be genuine. But part of me, a small part, couldn't help but wonder if some of it would be driven by guilt because I was hurt. Hadn't I gotten myself into this mess?

It was over. All over. I would start fresh, and even though I hadn't done right by them before, I would now. No need to compound the strain and reopen the wounds. Maybe one day, they would find it in their hearts to move on and forgive me for all of this.

My voice came out foreign, raspy with soreness and strangled with pain, but strengthened with renewed confidence. "No. Don't call. As soon as I'm out of here, I'm going to see them myself."

I remained in the hospital for a few extra days for observation, the doctor said, but the longer I stayed, the longer I had to worry when I didn't hear any word about Kareem. I remembered seeing him back at the mansion, lying face down in a pool of blood. The thought had my fear heightening that much more. Please God let him have lived.

Naomi had said he'd been severely hurt with a gunshot wound, one he had suffered trying to block Leo's bullet from me. To say I was riddled with guilt was an understatement. I thought of Kareem's daughter. How old did he say she was? Nine? Ten? Had he even told me her name? I know he mentioned how long it had been since he'd seen her. Three years I'm sure felt like three lifetimes. Shit, it had only been a few months for me and I had been ready to risk it all to get back to my family. I'd pulled him in to helping me, relied on him. And he was suffering for it. If that man died trying to protect me, I would surely suffer more than these physical bumps and bruises.

"He's had a few surgeries," Naomi updated me one day when I'd asked for the umpteenth time. "The bullet grazed a critical artery, and, though it didn't puncture, he suffered a tremendous amount of blood loss. But he's stable now," she added when my face fell at the news. "He's actually doing much better than he was. So now all we can do is hope for the best."

I didn't like the sound of that. So, every morning and every night I exercised what I knew was better than mere hope. I prayed, and I used my faith. My dad had taught me that much. God had certainly pulled me through, that's for sure.

So, I gritted through my pain and exhaustion and went as far as to lower to my knees on the side of my hospital bed. "Lord God, I know You know and grant the desires of the heart. I thank You for getting me out of that situation with Leo. But God, I come to You humbly now and ask that you please heal my friend Kareem. He has so much to live for so I pray with everything in me that You please see him through this alive so he can get back to his daughter. I thank You God."

That was where Naomi found me minutes later. I hadn't mustered the energy to climb back in the bed so I'd merely sat there waiting. For what? I didn't know. A sign? A voice? Something.

Then Naomi spoke. "He's awake," she informed me with a smile. "And he's asking for you." Naomi had a nurse retrieve me a wheelchair and wheel me down to Kareem's room.

To my surprise, Kareem was sitting up in bed alert. And most importantly, alive. Even though he was hooked up to all kinds of machines and had a slew of bruises and abrasions canvassing his body in different stages of healing, he was alive.

I sent up a silent prayer of thanks to God. His eyes landed on me, and we both exchanged a smile; obviously, he was just as relieved to see me as I was him.

"Damn, I'm glad to see you, Kimmy." His sigh was one of relief that brought happy tears to my eyes. "I was worried about you."

"Me?" I wheeled myself further into the room allowing the nurse to shut the door as she left. "You were the one in and out of critical condition. Hell, I was worried about YOU."

Kareem waved away my distress. "You know I was going to be all right."

"I didn't. Leo shot you." The reality only reaffirmed the horror of that night.

"Well, really, he shot at you," Kareem teased lightning the mood. "I just pushed you out of the way."

He tossed me one of those smirks of his and as much as I wanted to take it as lightly, a part of me felt like crying. The man saved my life.

I eased my wheelchair closer to his bedside and reached out to grab his hand. "Thank you," I said. "From the bottom of my heart. Thank you for everything."

Kareem leaned over in response, planting a passionate kiss on my lips. Slow and sensual. Loving.

He broke the contact first and rested his forehead on mine as we both tried to catch our breaths.

"Now what?" I verbalized the question but I knew he was thinking the same thing.

"I wouldn't be selfish enough to ask you to come to Côte d'Ivoire and Nigeria with me," Kareem said on a slight chuckle. "Wouldn't that be ironic?"

He was right. I had moved Heaven and hell to keep from going with Leo and Obi. What would I look like ending up there anyway. But this was different. This was Kareem.

He read my hesitation and for a moment, a brief moment, a look of hopefulness graced his handsome face. But my apologetic smile had him nodding his understanding. "You've been gone long enough," he said, already knowing my answer. "Your family in Atlanta needs you." He paused briefly. "I want you to know something," he said, and all of a sudden the tension in the room shifted. Gone was the humor and Kareem's seriousness instantly had me nervous. "I wasn't sure if I was going to tell you because I didn't want you to feel different about me. But you need to know."

"What?"

Kareem's eyes glanced to the door to make sure we were alone. Then he lowered his voice. "I took that nigga out."

I frowned in confusion, then slowly, so slowly my eyes rounded with clarity. "Tyree."

His nod was slight. "I figured to make it look like a suicide but Kimmy, he had to go. He had too much of an upper hand. And when I found his cell phone with the video—"

"What video?"

"You and me on the wedding night. He was going to show that to Leo and get both of us killed. He had been looking for a way to get rid of you. And this was his chance. Especially considering he wanted me to set you up and though we were sleeping together, I kept telling him you were refusing me. So, he had nothing. Or so I thought until I found the video."

I mulled over his words. So close. Damn, we had gotten careless and had been so close to messing up everything.

"It was a risk, I knew," Kareem went on at my continued silence. "But he knew too much."

I didn't know what Kareem expected me to feel but sadness sure as hell wasn't the emotion. Relief was more like it. Tyree was accountable for all of my torture, all of my misery. Good fucking riddance.

I smiled then and pulled Kareem in for another kiss. "That's the nicest thing anyone has ever done for me," I teased.

Kareem laughed, obviously relieved his little confession hadn't bothered me one bit. "I'm going to miss you." He used his thumb to brush my lip, causing a shudder to ripple through my body.

"You can always get your daughter and come to Georgia," I suggested. I was only half-joking but he seemed to be considering the offer.

"You never know," was all he said, and he pulled me in for another kiss.

Chapter 23
Kimera

"*My love.*"

A hand touched my shoulder and startled me awake. *Please God, not him again.*

My eyes darted around in a panic, settling when they rested on the plane's coach interior, nearly empty with the early morning flight. I was even more relieved to see my riding companion, Detective Terry's reassuring smile from the aisle seat beside me. I had to smile at my own foolishness. I would not have considered myself traumatized but I knew it was probably going to take a while before I would be able to get a peaceful, 'Owusu-free' sleep. That was one reason I had insisted on downsizing to coach, despite the first-class tickets I could afford. The way I saw it, I had had enough luxury (and the costs associated with it) to last a lifetime. Any disassociation with that lifestyle, the better. I was now more than appreciative for the simple pleasures.

Detective Terry used those brilliant blue eyes of hers to gesture towards the window. "We're descending," she announced.

The relief swelled and I looked from her to Leo Jr. sleeping quietly between us, his head against Detective Terry's arm, his lips partially open as his soft snore signaled his deep slumber. Jamal was nestled in my lap, and had apparently slept through the entire flight as well. I turned to the window and took in a grateful breath at the sight.

The familiar Atlanta skyline broke through the clouds and suddenly my excitement turned to anxiety. It had been, damn how long? Three months since I had been gone. Any other time, three months didn't sound like much. But three months as a prisoner with Leo, shit felt like a lifetime. I hated to admit, I had started to lose hope of ever being completely free from those ties that bound me to the Owusus. It had been a shot in the dark trying to write a letter for Lupé to send home to my family and even though she didn't, Kareem eventually informed me that he had made sure to mail it off anyway. And for that I owed him my life. And Adria for taking it seriously.

Adria. Damn, I was so happy to know she was alive. She would be waiting for me, for us, at the gate and seeing her would be the first semblance of reality that I was yearning for. That I was really home and this entire ordeal was finally over. I had been in the hospital for a few days and we hadn't talked very much but through Detective Terry and her team as they made plans for my travel. But I was assured, much to my surprise, she would be there waiting. All ill feelings aside. I was safe and so was she. That alone settled my anxiety.

The boys woke up, cranky of course, as soon as we touched down, and Detective Terry and I shifted between them and gathering our belongings from the overhead compartment. A few parting words from the pilot and before I knew it, we were making our way through the tunnel and up the ramp towards the gate.

As soon as we made it down to baggage claim, Keon and Adria both rose from the seating area. My smile bloomed, and I felt the first few tears spurt free. Adria was nearly in a dead run as she pushed through the other passengers until she was able to reach me. She threw her arms around my neck, and I could only stand there as we both shared a joyous cry. Damn, it was so good to see her.

"I'm sorry, girl," she pulled back and used her fingers to wipe her tears from her cheeks. "I'm just so happy to see you." She fingered my hair, now dangling longer than usual at my neck.

"I'm cutting it as soon as I can," I said reading her mind. I took a good look at Adria. She had definitely lost weight since the last time and though I wasn't sure if it was intentional or not, at least she looked happy.

Adria turned her attention to Jamal in my arms and without a second thought, scooped him up and nuzzled his neck. Jamal giggled and reached for her face, cupping his mouth around her nose. "Aw, I missed you too," she gushed.

"Mama?"

The voice was tiny, uncertain and I looked down at Leo Jr. standing puzzled by the new people and attention. Poor thing almost looked frightened. I bent down to pick him up, settling him on my hip.

"Adria, this is Leo Jr.," I introduced as the boy stared curiously. "Leo Jr. this is your Auntie."

I could see something in Adria's eyes, really brief and subtle, before she smiled. Was it hesitancy? I know Leo Jr. was yet another reminder of my indiscretions, and no he wasn't biologically mine but blood couldn't have made this child any more of my son. I was sure that was probably going to be a little bit of a shock at first to everyone.

But to my surprise, Adria used her free arm to wrap around Leo Jr. and plant a sloppy kiss on his cheek. "Hey, LJ," she greeted.

Leo Jr. frowned at the nickname. "I'm Leo," he corrected with a confused pout, his chubby two-year-old finger pointing to himself.

Adria laughed. "Really? Because I was going to take LJ to get some ice cream."

That brightened up his face and Leo Jr.'s grin split. "Okay, I'm LJ."

I pulled Adria in for another hug and at the same time as if we were one half of the same brain, we both whispered in each other's ear, "I love you, Sis."

———◦————

Adria was thrilled to take the kids to the park and eat pizza and ice cream while Keon drove me to visit my mother. I had to admit, it was weird sitting there next to my brother again. Even weirder when he reached over the console to hold my hand as we rode in silence.

He had filled me in on the loss of his twin girls, and I felt sick to my stomach knowing Tyree, hell if I had to admit it, that I was the cause of his daughters' deaths. He skirted around some things going on with Adria, I made a note to myself to catch up with her about it later, but he did assure me they were getting their marriage back on track. A shock to me because I didn't even know their marriage had gotten off the rails. Then, could I really be that surprised? Nothing had been the same in the past couple years. Hell, nothing would ever be the same. Tragedy had snatched my family apart at the seams, but that same tragedy was slowly piecing us back together. But at least I could feel good knowing they were trying to get it together and I would be sure to encourage that in any way possible. My brother and best friend belonged together. Soulmates. Speaking of soulmates . . .

"How is Jahmad?" I didn't care if the question sounded entirely too desperate, too obvious. Keon knew our history and though I was fearful of the response, I needed to know, for my own sanity.

My brother paused but didn't take his eyes from the road.

"He's grieving in his own way," he answered finally. "But he was shocked as hell to find out what had happened to you and Jamal."

He hadn't meant for the words to warm my heart, but they did. I smiled. "I'm going to see him."

"Kimmy . . ." Keon stopped at a red light and shifted in the seat to look at me directly. "So much has changed. I don't want you to get your hopes up."

He hadn't said it, but I read his concern for what it was. Jahmad had moved on, I'm sure with CeeCee, though it honestly didn't matter at this point. I was a thing of the past and me reinserting myself back into his life wouldn't do anything but cause more confusion. And the last thing I wanted to do was open a sore he had managed to heal. We all needed to do some healing anyway.

Keon didn't say anything else nor did I inquire further. I just nodded, my smile still in place. Surprisingly, I was at genuine peace and maybe even a little lifted knowing Jahmad had found his happily ever after. I felt bad enough knowing my disappearance had damaged Adria and Keon's life. So Jahmad's moving on wasn't good news for me, but good news nonetheless. He deserved it.

I gave Keon's hand a reassuring pat. "I know," I said simply and that was enough for our mutual understanding.

Keon dropped me off at an assisted living facility called Golden Gates. I asked did he want to go in with me, but he declined, stating I needed this little bit of time alone. As much as I would have rather had him by my side, I knew he was right.

My mother's health had severely deteriorated over the past few months. I didn't even recognize the woman lying in the bed. She looked weak, nearly pale against the pastel pink-colored sheets. As if she wasn't even the First Lady. Then again, she hadn't been the same since my father passed. Really since the whole ordeal with me began, if I could be honest. None of us had been the same. As we all went through our own private mental damages, it was clear my mother suffered the most, mentally, physically, and emotionally.

Her eyes were closed and at one point, I wouldn't have even known she was breathing with the exception of the subtle rise and fall in her chest. A ghost of a smile flitted on her lips, and I wondered what, or whom, she was dreaming about.

A woman, who I assumed was my mother's nurse, sat beside the bed with an open book in her lap. She looked up as I peeked through the bedroom door and smiled, gesturing for me to join her in the room.

"Hi," I greeted. "I'm—"

"Kimera Davis, right?" The woman finished my sentence while extending her hand. "Keon called and told me y'all were right outside. I'm Jackie, Ms. Davis's nurse."

I shook her hand and looked again to my mother, lowering my voice. "How is she?"

Jackie's sigh was slight, but optimistic. "She's had better days," she admitted. "But I'm sure she'll be happy to see you."

"Thank you."

Jackie moved to the door. "I'll be right out here in the living room if you need me," she said and closed the door behind her with a quiet *click*.

I remained in place for what seemed like forever before I was able to will my legs to carry me to the side of the bed. Not wanting to wake her and risk disturbing her peace, my steps were slow and hesitant.

Gently, I lowered myself into the seat that Jackie had just vacated and picked up the book she had left open on the nightstand. Of course, the Bible. Did I expect anything else for the First Lady? The book was open to the fourteenth chapter of John. In neon yellow highlight were scriptures one, two, three, and four. I read them silently to myself, blinking back tears at the words I recognized.

"That scripture was from your father's eulogy."

I jumped at the sound of my mom's voice. As soft as it was, it was still enough to crack through the silence. I kept my head bent low so she couldn't see my face. Couldn't see my tears. She hadn't even needed to remind me. I remembered vividly her standing at the pulpit dressed in her black, her birdcage veil shielding her devastated expression as she sung her praises for the love of Mr. Davis, the pastor, the husband, the dad, and the man.

I looked over at my mother. Her eyes opened and her smile grew at the sight of me. She lifted her hand in my direction and I grabbed hold of it, almost desperately. It took everything in me not to squeeze for fear of hurting her.

"Mama, I have missed you so much," I said, tears clogging my voice. "I'm so sorry for everything. I—"

"Ssshhh." She silenced me. "It's all right. We're all right. I'm just so glad you're back and safe."

"I was going to bring Jamal. I promise to bring him later. Just wanted to see you myself first."

Her smile fell a little, replaced by a brief flicker of confusion. "Jamal," she questioned.

"Yes, ma'am. Your grandson." Apparently, my clarification still didn't register, and it pained me to watch her expression reflect just how foreign her mind was to her now. The signs of my mother's deteriorating mental state had my heart crying, but, still, I smiled anyway and just shook my head to dispel the perplexity. "Never mind," I said, rushing on. "How are you feeling?"

"I'm doing so much better now," she said. "I'll be glad when Keon lets me out of here so I can go home."

I knew that wasn't happening. Still, I nodded along.

"Your father is doing well too," she went on. I kept my lips closed so as not to question her thought process. Keon and Adria had already told me she often spoke about my father in present tense. In her mind, he was still alive and well. Everyone had agreed that alone had brought her a sense of peace so to let her have her reality, no matter how false. She needed that right now.

Part of me wished there was one I could escape to as well, and there were some memories and experiences I would have loved to forget. I hated losing my mother to this, but that seemed to be the only thing keeping her whole.

Mama's sigh was heavy as if took a great deal of strength. I swallowed and, when I felt sure my voice wouldn't crack with the weight of my burdens, I tightened my grip slightly on her frail fingers, hoping she felt my love through our contact. I whispered, "We love you, Mama. It's okay. We're okay. You can go home now." I knew that was all she needed to hear.

I left our fingers connected as I dropped my eyes back to the highlighted scripture open in front of me. I hadn't meant to read out loud, but it was as if my heart needed to feel them and the words tumbled from my mouth as if on their own. "Let not your hearts be troubled. Believe in God; believe also in me. In my Father's house are many rooms. If it were not so, would I have told you that I go to prepare a place for you? And if I go and prepare a place for you, I will come again and will take you to myself, that where I am you may be also. And you know the way to where I am going."

Chapter 24
Kimera

I eyed the headstones and sighed in relief when I saw my dad's. *"Life is not a dress rehearsal. To God be the Glory."* My lips curved at the quote. "Words to live by," I murmured.

I took my time, shifting to kneel at the granite. I removed the fresh bouquet of flowers from the plastic bag and tenderly sat the gorgeous blossoms against the tombstone, the crisp white-and-red petals an appreciative contrast against the rigid gray. My dad wasn't even a flower person. But because he always told me to "stop and smell the roses," the gesture seemed fitting.

"Sometimes, I wish you were still here," I said, resting my hand on the ground. "Other times, I'm glad you're not. Not because I don't want you to be, but because I know you would hate me for what I am, if that makes sense." I sighed. "I'm ashamed of things I've done, Daddy. Disgraceful things. Things that embarrass me to even think about, honestly. And I guess it hurts even more because I feel you would look at me a certain way. Not judgmental, at all. Just disappointed. And I never wanted to disappoint you, Daddy. I always wanted you to be proud of me as your daughter."

I lifted my head, eyed the rows and rows of markers in systematic succession. "And you're right," I went on. "I was almost right out here with you, Daddy. A few times. And that scares the shit out of me. I won't detail it to you. You would probably roll over in your grave if you knew everything. But, just know that I have changed. I hate it took me as long as it did and I hate it took what it did for my wake-up call. But, I'm still here. I have another opportunity at life, and I'm going to do it right."

The wind picked up, brushing my hair from the neat ponytail at the nape of my neck. I pulled my blazer tighter. "Everyone is doing okay, too. Adria comes to visit you all the time so I'm sure you know all about everything with her and Keon. She got on drugs Daddy, but she's doing so much better and she and my brother are in therapy. Working on piecing together their marriage. They owe it to God, to themselves, but they also feel they owe it to you, Daddy. You officiated their marriage. That meant something. She and I are also working on rebuilding our relationship. Even been talking about opening another Melanin Mystique." I chuckled. One day at a time. "You have two grandboys now. Not just one. Though I can never really see too much of that oldest one, Leo Jr., or LJ now. Adria has him ALL the time. I think she believes that's really her baby. Jamal is doing great too. Getting so big."

What about you, baby girl?

I smiled. I could almost hear the question as if my dad had uttered the words out loud. "I'm hanging in there, Daddy," I answered. "One day at a time. But my story is one for the books, that's for sure. I'll have to give you all the details one of these days."

I touched my fingers to my lips and laid them on the earth once more. Then, I climbed to my feet. I was completely healed but still, my movements were slow as if I were savoring each and every thing. "I love you, Daddy. I think that's what I needed to say."

I paused, my eyes trailing to the space next to my dad's. A small smile touched my lips as I nodded my head in that direction. "You take care of him, Mama," I said to my mother's grave. "I know he hasn't been doing right without you."

And as if surrounded by their joint chuckles in amusement, I turned, swallowing my grief, and headed back to the parking lot, leaving my parents to rest in Heaven together. Two halves of one soul, reunited.

I felt like a fool, sitting there trying to psych myself up to go inside. I was meeting up with Adria soon, but I had one more stop to make first. Funny, I had survived jail, murder, kidnapping, and everything else that could happen, did happen to me. So, with every life-threatening circumstance that I had been through, my ass was scared to turn off the car and walk up to a house to speak. The irony.

I could leave, I reasoned. Just pretend I was never here, turn around and go back home and no one would be the wiser. But that would be a punk ass move. Wasn't I stronger than that?

My phone rang, a welcome relief to my mental war, and I grabbed it from my purse. The name on the caller ID brought a smile to my face.

"Hello?"

"Kimmy," Kareem greeted. "How you feeling?"

I felt silly telling him the truth, especially considering it wasn't that big of a deal. "Feeling much better now that I'm hearing from you," I admitted. "Did you touch down safely in Ivory Coast?"

"Yeah, we flew into Abidjan first. Twenty-four hours later."

"Oh, you need to get some rest."

"Nah, later for that," Kareem said with a chuckle. "My first stop is seeing my daughter. I can't get there quick enough."

I smiled, my heart swelling. "I'm so glad you made it safely. She's going to be so excited."

"Yeah." Spoken like a true Papa Bear. "How are the boys?"

I thought of the numerous toys piled into my apartment. There was barely enough room to walk around. "They're doing great. Loving getting spoiled by their aunt and uncle, that's for sure."

"I bet. And you?"

I sighed. "I'm hanging in there. One day at a time. It's so good to be back home."

"I feel you." Kareem commented to someone in his background before coming back to the phone. "So, hey, let me go. I'm about to catch this ride. You sure you're good? Need anything?"

"I'm good. Got everything I need right here. And Kareem. Thank you."

A pause and I could almost feel him beaming through the phone. "No, thank YOU, Kimmy. For everything. I'll check on you again soon."

We hung up and I couldn't wipe the stupid grin off my face. Kareem was a great friend and after everything we had endured, our bond was too deep and too strong for us to just part ways and never speak again. He had saved my life. In more ways than one. Anything more than that, well, in his words, you never know.

I glanced at the house again. Our little conversation had given me a little more motivation.

Cutting off the car, I grabbed the gift bag sitting on the passenger seat and stepped out. The driveway was already packed with visitors, so I had to maneuver around to make my way to the front door.

I probably shouldn't have come. I climbed the stairs to the porch, my hands shoved in the pockets of my jacket. I racked my brain for the appropriate words, but my mind drew a foggy blank. I had changed so much that I barely recognized the woman I had grown into. And that meant starting over and coming to terms with forgiveness and acceptance. That was probably the hardest pill to swallow. A collection of emotions marinated in the pit of my stomach. Anger and hurt was prominent but I also recognized a trace of grief weighing heavy on my heart. But better now to get this over with.

I pressed the doorbell, listening to the chime echo inside. The crinkle of the gift bag in my hand had me blowing a heavy sigh, struggling to calm down as I listened to the bustle of footsteps on the other side of the door. *Relax.*

The locks rattled noisily and CeeCee pulled open the door. I was surprised to see the expression on her face was more expectant than anything as her wide, pregnant frame filled the doorway. Though she had picked up some weight since the last time I'd seen her, the thickness combined with her glowing skin radiated a different kind of beauty that looked good on her.

"Kimmy," she held out her arms and I leaned in for the hug. "I am so glad you came."

"Thank you for inviting me, CeeCee. But I actually just came to drop off this gift and grab Jamal."

CeeCee looked genuinely hurt. "You sure? You don't have to go. I would like you to join us for the shower, but don't want to make you uncomfortable."

"Oh no, nothing like that," I assured her. "It's just a little soon for festivities for me. And Adria and I have some plans."

CeeCee nodded. "I understand."

"I tell you what," I added to lift her spirits. "Maybe next week we can do lunch."

It worked. CeeCee's face brightened. "I'd like that." We hugged again just as Jahmad walked up with Jamal on his hip. He put his arm around CeeCee and gave her a kiss on the forehead.

"Everything okay?" he asked, looking between us.

I gave him a confident smile. "Doing great."

"Thanks again, Kimmy," CeeCee said. Her smile was big and she looked like she had tears in her eyes. "Call you next week?"

"Talk to you then."

She left and Jahmad could only lift a brow. "Wow. Really?"

"Hey, we're all grown here and life is too short for childish games."

"Oh wow, look at Kimmy. All grown up."

I laughed and swatted his arm at the sarcasm. "Shut up." I held out my arms to Jamal and hoisted him onto my hip. "Hey, hand-some. You had fun with DaDa?"

"DaDa!" Jamal squealed.

"Love you, little man," Jahmad said and kissed him on his cheek. I swelled with pride. No, Jahmad wasn't his biological fa-ther, but this man was Jamal's dad in every way that mattered. And I loved him for it.

"Okay, we'll see you next time," I said. "Y'all have fun."

Jahmad threw his hands in the air and mimed like he was cheering. The gesture was clearly sarcastic and I couldn't do any-thing but laugh. "Yeah, just like that."

Jahmad waited while I carefully buckled Jamal into the car seat and I hopped in the driver's seat myself. He waved and I smiled and waved back.

Lord knows I still loved that man, and I knew he still loved me. But I knew who the better woman was for him. And I was willing to step aside and let him be with the more deserving. I had spent too much time tangled up with Leo. Now I was enjoying being single. Just me and the boys. That was enough for me. I had been through worse and I was stronger now. Much stronger. And now even more so because I needed to be strong for my boys. I didn't know what the future held but I would make sure to take advan-tage of each day I lived to see another.

Adria and I had gone to the therapist together the day before, and I had taken Dr. Evelyn's words to heart. *Immerse yourself in you.* And that's what I intended to do. I'd had enough of playing the wife. Now I was going to pour completely into myself.

I had never understood polyamory until I had been with Leo, and though he completely misconstrued the entire relationship (and damn near killed me in the process), I did learn something that was for sure. Having one person was like saying, "you're my sun, moon, and stars," while having multiple people was saying person one was your sun, person two was your moon, and person three was your stars. And look at me. I had two children whom I loved with all my heart. That I didn't even think was possible. So, could it be possible to love more than one person?

I thought of Jahmad and CeeCee. Jahmad loved us both, that much was certain. And whether a man with several wives or a woman with several husbands, I could never see myself settling into that type of relationship again.

I glanced at Jamal in the backseat and grinned. "Hey, little man. What's say we get brother and Auntie Adria and go to the zoo?"

I was met with spit bubbles and what sounded like a little business in his diaper. Satisfied, I nodded as I let back the sunroof.

"Yep. Sounds like a plan to me too."

I would save all the relationship shit for another time. Right now, I had other roles to play.

THE HEARTS WE BURN

Briana Cole

ABOUT THIS GUIDE

The suggested questions are included to enhance your
group's reading of Briana Cole's *The Hearts We Burn*.

DISCUSSION QUESTIONS

1. The Hearts We Burn alternated between perspectives (Adria and Kimera) and intertwined a few flashback sequences. What difference did this structure make in the way you read or understood the story?

2. If you could hear this same story from another character's point-of-view, who would you choose?

3. Which parts of the book stood out to you? Are there any quotes, passages, or scenes you found particularly compelling? Were there any parts of the book you thought were incredibly unique, out of place, thought-provoking, or disturbing?

4. Which one of the characters could you relate to the most/least?

5. What do you think of the book's title? How does it relate to the book's content?

6. How did you feel when Adria got involved with her drug dealer? How do you think she felt having to resort to drugs to find relief from her pain?

7. Leo felt compelled to hide his true self because of his father. Did you feel sorry for him? After learning more about his father, do you feel Leo's actions were justified?

8. How do you picture the characters' lives after the end of the story?

9. What changes/decisions would you hope for if the book were turned into a movie?

10. If you have read the other two books in the Unconditional series, were you able to guess what would happen in this book?

Meet Kimmy and Adria for the first time in *The Wives We Play*

Available wherever books are sold.

Chapter 1

Something told me tonight was going to be special.

I could hardly contain my excitement as I followed the host through the maze of linen-draped tables, each topped with a single candle and surrounded by overdressed patrons. The ambiance was certainly set for romance and luxury, and I blended right in with my Tom Ford copper-toned sequined dress, which hugged each and every petite curve of mine. A gift from my man, of course. Lord knows I couldn't afford a $6,000 dress like this if I had to make the money myself.

Another thing I couldn't help but notice was my brown face was one of only a few in the entire restaurant. A crowd of crystal blue eyes against porcelain white skin turned curious gazes in my direction, no doubt wondering who the hell I had to screw to even be allowed in the building. I had become used to the questioning looks when alongside Leo. He was a man of power and great wealth, and me, well, I was just the arm candy. The trophy. And that was just fine with me. Especially considering my boyfriend already had a wife. Just let me look good and spend his money, and I was content with keeping my face made up, my body in the gym, and my legs spread in exchange.

The host showed me through a sheer curtain to a round booth.

It was dimly lit and entirely too large for a party of two, but I knew Leo didn't mind paying extra for privacy and comfort.

"My love." He rose to greet me and, as customary, I held out my hand. Leo turned it over and planted a gentle kiss on my palm. I loved when he did that. His eyes swiped over my body with an approving nod. "You look like a masterpiece."

I grinned at his words. The man could charm me clean out of my panties. "I know," I gushed, placing my hands on my hips. The gesture had the already mid-thigh hemline rising just a bit. "And, my oh my, don't you look completely edible." The cream linen suit seemed to radiate against the stark contrast of his black skin. His locs were fresh, and he had taken care to have them braided to the back. It had been a minute since I'd seen them down, so I didn't realize they reached past the middle of his back. Leo usually kept his locs piled high in a man bun on top of his head and out of his way. He smiled, his dimples creasing his cheeks and barely noticeable underneath the fine hairs of his well-trimmed goatee.

"So," I prompted as soon as I slid into the plump leather cushion of the booth. "You certainly went all out this evening."

"It's a special occasion."

My nose wrinkled in a curious frown. We usually didn't do the anniversary shit. That was for serious couples. Not us.

Before I could open my mouth and ask what he was referring to, our waiter appeared at the side of our table, a linen cloth slung over his arm, a bottle of wine in his hand. He greeted us and began to pour the rich red liquid into our glasses. No need to ask what kind of wine it was. Knowing Leo, it was delicious and expensive and that was all that mattered to me.

I hadn't even bothered to look at the menu. Leo ordered the same thing for both of us, some fancy dish I couldn't pronounce. We handed over our menus, and I waited until we were alone again before I spoke up.

"Special occasion?" I reiterated. "For us?"

"Just period." Leo reached across the table and grabbed my hand in his. He used his thumb to caress my knuckles. The excitement was all but twinkling in his chocolate irises and I felt my own anxiousness beginning to bubble up right along with this silky wine. My mind began to hum with possible scenarios of where this was going. But for some reason, my thoughts kept settling on him handing over the keys to either a house or a car. Hell, maybe both.

"How long have we been together, my love?"

"Few months."

"How many? Do you know?"

I didn't. I hoped that the question was rhetorical, but he waited patiently while I fumbled through the previous months and events we had shared. "Like around three or four, right?" I guessed.

"Eight," he corrected with a gentle smile. "Eight months, two weeks, and five days, to be exact."

I strained against the smile on my face, hopefully masking my apathy. What was he getting at? Was that too soon for him to buy me a house?

"It has been probably the best eight months of my life," Leo went on, almost to himself. "I hope you know just how special you are to me."

My smile widened. "Of course I know, sweetie."

"Well then, you should know me well enough to know I don't make rash decisions. I'm very strategic, calculated, and usually once I set my mind to something, I just go for it. No questions. No hesitations."

I nodded as my heart quickened. If it was a car, I hoped he had gotten it in red. Something sporty and flashy. I liked flashy. And I hoped he'd paid the insurance up. He knew damn well I couldn't afford insurance on any vehicle after a 1995.

Leo blew me a kiss before rising to his feet. He still held my hand in his and pulled me up out of the booth with him. His eyes slid past mine and nodded in greeting to someone behind me. Confused, I turned and eyed the woman who approached.

We had the same taste, apparently. She too wore Tom Ford, but her dress was black, ankle-length with a sheer side panel that revealed just the right amount of skin to be classy. A high weave ponytail cascaded down to touch the small of her back. She was taller than I am, a little more curvaceous, and chocolate skin as rich and as smooth as a piece of black clay pottery like you could find on a vendor table at some art festival.

She held out her hand in my direction. "Kimera," she greeted with a huge smile. "I'm Tina Owusu."

Owusu? I glanced to Leo and back to Tina, my head reeling with the strange yet familiar visitor. I ignored her outstretched hand, instead turning my back on the woman to narrow my eyes at Leo.

"This is your *wife?*" I snapped, jutting the manicured nail of my thumb in her direction. "Did you really invite your wife to dinner?"

"My love, let me explain."

"Explain what?" I pulled on my hand to release it from his grasp, but he tightened his grip.

"It's not what you think."

"It's not? Well, what the hell is going on, Leo? Care to explain this shit to me? Because I'm not understanding."

Leo, still clutching my hand, dropped to one knee. And my heart dropped just as fast. I didn't even see him reach for the velvet box. Before I knew it, it was in his hand, the marquise-cut diamond glistening from the white cushion. I couldn't do anything but stand there speechless. Not because he was proposing. Hell, I had been proposed to a number of times, and usually I knew it was coming. But, no, I was shocked as hell because Leo's wife was still standing right there, waiting for my answer just as patiently as the man kneeling in front of me.

I took a step backward, bumping my hip against the nearby restaurant table. Somewhere, the jazz music had died down, and I felt as if all eyes were focused on me and Leo, still on one knee in his crisp linen slacks. I wanted to slap him. Slap him for putting me in this awkward situation. For making a mockery out of this whole thing.

Sure, I knew he had a wife. Well, let me correct that. I knew *now* he had a wife. When Leo first strolled up to my line at the bank where I worked, I didn't know he was married. I just saw a sexy-ass man with a complexion that looked like something fresh off an African culture oil canvas. His smile was slow and deliberate underneath the mustache as he made no move to hide his eyes wandering up and down my body. I felt the blush warm my cheeks and, smirking, I averted my eyes and busied myself with the Post-it notes on my counter.

"You shouldn't do that," he said, his accent seeming to caress each syllable.

"Do what?"

"Look away," he said. "Most pretty ladies like it when they see a man appreciating."

"Well, most men don't make it so obvious that they are appreciating," I said with a flirtatious grin.

"Well, I'm not most men." He held out his hand across the counter. "I'm Leo."

I paused before placing my hand in his. He took his time lifting it to his face. To my surprise, he turned it over and placed his lips gingerly against the tender flesh of my palm.

That had been all it took. The sexy Leo Owusu had plenty of charm and family money, and he hadn't been shy about lavishing both on me. I wouldn't say I was the kind of girl that would go weak at the knees over material shit. Well, let me stop lying. Yes, I was. The pot was damn lovely.

So when Leo finally revealed the truth, that he indeed had a wife, I had to say I really wasn't shocked. To tell you the truth, I knew my attitude was more of nonchalance. It didn't concern me. What he did in the confines of his own vows wasn't my business. He claimed they had an open marriage and that she knew about me. I'm not going to lie; that did seem awkward, but I quickly swallowed that pill too. The way I saw it, at least we didn't have to sneak around and shit. And after he assured me and reassured me I wouldn't have to worry about no bitch trying to catch me outside with fists and Vaseline, I was actually relieved.

"Kimmy." Leo pulled me back to the present and I again looked from him to the ring box he held in his outstretched hand. His wife, Tina, watched me closely, and it made me nervous as hell when she remained quiet and expressionless. She had drawn back the privacy curtain and now the entire ordeal was on public display like a Lifetime movie. I could feel a multitude of eyes from the restaurant patrons zeroed in on our little "romantic" scene. Anxious smiles and even a few phones were pointed in our direction to capture this moment. And here I was, frozen in embarrassment with a collection of curse words already gathered on my tongue. *What the hell did he think he was doing?*

"I want you to be in my life forever," Leo poured on the charm at my continued silence. "Marry me, Kimmy."

I knew my next move was about to be on some classic Cinderella shit, but I no longer cared about the audience. Or the appearance. Unable to do anything else, I turned on my heel and half ran toward the exit. I was slowed down by having to dart and weave through the maze of occupied tables and nearly stumbling in my six-inch stilettos. Anger propelled me forward, and I pushed through the glass door and inhaled the crisp night air.

The vibrant roar of downtown Atlanta traffic greeted me, and I welcomed the noisy relief. After the stunned silence, I needed the chaos to drown the confusion. What the hell was Leo thinking? First, he invites me and his wife to dinner tonight, only to propose with her standing right there? Looking on like this was completely normal. Who the hell proposes to the side chick?

"Kimmy."

Shocked, I turned back toward the building. I surely hadn't expected Tina to come after me. But there she was, seemingly gliding in my direction like she was in New York Fashion Week. I had noticed before that she was just average looking. The kind of Plain Jane face that didn't really give definition toward the pretty side or the ugly side but teeter-tottered somewhere in the middle, despite the makeup. Yet the diamonds that glittered from her fingers, ears, and neck had her moving with cocky arrogance like she was above any and everybody. I didn't like the bitch.

"Kimmy," she called again as if I weren't looking right at her.

I rolled my eyes. "Kimera," I corrected with a frown. "You don't know me like that."

She smirked, and her warm chocolate complexion appeared to glow with the attitude. "You have been sleeping with my husband for about eight months now. Trust me. I do know you like that." She took a step in my direction, apparently trying to see if I was going to storm off, but curiosity had me planted on the pavement. She closed the distance between us, and I could smell her Flower Bomb perfume permeating in the air. Well, to be honest, I couldn't tell if it was hers or mine, because Leo had bought me the exact same fragrance. *What were these people into?*

"What do you want?" I asked when she made no move to speak.

"I just want you to come back inside," she said. "Accept the proposal. Leo is serious."

"Did he send you out here to come get me? Seriously? His wife to come beg another woman to marry her husband? What kind of shit is that?"

Tina blew out a frustrated breath. "He was afraid that I may have been the reason you declined his offer."

"You think?"

"That's why I wanted you to hear it from me. You both have my blessing. I don't want to stand in your way."

I was so confused. I felt the beginnings of a headache throbbing at my temples. Shit was baffling me.

"So wait. Are you two divorcing or something? And why the hell are you so cool with this?"

"Divorcing? Who? Me and Leo?" Tina let out a snarky chuckle. "Girl, no. 'Til death do us part. I will always be Mrs. Owusu. But I am willing to share with you."

"Share? Your husband? Haven't you been doing that for the past few months?"

Now Tina's smile was genuinely humorous. "Touché. But now I'm offering you a chance to make it official. Because at the end of the day, what do you have to show for it? Some jewelry and some furniture in that raggedy-ass room in your parents' house?"

A fresh swell of anger had me tightening my fist; the urge to punch this smartass bitch in the jaw was overwhelming. Tina clearly sensed my intentions and held up her hands in mock surrender. "No offense," she said, though her tone was clearly one of an offensive nature. "I just mean that being the woman on the side only gets you so many benefits. You want to be the temp all your life, or you trying to actually get hired permanently?"

I was fed up. The bullshit she was spewing was absurd, not to mention unbelievable. How did they really expect to pull this off? And why? Where was Leo, and why had he sent his wife to handle this ridiculous sales pitch?

"Y'all idiots are crazy and deserve each other," I mumbled.

"Leave me the fuck alone." I was already turning and marching up the sidewalk.

"No, you're the idiot if you don't take him up on this offer," she called to my back. "I suggest you think about it and we'll be in touch with the details."

I kept walking. Since when did logic make me an idiot? And what the hell was there to think about? The certainty in her voice had me quickening my steps, even as her words continued to reverberate.

Connect with U s

Visit us online at
KensingtonBooks.com
to read more from your favorite authors, see books
by series, view reading group guides, and more.

for sneak peeks, chances to win books and prize packs,
and to share your thoughts with other readers.

facebook.com/kensingtonpublishing
twitter.com/kensingtonbooks

Tell us what you think!

To share your thoughts, submit a review,
or sign up for our eNewsletters, please visit:
KensingtonBooks.com/TellUs.